The Way Things Look to Me

Roopa Farooki

W F HOWES LTD

This large print edition published in 2009 by
W F Howes Ltd
Unit 4, Rearsby Business Park, Gaddesby Lane,
Rearsby, Leicester LE7 4YH

1 3 5 7 9 10 8 6 4 2

First published in the United Kingdom in 2009
by Pan Books

A CIP catalogue record for this book is available
from the British Library

ISBN 978 1 40745 166 4

Typeset by Palimpsest Book Production Limited,
Grangemouth, Stirlingshire
Printed and bound in Great Britain
by MPG Books Ltd, Bodmin, Cornwall

FSC
Mixed Sources
Product group from well-managed
forests, controlled sources and
recycled wood or fiber
SA-COC-1565
www.fsc.org
© 1996 Forest Stewardship Council

The Way Things Look to Me

ALSO BY ROOPA FAROOKI
FROM CLIPPER LARGE PRINT

Bitter Sweets
Corner Shop

To my sisters, Preeti and Kiron –
for all the ways we are different, and
for everything that we share

And for our Nanu, Firdousi Khanum,
in memory

There were doors all round the hall, but they were all locked; and when Alice had been all the way down one side and up the other, trying every door, she walked sadly down the middle, wondering how she was ever to get out again.

Lewis Carroll,
Alice's Adventures in Wonderland

I'm working on making myself all-seeing. It's about arriving at the unknown by disordering all the senses. It's wrong to say: I think. I is someone else.

Je travaille à me rendre voyant. Il s'agit d'arriver à l'inconnu par le dérèglement de tous les sens. C'est faux de dire: Je pense. Je est un autre.

Arthur Rimbaud

AS IF HE WASN'T THERE

Asif Declan Kalil Murphy has a brooding resentment of his name, and by extension, of his deceased parents, although he resents them for many more things than his name, up to and including their untimely departure from life. The trouble with his name, he thinks, is that it promises so much more – it promises that he will be interesting and exotic and larger than life, Irish charm and whimsy blended with South Asian mysticism and romance. Asif finds it impossible to live up to his shining name, and so shudders moth-like just beneath it; avoiding introductions and hiding behind initials. He finds it much easier to be A Murphy, a Murphy like any other, just one of the crowd of immigrants of Irish descent littering north London. Or better still, simply AM; I am what I am, thinks Asif, as his tube rumbles into the disappointing depths of Finchley Central, where the rain has made the edges of the platforms slippery, and there is a strong smell of ammonia from an unidentified source. I am what I am, he muses, not special or flawed or creative, just unimpressive, dull as dishwater, little old neutral

1

old nothing old me; at a certain point, he thinks, he really needs to stop blaming his parents. But not just yet. He's still young, he's just twenty-three years old, and he suspects that he has years of grievance left in him. He's an accountant like his British Asian mother before him; he lacks her strong will, but he has inherited her fickle constitution; his father was a hero who died on a peace-keeping mission several years before his wife's congested heart was to claim her; Asif knows that he has nothing approaching his father's courage, but he shares his sense of duty, and propensity to follow orders. It seems a bad joke that the very things that got Asif's father killed are the things that deny Asif his own life; Asif is not the sort to swear, but he admits to having experienced a secret, soaring thrill the first day he heard the Larkin quote, from Lila, of course: 'They fuck you up, your mum and dad. They may not mean to, but they do.' It was so brilliantly and starkly true. Like a song he'd been humming his whole life had finally been put to words.

He walks up the steps at Finchley Central, and away from the gritty high street down the narrow, tree-lined roads towards the family home that he has inherited from his begrudged parents and that he shares with his youngest sister, Yasmin. The higgledy-piggledy streets are untidy and the knobbly, sore-looking trees are not slightly picturesque, but despite this, the walk to and from the tube is his

2

favourite time of day. It's when he doesn't have to be at work worrying about his performance and whether he'll Consistently Meet Expectations or Consistently Fail to Meet Expectations at his next appraisal, and when he doesn't have to be at home worrying about pretty much the same thing, waiting to be appraised wordlessly by Yasmin's NHS-assigned specialists instead. During the walk he is in between things, and no worse than anyone else; certainly not any different. During the walk he imagines that he has secret superpowers, as he is invisible, in his smart suit and precisely ironed shirt, and good shoes and tattered briefcase, which he inexplicably carries like a prize, as one might a broken nose, as though it has a scent of history about it; he is the sort of pleasant-faced young man that no one would notice.

His mobile phone rings as he turns into his street, and he stands at the corner shop in full view of his house, watching the curtain in the upstairs window twitch. Yasmin is looking out for him, as she always does between 6 p.m. and 6.30 p.m. He knows from past experience that if she doesn't see him there, she panics, and so he never digresses from his usual path without warning. He has got so used to seeing the curtain twitch in the upstairs window each and every evening that he wonders whether he'd panic himself if he didn't see it, as though Yasmin's symptoms might be contagious; after all these years of accommodating her infuriating demands for consistency and routine, her habits and neuroses, it would hardly be surprising if he unwittingly adopted some himself. He searches for his phone in every pocket, with mounting panic, until he finally locates it; he is relieved to see that it is just his other sister calling, and answers hurriedly, aware that Yasmin is waiting and watching. 'Hi Lila, what is it?'

'I'm fine, thank you for not bloody asking. You're losing your manners spending all your days locked up with Yasmin, I've always said it would happen.'

'I don't spend my days locked up with Yasmin, just the evenings. I spend my days locked up at work,' retorts Asif, feeling guilty that Lila has managed to sum up so swiftly and with so little premeditation what he has been wondering himself.

'At Accountants' Anonymous?' sniggers Lila, pleased with her joke. 'Same difference. I'm returning your call from yesterday afternoon.'

'Oh good, you got the message. That bloke who took the call seemed really out of it.'

'Mikey? He owns the record shop. He *is* always out of it; I think he did too much dope as an adolescent or something. Still does. Has a fantastic arse though, I'm considering sleeping with him when I'm single again.'

Asif, becoming rapidly appalled at how quickly he can lose any sense of conversational control with Lila, ignores the merits of this unknown Mikey's arse and asks, 'So you're coming round tonight, at eight-ish? I'm getting a curry in for us.'

'What? As if, Asif! Spend a Friday night in with

you and sodding Miss Spock. Not bloody likely.' Lila begins to laugh, and then, realizing that her cackle sounds self-consciously cruel, like a cartoon villainess, stops abruptly. 'I'm seeing Wesley tonight, anyway.'

'That's nice. Where are you meeting up?' asks Asif with pointed civility, watching the curtain twitch a little bit more.

'The Central,' admits Lila grudgingly. The Central Bar is only ten minutes' walk away from the house, a fact that hangs unspoken in the air between them.

'Then come around at eight anyway,' asks Asif at last, trying to sound business-like rather than pleading; he often gets lost between these two tones when making perfectly reasonable requests at work of the office support staff. 'You can bring Wes if you want. Or leave him there for half an hour if we embarrass you. Yasmin has something important she wants to discuss with us; she wouldn't tell me what. Something to do with school, I suppose.'

'Why is it always about Yasmin?' mutters Lila. Asif doesn't answer, as, of course, she knows why already. 'OK, I'll pop around, but just for half an hour. And get me a veggie samosa please.' Asif smiles; both he and Lila know that she doesn't really want a samosa; asking him for one is her way of saying that she'll be there, it's her promise, wrapped up in pastry and stuffed with steaming and aromatic vegetables. His smile fades a little when he sees the curtain at the window has stopped twitching; he hopes that Yasmin

5

isn't sitting in the corner sulking because he took so long on the phone.

When he walks into the house, it is exactly fourteen minutes past 6 p.m., so Yasmin has only had to stand at the window for fourteen minutes that day. He tries to convince himself that he doesn't need to worry about Yasmin; she'll probably be a complete delight all evening, and will behave beautifully when Lila and Wes come round. As if, Asif, he mocks himself, the childish mocking that Lila so perceptively started almost as soon as she could talk, and has never tired of since. Of all the inspiring Asian names available, why did his parents call him an unanswered question, 'As if?' The idea of something still wanting, a road untravelled, an unfinished comparison, which of course it was. They had expected a girl, whom they were going to call Kalila, which is how he had ended up with his third name. Asif Declan Kalil Murphy. A Murphy. AM. Little old nothing old As If he wasn't there.

When Asif enters his house, he goes through to the kitchen, and sees Yasmin washing up plates at the kitchen sink; her hair is pulled back in a sensible ponytail, and she is wearing a grey T-shirt and her soft, baggy jeans. She seems so normal that it almost looks contrived, as though she has made preparations for a stranger to come in and say Hi-Honey-I'm-Home.

'Hello Asif,' she says with polite, almost rigid

formality, but she does not turn towards him or acknowledge him in any other way. He is home as he always is, and that is enough for her. There is something a little bit wrong with the scene that an outsider would take some time to work out, a bit like those spot-the-difference pictures in the backs of magazines, where you have to find the tiny mismatch, a different detail in the background greenery, a strand of hair misplaced. Asif is used to Yasmin, and doesn't need any time to work it out; he can see that the plates that she is scrupulously washing up are already clean, she has probably just taken a stack straight out of the cupboard or dishwasher. Sometimes Yasmin irons already ironed clothes, although he's not very comfortable with her using the iron if he's out of the house, for obvious reasons. And sometimes she launders already clean bedlinen. Just for the calm, soothing feeling of fulfilling domestic routine; the beautifully ordinary things that their mother used to take care of, when not taking care of Yasmin.

He doesn't comment, but puts his briefcase down, and tells his sister, 'Lila's going to be here for 8 p.m. just like you asked.'

'Great, thank you,' says Yasmin mechanically, putting the last clean plate in the rack.

'She might bring Wesley,' Asif adds. 'Or she might leave him at the bar and come by herself.' He sees Yasmin's shoulders stiffen, not because she dislikes Wesley, but because she dislikes the uncertainty of whether he will be there or not.

7

'Great, thank you,' she says at last, and this time she remembers to face Asif, and looks him deliberately in the eyes. Yasmin's own eyes are hazel, clear and rather pretty; specialists have occasionally commented on Yasmin's pretty eyes, something which Asif thinks is wholly inappropriate. He never leaves her alone with anyone whom he doesn't know and trust, specialist or not, and especially not with any overqualified creep who remarks on her looks; Yasmin has never had a boyfriend, and he worries that her inexperience, youth and vulnerability would make it too easy for the wrong sort of man to take advantage. After Yasmin has held his gaze for a count of Mississippi One and Mississippi Two, just as their mother taught her to do, she takes the plates out of the drying rack and puts them back in the sink, to wash up all over again.

Asif watches her for a moment, and considers asking her about her day; smarting slightly about Lila's earlier offhand remark, he wonders whether he should remind Yasmin about it being good manners to ask how someone is when she speaks to them. But then he'd have to remind Yasmin to listen to the answer as well, and to respond to it. It suddenly seems too much like hard work, and he doesn't feel up to it, he'd just like to have a beer and watch the TV for a bit. The rest of the evening stretches out painfully before him, another evening in which he has to entertain Yasmin, or rather, let her entertain herself, while he watches over her.

His little sister's warden. Fridays are the worst, as he knows he won't be escaping the next morning, but will have to be there for the whole, aching weekend, making nutritious dinners which will probably be rejected in favour of neatly compart-mentalized ready-meals, planning improving activities to get Yasmin out of her room and away from her TV and computer for at least a little while. He imagines that this is what single mothers feel like. He realizes uncomfortably that he would rather be anywhere than here.

Asif tries to console himself with the fact that at least Lila will come round tonight, but he knows that she will only stay for a little while. She doesn't consider looking after Yasmin to be her job; she doesn't even think that Yasmin needs looking after, as though it is all some elaborate game that Yasmin has played for the last nineteen years in the inter-ests of being bloody-minded. And so Asif is left to do the looking after, and the coping, and the caring; as he has his whole life, and especially now that his parents are dead. No wonder he hates them; resents, he corrects himself sternly, I resent them. It's OK to resent your dead parents, but it's not OK to hate them just because they're dead. It feels like just the sort of fine distinction that he'd have to explain to Yasmin.

Asif orders the takeaway and gets his beer out of the fridge; there is a photo of his mum with the three of them as children on the fridge door, with little Yasmin on her lap, but sitting scrupulously forward, to avoid touching her siblings. Lila and himself are pushed out to the side. When he was a child, he used to believe that his mother was the most beautiful woman in the world, practically bridal with her permanently fresh-faced and dewy complexion. Now, as he looks at the photo, he can see that she is smiling with unnatural, strained calm, her expression almost assessing, as though she is daring someone to criticize her or her offspring. He hears his mother's voice, 'Engage with her, Asif; you need to engage with her, or she'll never learn to . . .'

'To what, Mum?' Asif had replied with adolescent annoyance at her deliberately trailing off. 'To be normal?' The look his mother had given him was so disappointed that he'd almost rather she'd hit him; as she sometimes had Lila. A disciplined slap to show where the acceptable boundaries were; a slap issued with sadness rather than anger, along with the quiet command, 'Go to your room and think about what you said.' And how Lila had sobbed that obvious, overused phrase, clutching her sore face, a phrase which probably haunted her now, years later, 'I HATE you, I wish you were DEAD,' before running upstairs.

Sometimes he thinks he should take the photo down, but it seems to him that would be an act of defeat; as though his mother would just say I-told-you-so from the safe distance of her harp-twanging cloud. How easy, it would be, not to engage with

Yasmin. Just to share the house as indifferently as flatmates who've come together through an internet ad, and to coexist like toddlers sharing a set of toys at a nursery, sitting side by side but not playing together. Leading parallel lives, never having to connect. She could sit at her computer, and watch the same episode of *The Simpsons* and wear the same clothes all week without him commenting, and he could go to work and go to the pub and snog a kind-faced stranger and come back drunk and pass out on the couch without having to notice whether or not she'd eaten or done her homework or kept her medical appointments. Engage with her, Asif, his mother tells him coldly. Yasmin's not sorry for herself, so why are you?

Asif sighs; he is unable to be disobedient, even to a memory. 'Thanks for washing up, Yas,' he says. 'So, how was school today?'

'School was fine,' says Yasmin automatically, abruptly putting the last double-washed plate in the rack, and walking away from the sink. She looks at Asif, Mississippi One, Mississippi Two, and then leaves the room, and heads upstairs.

'Did anything interesting happen?' Asif perseveres, calling up the stairwell.

Yasmin pauses and looks at her feet; lots and lots of things have happened today: Tilly came into History class ten minutes late, and had a red bruise on her neck that she tried to hide with a fringed purple scarf, and there was a spider in the corner of the Great Hall where they had assembly,

11

descending on a silky line which caught the light, and they sang one of Yasmin's least favourite hymns because it had five typos in the hymn book which always annoyed her, and one of the first years had cried in the loos and Yasmin had remembered to ask what was wrong but had forgotten to listen to the answer and left when the bell went for her next class, and she had walked around the playing fields eight times clockwise and eight times anticlockwise at lunchtime, and she had gone to the canteen and had orange juice and grated cheese and bread for lunch, and Mr Hutchinson had read *The Pardoner's Tale* at the afternoon sixth-form lecture in what was meant to be a Middle English accent, but she had counted thirty-one inconsistencies in his pronunciation, and his lip had had a bubble of spittle on it when he'd finished, and in French class they had started reading Camus' *L'Étranger* which starts off with the line '*Aujourd'hui, Maman est morte*,' and the opening chapters are meant to shock you because the character's mother had just died but he still went on a date with a girl while he wore a black armband and watched a funny film starring a famous French comedian, but it hadn't shocked Yasmin at all, as she had wanted to watch *The Simpsons* after Mum's funeral and only hadn't because of Lila . . .

Yasmin looks up from her feet and down the stairs towards Asif, as she tries to work out if any of these might be classified as 'interesting'. Just a few seconds have passed since he has asked his question, and all these images and many others are melting and swirling with insistent lucidity around her head, each with their own texture and shape and taste and music, each recollected moment as present and loud and impressive as the next, as though demanding that they get plucked out and chosen, even though she knows that they are probably Mostly Irrelevant. Her gaze fixes and focuses upon the drink in Asif's hand, and she says with no further hesitation, 'Yes, I had orange juice at lunchtime. They normally run out by the time I get to the canteen, but there was still some today.' She feels satisfied with herself for this small achievement; he has asked, and she has replied, the perfectly ordinary tennis of conversation, a matter of returning the ball with appropriate speed, and not letting it bounce out of play; there are no spectators at this rally, but if there were, they would be looking left and right and left again, as Asif's words and then her own go thwack-thwock across the invisible net of each other's consciousness. Her response isn't slightly interesting to her, but she hopes that it is interesting to Asif.

Asif smiles at her encouragingly. 'That's nice. Our office canteen doesn't even have orange juice. Just lots of complicated mixed fruit smoothies. You've been there, you remember, don't you?' Yasmin smiles back, to make him happy by showing that she is, but as she is distracted by the importance of returning his smile, she doesn't really register what he says, and realizes that she has let the ball

13

bounce out of play; asking him to repeat himself would bring attention to this, so instead she makes an assenting sound that follows, rather than accompanies her smile. It seems to Asif as though she is agreeing with unnecessary solemnity to what he has just said, effectively closing the conversation, so he attempts nothing further as she carries on upstairs. A moment later, Asif hears the familiar theme tune to *The Simpsons* playing from her bedroom, a sound he used to love and now heartily loathes.

THE PLACE SHE USED TO LIVE

As Lila turns the corner towards the house in which she grew up, she feels a furious, familiar itching along her upper arms and shoulders that makes her shudder; she longs to scratch, deep frenzied scratching that rips the bubbling skin, she longs for the mixed-up relief that drawing blood would cause. She digs her nails, cut aggressively short on doctor's orders so that there isn't a trace of white to them, to avoid her scratching in her sleep, into her soft, strong palms; her palms don't tend to tear or bruise, and consequently take a lot of punishment. Lila's skin horrifies her on a daily basis, with its itching and flaking and inexplicable cracking and thickening, but she restrains it viciously, scraping off each offending flake and stripping her surface with minute, tweezering surgery and harsh scrubbing every morning, until she is shiny, sore and new. She wears a lot of make-up, too much make-up, which turns the raw smoothness into a rosy glow, and she is so skilful that sometimes people actually compliment her radiant complexion. Her throbbing itching appals her, her oozing physical

15

surface appals her, but she just about manages to control them, with fierce will and brutal care; sometimes, she feels that these are the only elements in her wayward life that she does control.

Wesley is waiting for her at the end of the street; 'I thought we'd go in together,' he explains as he kisses her hello. 'Wow, you look great,' he says, admiringly. 'We should go somewhere better than The Central tonight. How about Nobu?'

'Sweet of you, but I couldn't face the tube into town tonight,' says Lila, dismissing the compliment. She always looks great; she knows this, as it takes her a great deal of work; she almost resents her proficiency, and her success in hiding her flaws. Just that morning, her hair had been scraped back while she scrubbed and scrubbed around her eyes, where the dry skin had seized up and tightened so severely that one eyelid had lost its usual fold, giving her a mad, wonky look that wouldn't pinch back into place. She had spent one hour and fifty-three minutes at the sink that morning, trying to get her proper face back, and finally succeeding, as she always did.

'Are you hinting that I should cough up for a cab?' asks Wesley with amusement.

'You know I don't drop hints,' replies Lila, so flatly that it sounds almost flirtatious in intent. In fact, she is annoyed that she remembers to the minute how long it took her to scour her face earlier, it implies a precision verging on obsessive; she

16

wonders if she is copying Yasmin's symptoms, as though she somehow envied them. It's not how we're alike, but how we're different, that's what matters, thinks Lila, as she slips her supple palm into Wesley's in a possessive, girlfriend way that seems to her to ape affection rather than display it.

'Hi there,' says Asif, answering the door. He shakes Wesley's hand, 'All right mate,' and kisses Lila on both cheeks. Yasmin is in the living room, a plate of bhajis and pakoras on her lap; she shakes Wesley's hand calmly, and when Lila hugs and kisses her with overbearing enthusiasm, she holds herself still with the stoicism of a child being embraced by a bosomy, over-perfumed aunt. Lila deliberately makes no attempt to allow for Yasmin's Asperger's when it comes to physical contact. Her exuberant cuddling and kissing is so insistent that it is on the verge of being callously bloody-minded; but it is possible that Yasmin can thank Lila's scary, loving jostling for getting her used to being touched.

'You look nice,' says Asif, politely, and a bit unnecessarily. Lila always looks beautiful, but in the exact opposite way to their mother; reacting against her debilitating eczema, Lila makes sure that she is exquisitely polished, and she is always self-consciously groomed and dressed, with a care that contradicts the careless nature of the rest of her life, epitomized by her unfinished education, her non-existent career where she drifts from one unskilled job to another and her rubbish-tip flat, where she lives in a cluttered squalor that only her besotted string of short-term lovers would find picturesque. Whereas their mother had wonderful skin, which never had a wrinkle until the day she died, and never needed the slightest cosmetic enhancement; her thick hair had a slight wave and although it was shoulder length, she didn't even own a hairdryer, and usually just twisted it up out of the way. Once, when she was pregnant with Yasmin, their mother had gone to a family wedding, wearing a plain cotton sari with her hair pulled back in a bun, and she had caused a sensation. 'That girl's stunning,' said one of the Punjabi guests, heavily bejewelled and kohled, with twisted and teased hair. 'And she's not even wearing a scrap of make-up,' complained another, as though it was somehow the height of bad taste to look so good with so little effort. Little Asif's pride in his mother that day was something that filled him up like one of the puffed pooris at the buffet table; her eyebrows like birds in flight, adorned with nothing apart from her wedding band and pregnant bump, she lit the room.

Although Asif's compliment is unnecessary, it is sincere. Lila has a habit of changing her image and hair colour drastically on a whim, sometimes, although not always, precipitated by a new relationship. In the last two years she has gone from being a dreadlocked grunge goddess, to coin-belted

18

hippy, to goth chick in leathers, to American preppy, wearing crisp white shirts under fitted sweaters with exquisitely low-key accessories. Asif quite likes this last look, accompanied by the chic haircut, which she appears to have adopted in honour of Wesley, as he is an Ivy-League educated New Yorker.

'What, this old thing?' Wesley replies wryly, deliberately misappropriating Asif's compliment and gesturing towards his outfit.

'I'll thank you not to call me old thing,' replies Lila pertly, misappropriating Wesley's comment in turn, as she sits down. She picks up her samosa from the coffee table where Asif has set up the takeaway. 'How's it going, Yas?' she asks.

'Fine,' replies Yasmin automatically. She is looking at Wesley's recently shaved head with admiring fascination; Wesley is black, and very attractive in a slightly gay way, with his impeccable grasp of casual-chic, and gym-honed physique. Yasmin is wondering what it would feel like, to spread her hands across the back of his well-shaped skull, to be held in those muscular arms where the skin flows over the sinews and flesh like melted chocolate. Would she feel safe, like when she was a small child on her mother's lap, or would she feel imprisoned, in danger? She envies Lila being able to be held with so little controversy, to be able to accept physical love with so little drama or difficulty.

'So what did you want to talk to us about? Meds or Mocks?' asks Lila, seeing the distraction

19

in Yasmin's face, and not wanting to be stuck in the house all night.

'Meds or Mocks?' repeats Yasmin blankly. Lila is always doing this to her, throwing out ambiguous phrases she thinks Yasmin ought to be able to understand.

'Medication or Mock exams?' explains Asif kindly, looking a bit crossly at Lila. 'Was it something to do with your treatment, or school?'

'Oh, neither,' replies Yasmin, before reconsidering. 'Or both. Or everything, really. Everything about me.' Asif and Lila glance at each other; it is very unlike Yasmin to be vague.

'It's about me, you see. They want it to be all about me; but now they've said they want to come and talk to you both as well. They heard about me through the school psychologist.' Yasmin pulls out her pink folder, and hands Asif a bound typewritten document. Asif reads it frowning, and passes it to Lila, who shrugs it away, her fingers now greasy from demolishing her vegetarian samosa. 'As if, Asif. Just tell me what it says.'

Asif says, with a little embarrassment, 'A TV production company wants to do a documentary on Yasmin; about her special abilities. They want to talk to us too, about it. The proposed title is "The World According to Yasmin Murphy".'

'What!' shrieks Lila in disbelief. 'What? I mean what . . . I mean why?' The frank incredulity with which she looks at Yasmin is almost comic; her reaction couldn't be any more sceptical if Yasmin

20

had announced she'd been awarded with Best Fringe Act at the Edinburgh Festival.

'Wow, that's great,' says Wesley to Yasmin, and Lila feels a flash of irritation with him; why is everything always 'wow' and 'great'? If a bloody bus ran over his foot, would it still be wow and great? 'Congratulations,' he says, giving Yasmin a warm smile, which irritates Lila even more.

'Congratulations? Why are you congratulating her? It's not like she's announced her sodding engagement,' she says meanly, and snatches the document out of Asif's hands, the paper getting shiny, transparent blotches from her greasy finger-tips. She scans it quickly, shuffling through the sheets. 'I mean, what the fuck is this? Look at these themes: Celebration of the gift of Asperger's? Humanity over Disability? And they want to show-case your "special abilities" – who do they think you are, sodding Raingirl or something?'

'You've called her it often enough,' mutters Asif. 'That's enough, Lila. We're meant to be discussing this with Yasmin.'

His attempt at calming Lila has the opposite effect; her eyes blaze as she snaps, 'Who died and made you Mum?' She realizes what she has said a moment too late, once the blasphemy has escaped to where she can't take it back. Just like her refrain of I-HATE-you-I-wish-you-were-DEAD all those years ago. Her temper abates immediately, and she sinks back into her chair.

Wesley tries to cover up his embarrassment by

21

making conversation. 'So, I didn't realize you had special abilities, Yasmin,' he says, glancing nervously at Lila. He looks like he's about to take Lila's hand, but on seeing her expression, puts his hand back on the table, where he taps his fingers lightly. Yasmin has not realized that his statement requires a reply, as it wasn't a specific question, and watches his fingers drumming on the table, a miniature Mexican wave as if he were playing a five-note scale; he has elegant hands, with squareish oval nails – squoval nails, as the nail salon on the high street calls them on their window display; she wonders if he gets professional manicures. She considers asking him this, when Asif responds on her behalf.

'Yasmin can do lots of things. Her memory's amazing; she reads really quickly, and remembers everything she's ever read, and every piece of music she's ever heard, even everything she's worn on a random day. And she can do fantastically detailed drawings of things that she's seen just for a few minutes. And she's great at languages . . .' He trails off, realizing that he does indeed sound like their mum, talking up Yasmin again, letting people know that she is gifted, not damaged, deserving of admiration rather than sympathy.

'And math? Are you good at math too?' Wesley asks Yasmin directly. She isn't thrown by his use of the American singular, as she has heard it on numerous imported TV programmes.

'No, I'm not very good at maths,' she says simply. 'That's why I'm not doing it for my A levels.'

22

'She's amazing at maths,' contradicts Asif. 'She can do some really complicated calculations in her head. Like the cube of . . . almost anything with three digits.'

'Knowing the cube of something isn't the same as being good at maths, is it, Yas?' asserts Lila, drawn back into the conversation despite herself.

'No, it's not,' agrees Yasmin.

'Still, they don't seem to be that interested in your mental arithmetic,' says Asif, flicking back through the document that Lila has left in an untidy heap on the table. 'Apparently it's been done before – everyone expects autistic savants to be maths geniuses, anyway. They're interested in what goes on in your head, your unique world view, all the things to do with your synaesthesia, drawing the connections between the different senses the way you do. I guess they're right, not many people with synaesthesia can describe it the way you can, they just don't have the communication skills.' He turns back to Wesley. 'Yas is always being complimented on her communication skills, you know.'

'I'm not as bad as I used to be,' confirms Yasmin. She continues with unusual fluency, as though repeating something she has practised, 'I think I could tell people about myself, so people know what it's like to be non-neurotypical. I've got a responsibility to teach them about me. Mum always said that my skills came with responsibility.'

'This is effing ridiculous,' says Lila. 'Yasmin, you're

not really considering doing this, are you? Making yourself some circus show freak for reality TV, having people follow you around while you perform tricks like a bloody monkey. It's demeaning! And it's a fraud – you haven't got any special abilities, not really, just a good memory. You've barely got Asperger's. There's nothing bloody wrong with you, and nothing bloody special about you.'

'That's enough,' Asif says, wishing he sounded less like their mother, but knowing that Lila wouldn't dare make the same jibe again. Why did he get stuck having to be the sensible one; why couldn't he throw his toys out the pram all the time like Lila, and be thought of as interesting and exciting because of it, instead of a boring pain in the butt? 'Yasmin has a diagnosis – you're not a specialist, you're not qualified to disagree with it.'

'Fine,' says Lila coldly. 'Well, if you've got such a great memory, Yas, tell me this? What were you wearing on . . . say . . . 20th May . . . 2004?'

Asif freezes in horror, his fork dangling halfway to his mouth with prawn biryani. Yasmin stands up abruptly, the plate falls from her lap and the savoury pastries scatter flakily over the carpet. Her fists are clenched, her face twisting as though she is about to scream or sob, but then she simply tears out of the room and up the stairs, where they hear Wagner's *Ride of the Valkyries* blast out at full volume. A few seconds later, all is silent.

24

'She's plugged it into her earphones,' explains Asif wearily to Wesley. 'What the hell's wrong with you, Lila?'

Wesley glances up uncomfortably at Asif. 'So I guess she didn't remember, what she was wearing that random day?' he suggests, as though Lila had been right to question Yasmin's abilities. 'Is that why she's gotten upset?'

'It's not a random day, it's the day Mum died,' Asif says quietly.

It is Wesley's turn to freeze in horror. 'God, you're a bitch, Lila,' he says.

Lila doesn't look slightly sorry. 'Oh just piss off, you smug sanctimonious prig,' she says viciously. Wesley gets up unceremoniously, regarding her with something like disgust, and then turns towards Asif with a look that wavers halfway between pity and accusation; he leaves the room without saying a word, and they hear the front door bang a few moments later.

Asif looks at Lila curled up sullenly in the chair, her legs drawn under her. She shows no sign of going after Wesley, so he simply finishes his biryani in a few mouthfuls, and then starts picking up Yasmin's pastries, and the flecks of flaky batter that have got stuck in the carpet pile. 'Oh, leave it,' Lila says in irritation. He says nothing and continues to tidy, as they both knew he would, just as they both knew what Lila would say next. 'I'll go up and apologize to Yas in a minute.'

'What about Wesley?' asks Asif.

25

'I'll call him tomorrow. He's right, I am a bitch, aren't I?' Asif shakes his head, and sits on the edge of Lila's chair, putting his arm around her. He and Lila shared a room when they were children, and it is very easy for her to snuggle against him, and for him to share his warmth with her, just as they did when they were very young, when it sometimes felt that they only had each other.

'You're not a bad person,' says Asif. 'Just a bit thoughtless, sometimes.'

'Bollocks, I'm just a bitch,' says Lila, into his jumper. 'I'm not making excuses, but there's something about being here, about being back home that brings it out in me. I just feel so . . . angry.'

'And you don't even have to live here,' Asif replies, trying to keep the reproach from his voice. He knows what Lila means, their home is a little like a gaol, and a little like a shrine to everything that went wrong when they were young. A childhood of uneven treatment without the satisfaction of actual neglect, wrapped up in four brick walls and topped off with the leaking loft extension; memories hardening into the present-day reality, of sobbing and snuffling 'It's not fair!' into a pillow at night, so no one would hear.

'I didn't want to turn out like this. To be so mean, and defensive, and everything else. But I don't think it's all my fault.'

'They fuck you up, your mum and dad,' says Asif with sympathy; the tension lifts and they both stifle a laugh at the old joke.

26

THE CRYBABY BABOO

Yasmin was a crybaby sort of baby. Asif and Lila didn't like her very much, and once the novelty of her arrival had passed, they had passionate and incoherent discussions about whether they could get the hospital to take her back. Asif was over four when Yasmin was born, and Lila was three, but spoke as fluently as her big brother. Sometimes more fluently; he had been a late talker, and so she would frequently correct him, to his confused humiliation.

Asif couldn't remember a time when Lila wasn't around, but sometimes would look at old photographs in wonder, seeing his parents and him alone, an adored podgy little prince, with dark brown downy hair and chubby pink cheeks from the potato-heavy diet that his Irish father swore by. In one photo, he was lying on the cream sheets of his parents' bed, dressed just in his nappy, asleep with arms stretched above his head and his legs bent in a bow, knees apart and heels together, while his mother looked at him with solemn pride, allowing herself the gentlest smile while her head was bent towards his; he was beautiful, made beautiful because he was loved by someone wholly and absolutely, and because he belonged to someone wholly and absolutely, like every other beautiful baby in the world.

In another photo, he was older and cackling gleefully, held upside down by his father, so Asif's stripy Tigger-emblazoned T-shirt fell back over his round tummy and showed his belly button, while his mother, heavily pregnant once more, held his hand and grinned impishly at the camera. Then there were the photos of him with Lila at home, cuddling up to the tiny bundle protectively, even tenderly, although with little regard for her newborn fragility, as though she were just another stuffed teddy or bunny in his burgeoning collection. But in no time at all, Lila was just as big as he, and just as articulate and demanding of his parents' affection. And then they were both pushed aside by the arrival of the new baby; the shouty, crying baby with a high-pitched shriek like nails across the nursery blackboard.

'Do you like the baboo?' he asked Lila conversationally, while they were sitting on the sofa watching their nursery rhyme video.

'No, I HATE the baboo,' replied Lila matter-of-factly.

'Me too,' confided Asif, untroubled by Lila's strong choice of words. Lila loved or hated everything. Their mum walked into the room with the crybaby baboo, which had started screaming the moment it had finished feeding. Mum looked exhausted, and asked Asif if he wanted to hold his baby sister for a little bit, to sit with her carefully across his lap, as though this were a great honour, but Asif shrank back on the sofa, and said 'No, don't want.'

'No, *thank you*,' corrected Lila.

'No, thank you,' repeated Asif obediently. Although he didn't really hate the baboo, he didn't want it too near him. The next room would do fine. But the baboo was never in the next room, unless it was with his mother, and he soon realized that if he wanted his mother to be near, the baboo would have to be near too. And the baboo was always attached to his mother in a weird way, and sucking with a concentrated look on its face, and sometimes with a slightly leering smile that made Asif feel a little sick; these sucking times seemed like the only times that the baboo was quiet.

It was still sucking on their mother almost two years later, when it was old enough to walk around and wear proper clothes, and sit in a high chair for meals and had all its own teeth; and then, of course, he didn't call it the baboo; he called the baby by her proper name, which was Yasmin, or Yas for short, and although she still cried, and worse, threw tantrums and banged her head to get attention, she wasn't a baby any more. She could even speak a little, although she didn't say very much apart from 'No!' and 'Poo!' and, most of all, her constant demand, 'Mama-Mama-Mama!'

He and Lila realized then, with childish despondency and adult resignation, at the tender ages of six and five, that crybaby, tantrum-throwing, head-banging Yasmin had stolen their mother, and that they were never going to get her back. And the small tragedy was that they were right.

THE COLOUR OF BROKEN MEMORIES

My name is Yasmin Murphy, and I don't remember very much about the morning that my mum died, which is odd, as normally I remember everything about a particular day. Everything. *Everything.*

For example, if we take another random day, like the 27th of March last year (I chose that day because March is the third month of the year, and three is my favourite number, because it is pink and a little bit billowy in my head, like candyfloss or clouds in the sunset, and twenty-seven is the cube of three, which is 3 X 3 X 3 or 3 to the power of three, which is why cubes are my favourite shapes, so the date isn't really random, but not much is. Most things have a reason but they're not always apparent to neurotypical people, and I'm not neurotypical), I could tell you that the temperature in my room was 17 degrees Celsius, and that I was wearing the black trousers which have an uneven stitch on the inside leg when the machine that made them must have jumped, and that I did up five buttons on my cardigan that day, the purple cardigan where the label is on the back of the neck where it scratches slightly, and that I made pin-prick holes on the cardigan as I was wearing an epilepsy awareness badge, and I could tell you all about the tinny, pointy feel of the badge in my hand, and its musty metallic smell that was a bit like copper change, which made me smile because I like the warmth of copper change, and the sensation of slight heaviness it gives in a pocket, and the sound it makes when it jingles, and I could tell you that the badge was slightly dented because it fell off and I stepped on it and then I pricked my finger trying to put it back, and creepy Mr Johnson looked too much at my chest when he read it and patted me on the shoulder, and I call him creepy because I don't like the way he shows his gums when he smiles and I don't like being touched by him, or anyone really, although now I'm older I can put up with it without having a Meltdown, like I used to.

I remember everything, but the things that I remember are Mostly Irrelevant, according to my older sister, Kalila, who prefers to be called Lila for short, so that is how I'll refer to her from now on. When Mum died, it's like someone cleared my hard drive, and I lost all the usual things that I remember. Instead, I only remember a few things, and I don't remember these very well – they're like pictures from a shaky old movie that runs in a loop in my head. I remember that Asif had water running down his face (crying, I know that's called crying, but I can't remember him actually crying out or making a noise, should it still be called crying if there's no cry and no noise?), and I remember that Lila's face was very pink like it is when she's been running, with red blotches around her eyes and on the high bits of her cheeks, and she was shouting in my direction and shaking me, but again, I didn't hear any noise, so it looked like her mouth was opening and closing like a goldfish's does. I remember sitting in the corner with my index fingers pressed hard on my ears, and humming to make the white noise that I like, but I don't even remember the sound of the white noise, and I'd like to remember the sound of it, because it would be comforting, and when I try to remember that morning, I don't feel happy and would like to be comforted. And I thought my eyes were shut tight, but they can't have been, because I definitely remember seeing Asif with the water-face, and Lila with the red-blotch eyes, but I couldn't tell you what they were wearing or the number of buttons they had done up on their clothes. I couldn't even guess, because I find it unnatural to fill in a gap of memory with something that would be a guess, because a guess is just something imagined, and although I have lots of thoughts, I'm not very imaginative. Lila says that I'm derivative, which I think she means as an insult, but it doesn't work, because insults make people feel bad, and I don't feel bad to be described as derivative, because that means

I derive what I think from real things, rather than just make them up out of nothing. And besides, a lot of people who think that they're being imaginative and making stuff up from nothing aren't really being original or creative, but are just copying from someone else and don't know that they're doing it, because they can't remember how or why the ideas came to them, because most ideas just go round and round in a big circle getting used and re-used like a pile of dishes, and most people can't name their sources, like I can. The colour of that broken memory is red with orange blotches, the blend of colours that I always associate with Anger and Loud Voices and Changes and having Meltdowns, and the music that accompanies the silence of the memory is a bit like Wagner's *Ride of the Valkyries*, and the texture of it is a slimy clammy surface like pond scum that looks solid but sucks your hand in if you try to touch it, and it feels hot and cold in a sickly, shivery way, the way it feels after you've walked in the rain for a long time without a coat, and then go into an overheated house.

The funeral was different – I remember everything about the funeral. Everything. I counted the number of panes in the mock stained glass in the crematorium decorated with non-religious images like trees and rivers and sunsets, and if you give me a pen and paper, I could still draw you every detail of them if I wanted, and that was almost five years ago. Some people said that I didn't care that my mum had died, because I was making shadow bunnies on the wall where too much sunlight was coming in. My mum didn't mind about the shadow bunnies, as she was hidden in her box, and if she hadn't been dead and decaying and soon to be burnt up, she would have liked to see me make them, as my mum used to play shadow puppets with me so I wouldn't be scared of shadows or bright sunlight. Asif wasn't crying at the funeral, and Lila wasn't shouting, and although there were Loud Voices with everyone singing, there wasn't Anger, but there were Changes, as I didn't go to school that day like I normally do. That made me a little bit upset, but I tried not to show it and I managed not to have a Meltdown, because although it is all right to be upset when someone dies, it is not all right to be upset if someone dying changes your plans for the day. That's what Asif told me, and he is usually right.

After the funeral, Lila was very quiet in that way of hers that is like being very noisy, because she was so quiet that no one could say anything at all, so I re-read a book (*The Encyclopedia of Greek and Roman Mythology*) because I thought that watching *The Simpsons* or playing Tetris would be too noisy; and then she broke that thick, fudge-like silence she had made, and asked me, 'Didn't you love Mum, Yasmin?' Then she realized that she had confused me with the negative 'Didn't' which I know now means 'Did you not' which really means to ask 'Did you', which is what she then asked me instead. 'Did you love Mum, Yasmin?' And I knew that she was serious and wanted an answer, as she had called me Yasmin. When she is cross and is just asking a rhetorical question that doesn't need an answer, she calls me something like 'Sodding Raingirl' or 'Sodding Miss Spock'. So I said, 'Of course I loved Mum.' ('Of course' just means 'Yes', and is a commonly understood way of saying yes emphatically, in the way that the French say 'Si' instead of 'Oui' to something that is asked with a negative, for example you'd respond to 'Mais non!' with 'Mais si!' rather than 'Mais oui!' if the conversation is something like: 'C'était bon!' 'Mais non!' 'Mais si!' which translates roughly as 'That was good!' 'No it wasn't!' 'Oh yes it was!')

I was only fourteen then, but I felt very grown up, as I knew it was the right thing to say, and Lila looked happier, and so did Asif who had just come in with sandwiches for dinner. I knew it was the right thing to say, in the same way that I knew it was right to ask 'Are you all right?' to someone who has just been hurt or fallen over, even though I could see that they have been hurt or fallen over, and are obviously not all right, which is why I still think it is a slightly stupid thing to have to say just to be polite.

And I wish I could honestly say that I knew what it meant, inside, to say that I loved Mum, but I really wasn't sure; even now, I'm not sure I know what love means, the kind of love that Lila was talking about, which is different to saying something like I love Mozart and custard tarts; it makes me a bit sad to think that I don't understand something so important to them, but I don't think that it's my fault. And I felt that if I said, 'I love you too,' to the both of them, that they would have stepped forward and come into my world, but I didn't, as I knew that only the words would be real, and they wouldn't be derived from anything real themselves. And then I felt bad, as I really, really, wanted to be held close and comforted, like when I was a baby in my mum's arms, but that longing was just a fuzzy memory in my head, as I knew that if anyone had actually tried to touch me at that moment, I would have shrunk away and maybe even screamed. And everything began to go red with orange blotches, so I just went into my room with my book, and shut the door behind me.

A WORK OF ART

Lila is at home in her rubbish-tip flat on the rainy Sunday morning following Yasmin's revelation that she is shortly to be filmed, and doubtless soon to be famous. Now she'll be everyone's favourite little super-freak, thinks Lila bitterly, as though stealing their mum wasn't enough for her; Yasmin's now set her sights on global domination like a wannabe popstar – today Finchley, north London; tomorrow the world. And it's not as though Asperger's is that rare, Lila continues to carp to herself, there are hundreds upon hundreds of gifted non-NT geeks out there, they just picked on Yasmin because she's a skinny nineteen-year-old girl, and with a bit of grooming and plucking would obviously be more photogenic than an unwashed, pizza-faced adolescent boy would be. 'Fucking perverts,' says Lila to herself, sloppily gouging ice cream out of a carton with her fingers, as she can't find a clean spoon. She'd tell them so, as well; she'd been told she could meet one of the researchers next week; she'd tell them that they were effing perverts trying to get ratings out of prostituting her little sister on national TV. And the whole basis of

their documentary was falsely premised, anyway –
'The gift of Asperger's', as if Yasmin's inconclu-
sively diagnosed Asperger's was the root of all her
useless party tricks. Her so-called gifts were just as
likely to be some sort of neurological accident; she'd
had serious epileptic seizures when she was younger.
Lila has read about a baseball player who suddenly
became a mnemonist genius with a simple trauma
to the head; if that was true, anyone could acquire
Yasmin's synaesthesia and savant qualities, all they
needed was a well-timed whack to the temporal
lobes in some controlled, diabolical experiment;
what a thought, shudders Lila, millions of little rain-
boys and raingirls waiting to be released from the
general public, like statues hidden inside their
uncarved blocks of rock. The ice cream is now too
liquid for Lila to scoop with her fingers, so she wipes
them on her T-shirt, and drinks the ice cream
instead, smearing a creamy moustache away with
the back of her hand, before she throws the carton
into the overflowing bin.

Lila lived in a tidy, minutely ordered house until
she was eighteen, where everything had its place,
and where seemingly random things, like a row
of coins along the radiator, her dead mother's
cardigan hung casually over the back of her easy
chair, could never be moved without invoking tears
and tantrums, or even worse, reproachful, injured
silences from her little sister. Since abandoning
Asif to be the sole carer of Yasmin, Lila has cele-
brated her freedom by becoming an obscene slob.

A filthy pig. An old-fashioned slattern. A slut. She takes a bizarre sort of pride in the mess, in the clutter so deep and wide and long that she could hide a body in it. Instead she hides there herself. The select few who have seen Lila's flat are amazed that she can emerge from it looking so fresh and lovely, like an orchid springing from a pile of manure.

In the flat, she wanders around in grey underwear with holes in it, and watches the snails climb up her damp, dirty windows from the overgrown window box, leaving slimy, viscous trails; she brushes her teeth in the kitchen sink after her ice cream, because she can't be bothered to empty the sink in the bathroom, where she has left some soy-sauce-stained garment to soak. Her shining hair is scraped back with an elastic band, and she scratches her arm with intense brutality, glad of all the freedoms she has on her own, when there is no one to witness her with disgust apart from herself and the odd parental ghost – she is sure that Mum is watching her with the opposite of pride, if she is bothering to watch at all; it seems somehow unlikely that her mother would take an interest after her death, as she never seemed overly concerned with Lila while she was alive.

Lila made up with Wesley on Saturday night, marking their rapprochement the traditional way with enthusiastic lovemaking, but she is not disappointed that he has plans and won't be coming over today, as even the rudimentary tidying that would entail, and the searching for underwear without holes, would be too much of a bore. She likes Wesley, but she thinks she likes her sluttish liberty quite a bit more; she would give him up first, of that she is certain.

The formality of melted ice cream breakfast and kitchen sink toothbrushing over with, Lila goes over to the canvas she is working on. 'Your paintings don't look like the things they're meant to represent,' Yasmin had said with her gift of infuriating accuracy while completely missing the point.

'This is the way things look to me,' Lila had answered defensively. 'If I'd wanted them to look like the things they represent, I'd have just taken a photo.' This had prompted Yasmin to launch into a dull monologue about digital image capture and pixels and resolution, another one of her temporary obsessions which had left her with an encyclopedic knowledge of tedious minutiae. From experience, Lila knew it was best to let Yasmin witter on until she ran out of material; interrupting just made it take longer, as Yasmin would simply pause and then carry on exactly where she left off. So she let Yasmin talk, while inwardly she was seething; just because she didn't draw like Yasmin, in painstaking architectural detail, didn't mean that her work had no value; had she imagined it, or had Yasmin accompanied her frigid verdict of Lila's art with a pitying look?

Lila doesn't know why her little sister still bugs her so much; they're both grown up now, after all, and Lila has her own flat and job and an impressive string of failed relationships at a relatively tender age. She doesn't have to spend any time with Yasmin unless she agrees to it, and yet, here she still is, obsessing over something that was once said, and probably not even with malice. Lila doesn't know why thinking of Yasmin still makes her feel so sad and petulant. 'Why is it always about Yasmin?' Lila asks her painting, a hulking landscape in oils, with tiny pieces of twisted metal and mud and twigs set into the paint in elemental serried ranks, like an army preparing for battle.

Lila is still feeling betrayed by what she said on the Friday, asking about the day that Mum died. She didn't mean to use her mother's death in a vindictive way, but that's what she did, because she is, quite evidently, an inescapably vindictive bitch, whether she wants to be one or not. It was a good thing for Yasmin that she had moved out; she might have strangled her sister by now if she'd still been living there; it was quite bad enough that she casually turned up and indulged in light emotional abuse. Lila's only excuse was that the particular date had recently been on her mind; she'd seen a Basque art exhibition the week before, and there was a painting called, *No one knows that my father died yesterday*, and it reminded her of Yasmin, as no one would have known by looking at her that their mother had died, on the day that she found out. When Asif had come back from the hospital, tearful and pale, Yasmin had barely paid attention to him when he had given them the news. She had carried on watching her *Simpsons* DVD and barely glanced at him. It was only when Lila had lost her rag and started shaking Yasmin and shouting at her that she had retreated into the corner and begun to hum; that was her usual reaction to distress, but it was hard to tell whether she was distressed because of Lila's aggression, or because it had finally sunk in that Mum was dead. Yasmin had claimed to love Mum, so why didn't she show anger, or loss, or pain, or *something*; how could these feelings be buried so deep inside her ponytailed little head that there was nothing of them to show to the light? What if there was nothing there at all – everyone assumed that Yasmin's mind had to be full of magical, wonderful, unspoken things – what if they were all wrong? What if there was nothing in her head but the machine which tick-tocked and kept her moving and functioning and calculating and memorizing, but which felt nothing?

Lila doesn't like her painting; it doesn't show enough anger or loss or pain either, and suddenly it looks a bit pretentious. The twisted metal is intended to be threatening but now just seems ridiculous, like piercings on a fresh-faced schoolboy, or a biker jacket on a staid asthmatic accountant. She suddenly pictures Asif with piercings and a biker jacket, and giggles to herself. As if. She suppresses the urge to call him and complain about her picture; she misses Asif since she moved out, he was the only still, sane point in her world. The place she went to for comfort. For sanctuary. When they were chubby children, not much more than toddlers, Yasmin's infant screaming would keep Lila awake and afraid, so she would tiptoe into Asif's bed, hugging his milk-scented, soap-scented, sleep-heavy body for comfort. Asif was lucky, as unlike her, he had always been clean, and he had always been good. Perhaps he knew that being good was just a matter of good fortune, as he was never smug about it, never proud of it even, and never seemed to judge her for her own bad luck.

The phone rings, and Lila waits until she hears a voice on the answering machine before she picks up. 'Wes? Hi babe, I thought you were watching the match today?'

'I was, but I miss you. I keep thinking about you. Would you like to meet up for lunch?'

'Not sure, I was going to finish off this rubbish picture that I've done, before I burn and dump it.'

'Pretty please? Trashing your exquisite works of art can wait. We can have lunch at my place, if you like? I'll grill us some Dover sole, with champagne and strawberries and cream . . .' His tone is both sensuous and pleading.

'At your place, you say,' muses Lila, so he just wants to fuck her again, how sweet. Irony and obviousness of intent aside, perhaps there is something genuinely sweet about his desperation, his eagerness for her. There is something undeniably nice about being desired. 'Sure, I'll come over in

44

about three hours, I want to have a bath first.' Wesley doesn't know that she will spend at least two hours soaking her scabby hide, scraping, softening and exfoliating, rubbing raw, and then moisturizing her skin to a flowing, glowing, satin sheen that will last Cinderella-like until midnight, before her skin dehydrates and starts to re-scab and re-scale overnight, by which time the pumpkin carriage of the 210 bus or a black cab will have delivered her home to her rat and mice footmen, nibbling the crumbling remains of food in her squalid kitchen.

'I'll be waiting, gorgeous,' says Wesley, and they both know that when she comes to his door, he really will be waiting, and that he'll say her name with worshipful reverence, and push his hands through her shining hair and kiss her violently, and that he'll stroke his palms up her smooth back, and groan as he pulls her hips into his groin, and that he'll slide his fingers inside her, and that they'll make agonizingly passionate, half-dressed love in his hallway, while the Dover sole dries out on the grill. Passion is one of the few things that makes Lila feel alive, which gets her through her humdrum daily miseries and self-flagellating introspection; it is probably one of the reasons why her relationships are so short-lived – once they start reading the papers in bed and she no longer bothers to shave her legs before a date, she knows the passion has left, and that she might as well too.

Lila removes her hole-ridden knickers and ice-cream-stained T-shirt, and gets into the bath. All the different images she has of herself, all the different lives she has tried on with different costumes, all the times she has reinvented herself, she always comes down to this, a naked figure in the bath. Perfected, in the way a body on a mortuary slab is perfected. While the water runs in, she looks at the soft insides of her thighs, inspecting the tiny, barely perceptible scars that run in neat parallel lines towards her crotch, too tidy to be stretch marks, although with the same silvery, apologetic appearance, as though they shouldn't really be there, like bashful gatecrashers at a party. Once the water soaks into the dry layer of her epidermis, she starts to feel that itching again, and suppresses the urge to scratch; she needs to wait for the dry, patchy skin to soften, so she can slough it off like a snake. She stares at her artist's scalpel in the ceramic mug by the bath, at the shining, sharp metal beckoning her, almost hypnotically, and finds that she really can't resist. She takes the blade and, biting her lip, with wide open eyes, carefully adds four neat cuts to the scars already there, with an artist's deliberation, and a surgeon's precision. She watches the blood blend prettily with the water in soft, gentle swirls, and the itch is forgotten with the tart delicious bite of the wound; she puts the scalpel back in the mug with her razor and comb. She knows she shouldn't have, but she thinks that Wesley will be too keen to get at her today to notice the cuts, just as he has never

46

noticed the silvery ghost-like scars, even when his mouth is pressed against them, his lips moving towards the moist join in her legs. She feels almost sorry that there is so little scarring, so little to show for her self-inflicted pain; she wonders what would happen if she rubbed ash in them, like the tribal people whose scars are designed to be a mark of honour, rather than shame. To make a decorative jewel, a tattoo, a work of art from her cuts; something incontrovertible that displays her loss, her anguish. Something that shouts to the world for admiration, for help.

When Lila is finally scrubbed and moisturized and dewily made up to natural perfection, sexy damp tendrils of her hair trailing delicately around the back of her neck, and her body so gleaming that she wears her skin like her ballgown, the elegant wrapper of soft trousers and crisp shirt barely consequential, she looks once more at her painting. It still doesn't look angry enough; it doesn't look damaged or lonely or unstable enough; it looks smug and safe and bizarrely ordered instead, and she just wants to slash at it, to cut it into neat ribbons. She realizes as she leaves the flat, aching for the sedative violence and numbing release of passion, for the explosive blankness of being in someone's arms, that Yasmin is right. The painting doesn't look like the thing it is meant to represent.

THE WORLD ACCORDING TO YASMIN MURPHY

My name is Yasmin Murphy, and I am not especially pretty, and not especially nice, but I am very, very clever, as I can do lots of things that other people can't because I have an Extraordinary Mind. But I have had to learn with great difficulty to do the things that other people find very easy, like looking someone in the eye when I speak to them, and shaking a stranger's hands when I meet them, and travelling on the tube at rush hour, and Showing Concern, and understanding what people mean, as opposed to just understanding the individual sentences that they speak. I have made great progress over the years since my first diagnosis, and everyone says that I'm not as bad as I used to be. But I still don't really 'get' other people ('get' in this context means 'understand' rather than 'fetch'), and probably never will; this doesn't make me a bad person, and as long as I pretend to 'get' people, that's all most people want anyway. That's why you smile when someone says something nice to you – not because you're happy,

48

but because you want to make the other person happy by thinking you're happy.

Most people are neurotypicals, or NTs for short. I am not neurotypical, and when I was six I was diagnosed as having Asperger's Syndrome. But as I said (I'm repeating myself now because I like repetition, I can watch the same episode of *The Simpsons* twenty-seven times in a row if I'm not interrupted), everyone says that I'm not as bad as I used to be, and many people that I meet briefly don't realize that I am different. This is probably because I usually don't speak to people as frankly as I am speaking now, as it makes them uncomfortable and they start to fidget. Instead I tell them normal things about my day if I am asked, and I try to keep the Mostly Irrelevant things to myself, as no one else cares about the details. But I am different; I'm special, and my mum taught me that special people have a responsibility to help other people learn about them. The documentary I'm going to do is meant to help people like me who aren't neurotypical, so they won't get bullied at school. Or be misunderstood. Or hurt themselves with little cuts on the arms or legs to release pain-relieving endorphins because they are depressed. Non-neurotypical people get depressed a lot; I am lucky, because although I'm not often very happy, I'm not often very sad. Even when people seem to think I should be, like when Mum died.

WHEN HE WAS GOOD

'You're a good boy,' Asif's mother had told him before she died. They were almost her last words, spoken casually just before she asked him to investigate where the doctor was, as she felt that unpleasant tightening around her chest begin again. Asif left her with the nurse, and when he returned, she was gone. A beautiful figure under crisp white sheets, thick hair with a slight wave fanned out behind her. Perfected. Her heart problem had come from nowhere; until the morning that she died, she had been an apparently healthy woman in her early forties, who looked after herself, and everything else, with strict control. It was only afterwards that they discovered how wasted and weak her heart muscle was, how congested the arteries; as though her heart had lived longer than she had, undertaking more work than it should have been called upon to do. If she had felt any symptoms before, she had never complained, never distrusted her own ability to retain control. Even of her overloaded heart, split too many ways, too tired and crowded to go on.

★   ★   ★

Asif's mother had not expected to die that day, so Asif might have been expected to forgive her for not giving their final moment its due, for not saying anything more valedictory and inspiring, for never saying goodbye. But just as he found it hard to forgive her for the abrupt nature of her passing, he felt equally cheated by the casual nature of their farewell. Why did she have to say that he was a good boy? Was that the very best she could say of him, her last gift to leave him? How mealy-mouthed, how petty of her, as though he was a wagging dog who had just fetched a stick, instead of her only son, who had rushed her to hospital while his younger sisters were at school, oblivious. Why didn't she say, why didn't she *ever* say, I love you? I love you, son. I love you, Asif. They said it in the movies all the time, on the TV, in books – how could she have not known the right thing to say to her departing child, who was on his way to fetch a doctor, when her heart was constricting and preparing to strike.

Asif could not remember feeling love from his mother, although he was sure that once upon a time he was loved, a time so long ago that it felt that it belonged to a fairy tale or myth, the time before his sisters had come along. He had only to look at the photos of his beautiful baby-ish self alone with his parents to know how he had been loved. But even though he had no memory of feeling it, he would have liked to hear the words, even if that was all they were. Just words. Because sometimes words mattered as much as the things they tried to represent; sometimes words were just as real.

Much as he disliked being called a good boy, he was to hear it many times over the days and months that followed his mother's death. His mother, controlled and organized until and beyond her end, had made arrangements for her children in the instance of her death, which she updated as they grew. Before Asif turned eighteen, her intention had been that the children go to her husband's people in Ireland, their closest living relatives, even though they only knew of them through cheery cards posted at Christmas, and, as some sort of private joke, on St Patrick's Day. Once Asif had turned eighteen, and Lila seventeen, their mother had decided that it was easier if the family remain where they were, supported by the trust she had set up for their education, with Asif and Lila as Yasmin's guardians, supervised by visits from the caring State. The anonymous relatives sent condolences, but offered neither financial support nor care-giving assistance; they were all but strangers to the family, not having visited even before Dad's death, and were probably relieved not to have to take responsibility for three bereaved adolescents. So Asif had to take Mum's place as head of the family, and look after fourteen-year-old Yasmin, and was unanimously praised as a good boy by every social worker, carer, specialist or educational professional he came into contact with.

'You're a good boy, Asif,' his economics tutor had said, when Asif broke the news that he would have to abandon his tripos degree at Cambridge, as he was needed at home to care for his sister. Asif didn't feel like a good boy at all, he felt like shattering the sherry glass that his tutor amicably offered him against the oak-panelled wall. He wanted someone, anyone, to tell him to stop being so bloody good, and to think of himself for a change; to abandon his sister to his father's unknown people in Ireland and get on with his life, to finish his degree and start a brilliant career and finally be a person in his own right. He wanted someone to tell him that he had already sacrificed enough of his childhood for his little sister, he didn't have to let her wreck the rest of his life. He wasn't good at all; he was mean, resentful, hypocritical; he found himself wishing his mum had died two years earlier, as then they would have all been shipped off to Belfast, and he could have deserted Yasmin there as soon as he went to college. The only person who told him to stop being so bloody good, who didn't condemn him for being a good boy, was Lila; and he loved her for it, even while he gave the appearance of disapproving of her thoughtlessness and varying unkindnesses towards Yasmin. And, of course, Asif never shattered the sherry glass, and never called upon the unknown relatives; he sipped his sherry meekly, and told the tutor that he'd been accepted at the London School of Economics to finish his degree, and he did as his mother wanted.

It was no one's fault, and he had no one left alive to blame; it was just the way it had turned out; like his mother, he would be responsible for Yasmin until the day one of them died.

OTHER MINDS

My name is Yasmin Murphy, and I don't understand other people's minds very well. Specialists have told me that I lack empathy; this means that I don't pretend to know what other people think, because I know that I don't really know, and I'm not good at guessing or making things up. And besides, I don't have any opportunity to guess or make things up about other people's minds, because my own mind is always busy doing something and demanding my attention. Teachers often say that I'm distracted or not concentrating, when I am actually concentrating a lot, but just on the wrong thing, on the inside world rather than the outside world.

I can't switch my mind off, like other people can; sometimes Asif comes home and has a beer and turns on the TV and then gets bored and looks like he's about to doze on the sofa, and if I ask him what he's thinking about, he says, 'Nothing,' and I think that it might be nice just to think of nothing occasionally. Sometimes I try to escape my mind, but it's difficult, because it's like there's a continuous stream of satellite television playing to me, and so I hum with my eyes shut and my index fingers in my ears to make a white noise for my mind to focus on to give me a break. And my mind is always storing new things, and it even stores what I was thinking the moment before, and the moment before that. So that when I'm in bed and want to go to sleep, I can't, because I've got Yasmin from one minute before, and Yasmin from two minutes before, and Yasmin from the day before, and the week before, and the year before all chattering away in my head, and the only ones that are really blurred and incomplete and not properly dressed in my mind are the ones from 20th May 2004. I sleep so little that the specialists had to prescribe me sleeping pills.

During a normal day, my head is so full of Yasmin Murphys that it hurts, which is why I sometimes bang my head when no one is looking; normally on the bathroom wall at home or at school, as bathrooms have locks so I won't be embarrassed by someone walking in on me. When I was little I hadn't yet learned to be embarrassed about doing inappropriate things in public, like head-banging or wetting myself or farting, and I would bang my head all the time, in a rhythmic, rocking motion, bang and bang and bang like the tick tock of a clock, or a metronome on a piano, until my head was bruised, and it hurt in a different, cleaner way. The brain has a gating mechanism that shuts out old pain when a new, more urgent pain comes along; I was too young to be told this, so I worked it out myself.

The fewer things my mind is exposed to, the easier it is. Which is why I don't like crowds, because when other people just see 'a crowd' I see two hundred and seventy-four people all wearing different clothes with different sounds and smells and textures. Which is why it was a relief, fifteen days ago, when I looked out of the window, and realized that I was seeing less than I used to. We have a walnut tree in our back garden, which is growing new leaf buds and has a bird's nest in it. And I saw the bird fly in and out of the tree, and I realized that I didn't know what kind of bird it was, because I couldn't see its markings or distinguishing features at all. So I couldn't say if it was a Northern European Mistle Thrush or anything – it was just a brownish-greyish bird. And since then, I realized that I was seeing less of everything, so everyone has been getting more attractive, as I can't see their imperfections, like pores, spots or wrinkles. Even I look prettier when I look in the mirror; my skin seems so smooth that I have to touch it to remind myself what it's really like.

It was a relief at first, but now it's a bit disturbing; because my sight doesn't just affect what I see – all the information I receive by my senses is mixed up in my brain, which is why I know what Lila means when I stare at her without intending to, and she says, 'Stop looking at me in that tone of voice.' She means it as a joke, but I understand. It is why I feel calm when I hear white noise, like the humming in my head when I block my ears, or the sound of the vacuum cleaner; the noise doesn't just blur the sound signals, it blurs everything else as well. I can't taste food if there is a loud, jarring noise, or concentrate on cutting a slice of bread if there is a strong smell. So now with my sight beginning to deteriorate, it's as though I don't hear quite as well, or feel quite as well. Instead of my other senses compensating for what I can't see, like they do in the books, they are all receding too. It's as though my world is shrinking, or slipping back into my head; as though my world might become nothing more than a place where memories were made. It feels as though the things which make me special might be slowly deteriorating, like Mum in her box before she got put in the oven.

I won't be telling anyone else about this, as what happens inside my head doesn't affect anyone else. I can't pretend to know what anyone else is thinking, so it would probably be Mostly or Wholly Irrelevant to them.

ACCOUNTANTS' ANONYMOUS

Asif and Yasmin are sitting down to breakfast on a Monday morning. Asif is already suited and booted and reading the paper, and Yasmin is still in her pyjamas, lavishly buttering her bread; it is a perfectly normal domestic scene. But once again, there is something that would cause an outsider to scratch his head, something a little strange, and which wouldn't be noticed straight away. The strange thing is the yellowness. All the food on the breakfast table seems to be varying shades of yellow, with just the odd splash of white that shows up the yellowness even more; the orange juice, the scrambled eggs, the lightly grilled toast, the pats of softened butter in a dish, the banana slices on the cornflakes. All perfectly usual things to have for breakfast, but just all yellow; it might be dismissed as mere coincidence, were it not for the coffee percolator in the corner of the kitchen, phut-phut-phutting away with little bursts of steam, as though demanding attention. Yasmin is studiously avoiding looking at it, whereas Asif glances towards the frothy dark nectar longingly, and a little guiltily, like a teenager at a party besotted with someone else's date. When Yasmin leaves the table, and goes upstairs to get washed, Asif waits until he hears the bathroom door click shut, and then all but leaps out of his chair and pours himself a cup. He sips it carefully, leaning against the counter and shutting his eyes with the bliss of postponed pleasure. After putting the breakfast things in the dishwasher, he pours himself a second cup, which he is practically forced to inhale, as he hears Yasmin come back down after precisely nine minutes. Sputtering a little with the effort of drinking too quickly, he hurriedly swills out the cup, and pops it in the dishwasher too.

'Bye Yasmin, have a good day at school,' he says.

'Bye Asif. Have a good day at work,' she replies automatically, her intonation so carefully mimicking his, with her conscientious effort to get the phrase just right, that she might be mocking him.

The yellow breakfast was Asif's fault; Yasmin had never insisted on having a yellow breakfast when their mother was alive, and had never stopped Mum having tea or coffee at the breakfast table. Nor had she ever stopped Asif, really. But once their mum had passed away, he noticed that whenever there were non-yellow things for breakfast, Yasmin wouldn't eat them, and would eat less of whatever else was there, until it got to a point that she wouldn't eat anything, if there was just one non-yellow item on the table, such as a cup of coffee. Whenever he asked her about it, she said that she just wasn't hungry; she didn't seem at all cross or demanding; it was as though she had genuinely lost her appetite.

He experimented, and discovered that when the table was only full of yellow things, she'd eat everything. It was an evasive form of passive aggression, which Yasmin didn't even seem to be conscious that she was doing. Their mother had always made sure that Yasmin ate a decent breakfast, just in case she didn't find anything acceptable to eat at school, or just failed to go to the canteen for lunch, and so Asif suffered agonies of guilt whenever he sent Yasmin off to school on an empty stomach, she was such a skinny little thing as it was. So when Lila moved out a year later, Asif capitulated to Yasmin's tacit demand, and only put out yellow-ish things; it wasn't as though he didn't like orange juice, or scrambled egg, or bananas or cornflakes. It just seemed easier. And he got used to not having his coffee until after breakfast.

He got so used to it, that during a work-away day, when his team all met up at 8 a.m. for breakfast at some Georgian mansion in Wimbledon, he was appalled to notice that he had only selected yellow things from the breakfast buffet, when all the multicoloured glories of fruit salad, baked beans and fried sausages were spread out before him, and that he had poured himself a juice rather than a coffee. It was as though Yasmin might have been humouring him rather than the other way around; as though she would be revelling in the freedom of eating Coco Pops and tea and straw-berry yoghurts, if that fussy old Asif wasn't around. Sometimes he wondered whether he was halfway to a diagnosis of AS himself, even though he knew logically that was impossible; you couldn't be a little bit non-neurotypical, just like you couldn't be a little bit pregnant, or married or dead.

Asif makes his way through the higgledy-piggledy streets, and descends into Finchley Central tube station with all the other invisible suits; some clutching their coffees in paper cups, some already braying importantly into their mobile phones. If they were that important, they wouldn't live around here, reflects Asif. He is just thinking that the office never calls him on his company phone, when it starts buzzing in his pocket, and then ringing discreetly; he drops his ancient briefcase trying to locate it, and then when he finally gets the phone, it leaps out of his hands with a gleeful life of its own, and he catches at it awkwardly, and answers breathlessly while the other smug suits watch him with amusement, his cloak of invisibility discarded with his comic strip clumsiness. 'Hello?' he asks.

'Asif Murphy?' demands a stern female voice, which sounds vaguely familiar but which he cannot place.

'Yes, Asif Murphy speaking,' he whispers with embarrassment, as he hates saying his name out loud in public.

'Clodagh here. Hector's got a client dropping in this morning, and needs to see the Gough Jenkins unsecured creditor files A–D; you signed them out of the file store on Friday.' No wonder Asif couldn't quite place her voice, he hardly ever had occasion to speak to Clodagh, a lipsticked dragon with a helmet of grey bobbed hair; she's Hector's PA and guards access to him fiercely. Hector is the Partner responsible for Corporate Recovery Services, and is so important that he never seems to do any work apart from striding noisily in and out of the office, smelling of luxurious cologne and lavish lunches, and cavalierly signing off departmental expenses and appraisals with the easy confidence of someone who knows that the details have already been scrutinized by his harder-working minions.

Asif replies nervously, 'They should be back in the file store now; I gave them to Terry to drop back in on Friday afternoon.'

'Terry?' asks Clodagh, sounding disbelieving.

It occurs to Asif that she might not know who Terry is, as he is not yet qualified and below even Asif in the office hierarchy. He starts to explain, 'Terry, the Receiverships Assistant. He sits round the corner near the photocopiers, black spiky hair . . .' The tube has finally come in, but Asif is too distracted to compete for a seat, and instead stands squashed just inside the sliding doors.

'I know who Terry is, Asif,' she says coldly, her tone adding 'Imbecile' so clearly that the word itself isn't necessary. 'He's not here today, and

63

neither are those files. I suggest you come in as quickly as possible and locate them. The meeting's at 9.30 a.m.'

'Sorry, was that 9.30? I'm losing the signal,' says Asif a little wildly, just before he does, and the tube hurtles underground. He's sure that she has probably hung up anyway. Bloody unreliable Terry. He probably dumped the files in the first convenient meeting room, and carried on chatting up Helena, a secretary at the Corporate Financial Services department next door. He checks his watch, he'll probably get into work for 8.45 a.m., which will give him a little under forty-five minutes to locate the files, assuming his immediate boss doesn't pounce on him for the latest adjudication spreadsheet. He feels very vulnerable as he puts his phone away in his pocket, and has a small moment of panic when he can't locate his briefcase in the crush. It is his father's old briefcase, dilapidated but irreplaceable, and he thinks he might have left it on the platform, but then realizes with a too-obvious breath of relief that it is rammed between his feet. He feels that everyone has been staring at him, even though now they are just looking dead-eyed and bored, as they scan the ads on the tube, shuffle uncomfortably, and try to read their papers or paperbacks. He is rammed up against another suit, a young man who doesn't look so different to him, except he has fair hair instead of brown. 'Bloody Mondays, eh, mate,' says the fair young man in an Australian accent. Asif nods, and looks at his feet, both comforted and humiliated by the unexpected sympathy. Sometimes he feels just as confused as Yasmin by the odd intimacy of the tube carriage, where disparate strangers are united by the simple fact of going in the same direction, where each person is close enough to kiss five others. Yasmin's dislike of the tube is one of the things that endears her to Asif, as it is something they share, and something that is reassuringly normal; everyone hates the tube.

Asif leaves Temple underground station with his back to the beauty of the river on a chilly winter morning. He strides as quickly as possible through the sharp air towards the grey monolith of a building which houses the multinational where he works. Accountants' Anonymous, Lila has called it with unnerving accuracy; as though it were some sort of self-help group. My name is Asif Murphy, and I'm an Anonymous Accountant, he imagines announcing during the department's monthly meeting; don't they always say that the first step to getting help is admitting that you have a problem? He walks past the massive marble reception desk, decked out with expensive imported flowers, and swipes his card to call the lift. A couple of people from Tax get on at the second floor; they are both from Asif's graduate intake, and took their conversion and intermediate exams with him. They greet Asif cheerfully with the comfort of superiority; Asif notes glumly how much more prosperous they look than him already; Tax always gets the best pay packages. Asif gets off at the fifth floor, and pauses at his desk only to switch his computer on, and deposit his briefcase, before charging around to Terry's patch. The files are nowhere to be seen, and he starts a methodical search of all the public areas in the department, and then the meeting rooms. The last one is Meeting Room 510c, which is rarely used, as it is tiny and windowless, and the lights sometimes flicker. He strides in and yelps with surprise.

'Oh Christ, I'm sorry,' he says, backing out. Sitting in the room is possibly the most beautiful woman in the world, breastfeeding a tufty-haired baby, which pulls itself off with indignant fury at the interruption, and screams with a wide open gummy mouth and tightly shut eyes. The beautiful woman's brown nipple is left briefly exposed to the air, but she calmly covers it with her hand, read-justs her shirt, and puts the baby down in a car seat next to her. The woman's hair is a shining, liquid curtain of dark silk, cut just below her jawline; she has bright brown eyes that tilt up slightly, as though catching the tail of a smile.

'For God's sake, Melody, calm down,' she says firmly to the baby, who obediently stops screaming, and starts sucking her fist instead, looking with intense concentration at the bright spiral of soft toys that hangs above her from the handle of the infant seat. 'Don't apologize. Have you got this room booked? I was told it was the most likely to

66

be free.' The woman picks up her pinstriped suit jacket, and shrugs it on.

'I'm really, really sorry,' repeats Asif. 'The room's free, I was just looking for some files. I didn't mean to disturb you.' The woman smiles, and under her frank gaze, her glowing maternal proficiency, Asif feels bathed in kindness, and has a sudden urge to confide in her, to tell her about the call from Clodagh, the unreliability of Terry, the threat of Hector, all the stupid little details of his morning that no one in the world would care about.

'I said don't apologize. She'd pretty much finished anyway, and it's not the first time that Melody's exposed my boob to the world, she gets distracted by everything these days. At least it didn't happen in the canteen, in front of the whole office having their Marmite on toast.'

Melody has been looking suspiciously at Asif, with twinkling slanting eyes like her mother's, as her chubby paws tug busily at her spiral toy. She finally succeeds in dislodging it, causing the colourful fabric coil, the unconvincing purple sheep and red cow and green lion to fall in a tinkling, rattling, squeaking pile on her lap. She explodes in laughter at her achievement, chortling so uproariously that Asif briefly thinks that she might be having some sort of attack. Every tiny feature on her round face is caught up in her giggles and her whole plump body bounces with pleasure.

'Your baby's gorgeous,' Asif says. He's seen smiling, laughing babies in adverts, but never in real life before; he finds it amazing that a baby could have so much capacity for happiness, for such uncomplicated joy. Yasmin, he remembers, was either angry or shouty as a baby, and drove the whole household to distraction.

'She looks like her dad,' replies the woman a bit dismissively.

'No, she looks just like you,' says Asif, before realizing what he's said. The woman smiles again, accepting the compliment with the ease of someone used to them, and picks up the infant car seat containing her still chuckling child.

'I'll get out of your hair,' she says, hoisting it up a bit awkwardly, waving Asif away as he steps forward to help. 'Melody's babysitter should be downstairs by now.' She walks towards the lift, and calls out, 'Good luck with finding those files.'

At 9.20 a.m. Asif admits defeat, and shamefacedly trudges to Clodagh's desk; 'I'm sorry, I've looked everywhere, I can't find the files that Hector wanted.'

Clodagh looks up at him, frowning. 'Of course you can't find them. They're with Hector. We found them in the file store after all. I left you a message on your voicemail. Didn't you check it?'

When Asif goes to his desk, sure enough, the little red light on his phone is winking. He hadn't noticed in his hurry. If he wasn't surrounded by people he'd bang his head on his desk in frustration; he goes to the bathroom, and does it against the mirror instead; strongly enough to feel it, quietly enough not to arouse suspicion from those outside. How-bang-stupid-bang-could-bang-he-bang-possibly-bang-be?!-bang-Bang-BANG; he remembers Lila's taunting childhood cry, 'You stupid, stupid, BOY!' as though his stupid-ness and his boy-ness were all wrapped up together in the same untidy parcel. He takes a leak, and breathes deeply before he looks at himself in the mirror once more; he is reassured to see that he looks just like anyone else, competent and unimportant. He strolls out of the bathroom and goes back to work; he has some figures relating to the Burrows Carlin receivership to deliver for lunchtime.

MILK AND LEMONADE

'If Yas is so clever, why does she still wear nappies?' asked Lila loudly, while she and Asif were playing in the corner of the garden. She was wearing jeans and a bubble-gum-pink T-shirt bearing the legend 'Pop Princess' with a crown and microphone motif; she was tall for nine years old, almost as tall as Asif.

'Shush,' said Asif, with a worried glance towards Yasmin, who was walking solemnly around the garden in concentric circles. The circles were getting larger and larger, which was why their mum had told them to play in the corner, where they wouldn't get in her way and cause a meltdown. As far as Asif could see, 'meltdown' was a word their mum had invented just for Yasmin; it allowed her to have a big screaming tantrum over nothing at all, and be soothed and cuddled and treated as though she'd hurt herself falling over. If Lila ever got cross or made a fuss over something stupid, she didn't get petted and looked after, she just got in trouble and sent to her room. Asif didn't like the idea of getting in trouble, so never got cross or made a fuss; sometimes he was so quiet and well-behaved that his mother didn't notice he was there; a model, mannequin of a child.

'Leah's sister is three years old, and she doesn't wear nappies any more. I don't even remember ever wearing nappies, so I must have stopped when I was a baby,' Lila continued. 'Yas is REALLY old to wear nappies; most people are at school when they're six, and NO ONE wears nappies at school.'

Yasmin stopped walking and turned towards Lila, but her eyes remained firmly down towards her own feet. 'I know you're talking about me, you're speaking really loudly, and I heard you say my name.'

'I told you to shush,' whispered Asif nervously to Lila, waiting for the dreaded meltdown.

'I was just saying that you were old to wear nappies,' said Lila defensively.

Yasmin nodded, now looking in Lila's direction, but not at her face. 'Yes, I am old to wear nappies. Most children stop wearing them at two or three years old. I still need them because I'm special, because my brain works in a different way and knowing when to go pee-pee isn't that important to it. And Mum calls them my Big Knickers, not nappies, but the box calls them 'Pull Ups' because you have to pull them up . . .' Yasmin carried on for about five minutes, and then stopped just as abruptly as she started, and began her circle walking again. Her mind was working furiously as she walked with slow, outward calm. Asif and Lila didn't realize that she was retracing the circles that

71

their mum had painted in whitewash on the lawn the previous summer, to teach Yasmin about personal space. Their mum had drawn them, as she'd noticed that Yasmin had no appropriate idea of this, and would sometimes stand close enough to a stranger to feel the warmth of their body, but would scream if a family friend came to give her a hug or kiss. Yasmin had stood in the middle of a small circle, which showed how close family could be to her, and then a bigger circle was drawn for friends, and then a bigger one for acquaintances, and then a bigger one for people like the postman, and then the biggest one for strangers. Their mother was careful to explain situations where the circles didn't work, like on the tube when everyone gets squish-squashed together, but that's only because there isn't enough room; she had to remind Yasmin that in a tube with lots of space, you shouldn't stand right next to someone.

Yasmin found these rules confusing. She tried to follow them, but felt they were counter-intuitive. She liked the warmth and the smell of pretty ladies in the street or shops, she liked to stand close to them, even if she didn't know them, and she liked the fact that she had nothing to say to them, and they had nothing to say to her, so they wouldn't bother her. She didn't like being pulled in a constrictive embrace by people she did know, and she didn't like being kissed with wet icky mouths and being inspected and asked about herself; the glare of attention made her itch, like sunlight did, and she'd rather turn her back to them and look at something else, like the bobbles of paint on the wall, or the leaves on a tree. She liked being close to her pretty mother above all; she liked the feel of her soft, sweet-smelling flesh; her mother didn't grab and squeeze her, but let Yasmin climb on her knee or on to her lap, where she could slip off just as freely if she wanted to. Sometimes, for Yasmin, the urge to be close to her mother was so strong that it was almost primal, it was a physical urge that felt more urgent than her need to pee, or sneeze or scratch; like a newborn's urge to suck. And yet at the same time, although she liked to touch, to put her hand on her mother's face or throat, to gather the warmth through her fingertips, she couldn't bear to be touched herself. She wanted to be close, she wanted even to be held, but without being touched, without the constraints of an embrace. It was something else that confused her, as though different bits of her brain were having an inconclusive argument, and pulling against each other.

'You think you're so clever, don't you, Yas?' said Lila with surprising bitterness for such a sweet-faced child, watching her sister walk in the largest circle yet, one that practically squeezed Lila and Asif into the flower-bed. She scratched the dry skin on the backs of her arms distractedly.

'Yes, I think I'm clever,' replied Yasmin, surprisingly unoffended by the interruption. 'I have a high

IQ and can beat Mum at chess and know all my times tables up to twenty and further, I can do times tables that aren't even in the books.' She paused, and said matter-of-factly, without any trace of vanity, 'I'm cleverer than you are and I'm only six.'

Asif looked at Lila's face with worry, hoping she wouldn't explode; it was just Yasmin being Yasmin. Lila's scratching had moved from the backs of her arms to the insides of her elbows, and became deeper and more aggressive; she didn't even seem to know that she was doing it, until Asif pulled her hand away with a gentle, careful gesture. Lila glanced at him, and then ran over to Yasmin, catching her in an aggressive bear-hug, channelling her unexpressed violence into extrovert, unwanted affection; 'Hoity-toity Yasmin! Hoity-toity Princess Yasmin, Hoity-toity Little Miss Yasmin,' Lila chanted, as she cuddled and nuzzled the struggling younger girl. Although Lila had shown some control in displacing her urge to hit Yasmin into a hug, Yasmin didn't seem to like it any better, and wriggled and screamed for Lila to let go.

'Lila, that's enough,' their mother called from the kitchen window, where she was making dinner. 'You know Yasmin doesn't like it.'

'Sorry, Mum,' said Lila, her face lighting up at this small attention from her mother, at the sound of her name being called. Asif, sitting invisibly on the edge of the flower borders, felt stupid for envying her.

'Yasmin,' said Lila, with a look of mischievous

74

cunning, 'as you're so clever, would you like to learn a little rhyme we're doing at school?'

'Yes,' said Yasmin promptly, as she liked rhymes.

'You have to do the actions with me: Milk, Milk,' she said, pointing to where her T-shirt covered her flat nipples. 'Lemonade,' she added, pointing to where her pee-pee came from. 'Turn around and chocolate's made,' she finished, turning and patting her bottom. 'Do it with me, if you want?' she suggested sweetly.

'Milk, Milk, Lemonade, Turn around and chocolate's made,' chanted Yasmin, mimicking Lila perfectly. They did it a couple more times, and Yasmin started repeating it incessantly, with the inappropriate gestures, and Lila started bursting with laughter. 'You're so funny, Yas,' she cackled.

'Lila, you shouldn't have done that,' said Asif, trying to sound firm, 'it's not a nice rhyme to teach to Yasmin.'

'It's funny! Everyone knows it at school. Don't be such a stupid boy, Asif.'

'I'll tell Mum,' threatened Asif weakly, knowing that he wouldn't.

'As if, Asif!' said Lila. 'Look at Yasmin, she's still doing it.'

Yasmin's chanting was enough to get their mum's attention, and she came out of the kitchen, an apron over her jeans and pink blouse; with her bare feet and loose hair, she and Lila looked disconcertingly similar, and Asif realized that Lila must have dressed deliberately to copy their mother that morning.

'Yasmin, who taught you that rhyme?' asked Mum, sitting on the grass so that Yasmin could sit on her lap if she wanted. Yasmin dropped immediately onto her mother's stretched-out legs, and pressed her face against her chest, breathing in her scent, and then just as quickly got up again, as though she had thought better of what she was doing. 'Yasmin, who taught you that rhyme?' Mum repeated patiently in exactly the same tone, as Yasmin had clearly been so distracted by her mother coming into the garden that she hadn't listened to what she'd been asked.

'Lila,' said Yasmin, looking at the ground, and beginning to retrace her circles, divorcing herself from any further discussion.

'It wasn't me, it was Asif,' said Lila unconvincingly, putting her hands in her jeans, and walking a little closer to her mother. She longed to be able to sit down in her mother's lap as easily as Yasmin had, but somehow, when Yasmin was around, it was tacitly understood that Mum's lap was for her alone. Because Yasmin was special.

'No it wasn't,' said Asif, coming forward on to the lawn, pleased that Lila had mentioned his name, pleased that he had something to say, however unimportant, and that Mum might finally notice he was there. He gave Lila a grateful glance, but she didn't notice or care for his gratitude.

'Shut-up-you-stupid-stupid-BOY,' she hissed at

76

him, unrepentantly, as though it were him rather than Yasmin who had given her away.

'Lila,' said Mum reprovingly, standing up and dusting her jeans. 'You know you shouldn't teach rhymes like that to Yasmin. You know she doesn't understand what it means. It's cruel of you to make fun of her.'

'It's just a rhyme,' Lila tried to explain. 'Everyone at school . . .'

'You should know better, young lady,' Mum continued. 'I'd like you to go to your room until dinner, and think about what you did.'

'But it's just a stupid rhyme!' exploded Lila furiously at the injustice of this. 'She can say that she's cleverer than me, but I can't even tell her a stupid rhyme in case she doesn't understand. It's not fair, it's NOT FAIR.' She stamped her feet to make her point, and when this got no reaction from her mother, she slapped her own face, with her mouth set in a defiant, fuming line.

'Stop that, Lila, you know that doesn't get you any attention,' Mum said. 'Now please go to your room. I'll come and get you for dinner.'

Lila slapped her own face once more, so hard that tears started to escape from her furious eyes, and ran to the kitchen door, the pale bottoms of her bare feet smeared with garden dirt. 'I HATE you, I wish you were DEAD,' she screamed, as she slammed the door and ran upstairs.

Yasmin had paid no attention to Lila, and continued to walk in circles around where her mother and Asif now stood, only looking up briefly when the door slammed, as though it were an event unrelated to her, like a car backfiring in the street. Asif's mum glanced down, and gave him a brief, capable smile, 'Don't worry, Asif. I know she doesn't really want me dead,' she said. 'I'll go up to her in about twenty minutes or so.' She called over to Yasmin, 'Come on Yasmin, time for your bath before dinner,' and Yasmin followed her into the house.

Asif was in the garden on his own. He knew that Lila didn't really want their mother dead; he suspected that it wasn't their mother she was talking about. And he saw from the sorrowful look in their mother's eyes, when Lila slapped herself and stamped and shouted, that their mother loved Lila, even when she was bad. Maybe even because she was bad, because that was how she got their mum to notice her, how she stole just a little bit of Mum's loving attention from Yasmin, who was so special and needed her more. He knew that Mum would go up to Lila's room later, and would stroke her hair and kiss her if Lila said she was sorry, and Lila wouldn't mind saying sorry even if she wasn't, because all she had wanted was this, to have Mum alone in her room, stroking her hair, and giving her a kiss. It was the definition of a mum, thought Asif, the one person who loves you if you've been bad.

The thing is, he thought, alone and ignored in the garden, how do you get someone to love you when you've been good? When you're so good you may as well be invisible. He realized, unhappily, that he'd never known any other way to be. It was always As If he wasn't there.

THE WOMAN IN THE MIRROR

Lila is in the record shop, standing behind the counter, her fingers lightly strumming along to the insistent beat of a new band's CD. She is thinking about her awful painting, which she had taken to the park and burned in cheerful defiance of the local borough's regulations relating to naked flames and wooded areas; she had been surprised that no one stopped her, as she hadn't made any attempts to hide what she was doing, and had chosen an open, clear bit of ground to make her painting's funeral pyre out of bits of old wood. The park, however, had been very quiet; it was one of those dismal February evenings, and the cold was so bitter that only the most arrogant and dogged of joggers attempted to brave it.

Lila had enjoyed burning the painting more than she enjoyed creating it. In fact, destroying it had almost felt like part of the creative process, the final treatment of cold air and flame like a varnish to seal and complete the work, fusing with the wood, metal and mud that she had already embedded in the painting. There was something primal, something quite literally elemental in the way that the wood embraced the flame, and the mud smears on the canvas went back to mingle with the dank clay earth underfoot. She had filmed the slow process of the painting's destruction, the buckling and warping and melting of the canvas, flakes of hot ash flying off into the air like fireflies and then descending as grey, ghostly specks; she watched the film later that evening, with a bottle of cheap red wine and pizza eaten from the box. She had considered putting on some music to accompany it, something dark and appropriate like *Don Giovanni*, but then decided that would be indulging herself too much, too clichéd and derivative.

Lila's feet are sore in her smart, low-heeled shoes, which match her achingly neutral, elegant outfit; she shifts her weight from one foot to the other, and then sits precariously on the wobbly stool behind the counter. She imagines the film being played backwards, and is strangely touched by the notion of her painting resurrecting itself from damp charred bits to smoking embers, and then finally laid down in smug entirety on its rough twiggy pyre, an unlikely and rather disappointing phoenix in a home-made nest. She is aware that she is a bit too proud of having destroyed the painting, a bit too preoccupied with her negative, anti-constructive act; perhaps this is how criminals feel, arsonists and vandals, perhaps they get addicted to the satisfaction of destruction, the kind of feral satisfaction that most people feel so rarely, only when they smash a glass during an argument with a spouse. Lila hasn't noticed Mikey, her boss, sidle in beside her at the counter.

'Hey, what are you thinking?' he asks in his over-mellow drawl. He beams lazily at her with the confidence of someone who's been told that he has a nice smile, and his loose, unkempt curls give him a cheeky, puppy-ish appearance. He is quite attractive, but in a posh student backpacker way, which seems slightly inappropriate and undig-nified for someone pushing thirty. As Lila smiles back, just to be civil, not enough to show her teeth, she wonders if there are any more irritating ques-tions in the world than the various versions of 'What are you thinking?'; possibly just 'Do you love me?' or worse, its evil twin, 'Don't you love me?', could compete with it.

Mikey appears to be expecting more of a response from her than a vague smile, and so she replies pertly, 'I don't give away that kind of dirt for free,' and pushes her stool back from the counter. Her elbow catches a pile of CDs that she was meant to have been labelling with discount stickers, and they crash to the floor. 'Shit, sorry,' she says, and starts to pick them up.

'No worries, I've got them,' says Mikey. He snorts with disapproval as he comes across a compilation CD of dated Ibiza dance anthems. 'Oh man,' he mutters. 'Might as well leave this one on the floor.' As he crouches before her, Lila is able to confirm that he really does have a superb bum; just as good as Wesley's. The fact that she is noticing this is a clear sign that she is definitely going off Wesley; the sex on Sunday hadn't been nearly as good as she had anticipated, and it had been far too quick; he had been much more concerned with attending to the Dover sole, which had, unlike her, been done to perfection. He had wanted to make love again after they had eaten, and Lila had only agreed out of politeness; he had gone to a lot of trouble with the meal and the champagne and the strawberries. The polite, leisurely sex was even worse than the quick sex at the door; at least there wasn't time to get bored during a quickie. 'So, how about lunch, then?' Mikey says casually, still disconcertingly at her feet, as though he's about to get on one knee and propose.

'Sorry?' asks Lila, who hasn't been paying attention.

'Lunch. Do you fancy going for lunch?' Mikey perseveres, his confidence waning with every word. 'Lunch with me, I mean,' he adds, as though worried that he hasn't made himself absolutely clear. 'I could shut the shop.' Lila has a brief fantasy; she imagines herself breathing huskily, 'Shut the shop but forget about lunch,' and dragging Mikey down on to the grubby parquet floor in the never-visited jazz section, for sweaty, passionate, urgent sex, her hands holding on to that fantastic behind while he pumps and grinds to the sounds of sweet soul music. She looks at him assessingly, surprised to find herself entertaining her unromantic, sluttish notion; she has condoms in her handbag, and he probably wouldn't refuse. After all, he'd asked her to lunch, and in Lila's experience, lunch was down payment on drinks and dinner, which was down payment on a snog, which was down payment on sex, probably by the third date. But the truth was that she didn't really fancy Mikey that much, and if she shagged him, she'd obviously have to get another job, or be stuck screwing her ganja-scented boss every other morning whether she wanted to or not, just to avoid hurting his feelings. Polite sex was the last thing she wanted. Which brought her back to the problem of Wesley. Why had Wesley suddenly become a problem, just after some less than impressive shagging? He was still one of the nicest men she'd dated, and it occurs to Lila that the things she liked about Wes to begin with are the very things that are starting to annoy her. When she'd first met him, she'd enjoyed his Ivy League civility, his wow-great enthusiasm and the fact that he worked out and could cook and dress better than she could; he was like a gay best friend who wanted to have sex; he was almost the ideal man.

'Sorry,' says Lila once more, a bit too firmly. She softens her rejection by adding, 'I'm already meeting someone for lunch, actually.'

'Yeah. Your boyfriend, I guess?' asks Mikey, looking

down to hide his disappointment; he busies himself with the CDs, which he stacks and labels with an efficiency that belies his self-consciously relaxed demeanour.

'I wish. Nope, I've got a blind date at the coffee shop with some tweedy little researcher; they're doing a documentary about Yasmin.' When Mikey looks blankly at her, Lila feels she has to add, 'My little sister.'

'I didn't know you had a sister – is she famous or something?' asks Mikey.

'No, she's autistic,' says Lila flatly, irritated by his interest. She then feels mean for packaging Yasmin into that convenient box, and not saying any more about what a wonderful person she is. She could at least have said that she had Asperger's Syndrome, which always sounded a bit better than autism. Oh sod it; it wasn't up to her to spread the word about Yasmin's special abilities, she was doing a good enough job herself.

'Wicked!' says Mikey inappropriately, before realizing what he's said. 'I don't mean wicked that she's autistic, obviously, just wicked that she's going to be on TV. Let me know if they want to use the shop for any of the filming, no publicity is bad publicity, all that crap.'

Lila smiles weakly, and goes to help a customer who has been waving to her from the World Music section. When she leaves half an hour later for her usual lunch break, she is buttoning up her jacket in the back room when she hears one of

Mikey's doped-out acquaintances say, 'I like your new bird, man. All neat and shiny like a Ralph Lauren catalogue – you just want to mess her all up. What happened to that goth-chick that worked here a couple of months ago?'

'That's her,' Mikey replies. 'Same chick, different outfit. She was someone else a few weeks before that, had blue hair and everything. The girl changes costumes like it's frickin' Halloween. Bit messed up, I guess, but fit as you like. If she wasn't seeing someone I'd be so into her.' Lila feels half vindicated, half compromised, torn between being flattered and belittled. She quietly opens the back door and leaves.

Lila goes to the coffee shop across the street, and sees the researcher waiting for her. He is immediately identifiable; everyone else is self-consciously metrosexual, but he's dressed like a geography teacher, with a duffel coat and screwed-up eyes, like he is concentrating on something, or just very confused. Lila had been intending to lay into him, but he seems heartbreakingly vulnerable surrounded by all the thrusting fashion and killer heels and designer eyeware; he looks as though he is just in his mid-twenties, not very much older than her. She waves to him, makes a face when he blanks her and doesn't bother to wave back, and queues up to get herself a coffee and a sandwich.

'Hi, are you Kalila Murphy?' he asks, as she takes a seat opposite him.

'Just her evil twin,' says Lila. 'Call me Lila, everyone

does. So you're Henry Taylor?' She holds out her hand, and when he ignores it, she raises her eyebrows and drops her hand noisily, letting it thump on the table with a dead weight.

'Thanks for meeting me,' says Henry. 'Would you like a coffee?'

'No,' says Lila, as she already has one, which she begins to slurp obviously. She doesn't meet Henry's eyes, as she is aware that she is shortly going to be irredeemably rude to him, and doesn't want to feel any sympathy for him that will stop her saying what she thinks. She notices that he has almost finished his coffee, and that the fingers which are holding the cup are long, slender and tapered, with nails cut as brutally short as her own. Pianist's fingers, her mother would have called them; Yasmin has them too, and plays the piano with a precision so intense that it could almost be described as passionate, even though she shows no emotion when she plays, except to stop crossly if interrupted.

There is an uncomfortable silence, which Henry tentatively breaks. 'Thanks again for meeting me, Lila,' he says, 'I really appreciate it.' When Lila says nothing, he carries on, speaking a bit quickly with embarrassment, and a touching eagerness to please that doesn't match his odd refusal to wave or shake hands. 'I know you don't want to be in the documentary itself, but your thoughts will be really valuable, you have a unique perspective as Yasmin's sister. It's such a fascinating and delicate proposal, we were thrilled to get the go-ahead on it, and want to get the balance just right. Humanity over Disability. Hope over Fear. Understanding over Ignorance. We want to show that people like Yasmin are a gift to us all.' Lila is open-mouthed with outrage at this pompous declaration; she wonders how much of a bloody gift he'd have found Yasmin if he had to grow up with her, but Henry either doesn't notice or ignores her reaction, and carries on, 'What we'd love to hear from you would be any stories or anecdotes from your childhood with Yasmin, from when she started to show the signs of being different and special . . .'

'I'm sorry,' says Lila, cutting across him abruptly; she's heard enough. 'I think you haven't understood why I agreed to meet you. It wasn't to contribute to your crappy documentary, and I don't intend to spout a load of heart-warming bullshit about Yasmin for you to spin into a shiny, happy story about AS. It was to tell you that I think it's a bloody awful, bloody irresponsible idea. Who the hell do you think you are, exploiting a kid like Yasmin, throwing her to the slack-jawed masses on a slow telly night just to get your ratings up . . .' Lila notices the researcher screw up his eyes even more, and she snaps, 'And can you cut out looking at me like that. It's really irritating.' She starts to scratch the inside of her elbow, which is also really irritating her, and stops herself, ramming her hand between her knees under the table.

'Well, this is awkward,' says Henry.

'Awkward for you, I'm not the one taking advantage of a messed-up orphaned teenager . . .' starts Lila, puffing up with righteous indignation. 'And I've asked you to stop doing that thing with your eyes . . .'

'Awkward for both of us,' interrupts Henry. 'I guess you haven't noticed that I'm blind.'

'Oh,' says Lila inadequately, pulling back into her chair. 'Sorry,' she adds. She raises a hand, and waves it tentatively across his face. 'But your eyes moved, you're not totally blind, are you?'

'No,' agrees Henry, 'I've got a little peripheral vision left. That's why I'm able to come somewhere like this without my dog.'

'Your dog,' repeats Lila, feeling very foolish; how could she not have noticed that she was insulting a blind bloke? She was getting like Yasmin; so self-absorbed that she couldn't even see what was right in front of her, across a steel table at a crowded café. 'No stick then?' she adds, just to lighten the mood.

'It's here,' says Henry, patting the inside of his duffel coat. 'It's retractable.'

'Retractable,' repeats Lila, once more. 'You're right, this is awkward,' she agrees. She waits a moment, fiddling with her teaspoon, and then asks, 'Would you like another coffee?' with the intention of being kind, as she notices that his cup is finally empty.

'No, thank you,' says Henry; his voice is perfectly

polite, but lacks the warmth and eagerness he has shown previously. 'But I would like to know why you think the documentary is irresponsible, why you describe it as exploitative? You have read the proposal, haven't you? We don't want to be sensationalist or misrepresent the truth for ratings; this sort of thing is never a commercial success, it's about integrity, about recognizing and celebrating difference with dignity. Yasmin could be someone who inspires hope in families who've had a son or daughter diagnosed with AS or autism. She could help people understand more about her condition, by showing how she experiences the world. That's why Yasmin's agreed to do this; she wants to show that it's possible for someone like her to overcome everyday difficulties faced by people on the autistic spectrum, to communicate comfortably with people and lead a normal life.'

'Normal? There is nothing normal about Yasmin's life, and there hasn't been since she got the diagnosis,' explodes Lila. 'She was a difficult kid, but then she suddenly became so bloody special and so bloody different just because she can do a few good circus tricks with music and memory, and claims to have the whole world in her head.' Lila adds, a little more calmly, 'It's irresponsible because Yasmin isn't different, and she isn't special; she's just a kid who's been spoilt her whole life because people assumed that she was.'

'So you believe that Yasmin's original diagnosis wasn't correct? Hasn't she been seen by countless specialists since then?' asks Henry reasonably. 'And do you think she's making up the way she sees the world? That would involve having an incredibly vivid imagination, which in itself would be fascinating for someone on the autistic spectrum. And what about the feats of memory, those are more than mere tricks . . .'

'There's no physical way of proving that she's on the autistic spectrum at all; it's just what a load of quacks came up with when she was a kid to explain why she was such a bloody, screaming horror the whole time. The savant abilities can be just as well explained by her childhood epilepsy; there've been lots of cases of people who acquire weird mental skills after epileptic attacks. And if you were honest, you'd admit that your bloody producers wouldn't give a sod for Yasmin's unique world view or high-minded educative intentions if she wasn't a fashionably skinny nineteen-year-old girl . . .'

'It helps,' admits Henry. 'But Yasmin's still a rarity, there are so few girls with AS, so to find someone who can communicate as clearly as Yasmin about her experiences is special.'

'Exactly! Did you know that less than ten per cent of people diagnosed with AS are girls? And the chances of being a girl with AS *and* savant syndrome are ridiculously small, and the chances of being a girl with AS *and* a savant *and* yet still being someone who can communicate well are so tiny as to be abso-fucking-lutely impossible! It's like saying – wow, that's bloke's blind, but he can still see, he's a bloody miracle! Well, guess what, if he can see, he's not so bloody blind in the first place.' Lila sees Henry's lips quiver, and she's not sure if she's mortally offended him, or whether he's suppressing a smile. She's aware of a stupefied hush from the tables around them, that she has said something so mercilessly inconsiderate.

Henry says nothing for a moment, his slim, pale fingers covering his mouth, and then speaks calmly, with the glowing, exasperating confidence of someone who completely believes that he is right, 'Yasmin might well be one in a million, but think how many millions of people live in the UK alone. Think about it, Lila; it's a vast, vast world, and amazing things can happen. Just because something is very unlikely, doesn't make it impossible . . .'

As he says this, Lila remembers the first time that someone described Yasmin as one in a million. It was her speech and language developmental therapist, when Yasmin was eight years old; Yasmin, who loved statistics, had seized on this with annoying certainty. 'I'm one in a million,' she had told Lila with a persistence that might have been considered taunting if it hadn't been coming from Yasmin, 'so there are statistically only fifty-eight of me in the UK, and I could meet each one of them for tea between today and April 16th, but I won't as I don't know where they live and I don't like travelling outside of Finchley if I don't have to . . .' She had gone on and on about it, and Lila had really wanted to hit her, but hadn't, of course. Just like Yasmin's IQ score, it was yet another figure that she could brandish around to show that she was special, and that Lila, by comparison, was anything but.

The old feeling of anger from that childhood memory flashes through Lila with a cutting intensity that surprises her, and she spits out, 'So have it your way, she's sodding Miss Spock and sodding Raingirl rolled into one; what the fuck do you people know about her anyway? I'm the one who's had to live with her and watch her get everything her own way, never mind the rest of us. I'm the one who's stuck with the spoilt brat for the rest of my life.'

'I take it that you're a very attractive person,' says Henry calmly, in response to the insulting tirade that has, once again, drawn glances from the other tables.

'Why do you say that?' asks Lila suspiciously.

'Because you don't seem to be a very nice person; I guess you have to get by on your looks.' Lila's jaw drops in shock, and she hears a muted cheer from the next table.

'Oh sod off, I don't need this shit,' says Lila, her voice breaking into an angry sob, and she storms out of the café. She turns into the anonymous Marks & Spencer's further up the road, and goes into the ladies' changing rooms to cry. She bangs her head against the mirror; 'Why am I such a fucking bitch?' she asks her reflection, which is blurry through her tears. The woman in the mirror looks wrong, in her perfectly neutral clothes. The doors to the changing cubicles line the wall, and she feels like Alice, trying to choose which one to enter along an endless corridor. If only she could try on the right clothes, she could try on the right life and go through the right door to the place where the normal people lived, where she would no longer feel embittered and bruised and scarred. As Lila silently weeps, the impeccably dressed woman in the mirror mimics her cruelly, mocking her with her sullen mouth and damp, swollen eyes; however much Lila stares her out, she doesn't go away. Lila feels sorry for the woman; she's ugly, inside and out. She realizes that it's not just Yasmin she's stuck with; it's herself.

GARDEN IN THE WILDERNESS

My name is Yasmin Murphy, and sometimes I am so full of things to say that I'll feel that I'll burst if I can't get them out, and will talk, and talk, and talk until I can see people fidget and move uncomfortably and want to go to the loo. And now I know to stop and take a break for other people to say something or go to the loo, even though I still want to say everything that I was thinking of, but when I was little I would just go on and on without stopping for anyone, and would scream and hit something if I was interrupted.

And sometimes I have nothing to say at all, because there is so much stuff in my head that I can't choose what to say, and so I just think it all instead, and it takes over so much that I stop whatever I was meant to be doing on the outside, which is why I like to do soothing and repetitive things that don't require my attention, like walking in a circle or washing up.

I don't think that I have a very tidy mind, because to have a tidy mind, it needs to be small enough to keep it neat and orderly and to have a place for everything. Like our garden, which has nine square metres of decking, ten square metres of grass, eight square metres of flower borders including the walnut tree, and one square metre with vegetables that Asif and I planted together; it is easy to keep our garden orderly, because if there is something Mostly or Wholly Irrelevant in the garden, like a weed or a lager can that someone has thrown in from the street, I can put it in the compost pile or rubbish bin. If I want to walk about our garden, in a circle around the lawn, or sometimes in straight lines up and down the decking, I don't have very far to go before I come back to where I started. My mind is not like a neat and tidy garden; it is a vast untidy wilderness, full of irrelevancies, but with lots of places to wander and get lost. Sometimes I do get lost, and fall into the past; I sit in my memory like a spectator and watch myself during a past event, and sometimes in my mind I have conversations with myself, with all my previous selves that I meet in my memory, which feel just as real as the conversations I have with other people. It is like having an imaginary friend, only I am not very imaginative, and so my imaginary friends are just the same as me.

Because of my untidy wilderness mind, which makes me talk too little or too much, I have always found it hard to make friends, and when I was little, I had no friends at all my own age. But a friend is just someone you talk to and do things with, so my mum was my best friend, and when she died,

Asif became my best friend instead. Lila wasn't my friend as she didn't do things with me as we don't like the same things because Lila is generally not very clever and as a child she was sometimes very stupid. I had my last epileptic fit when I was eight years old, and I remember her just standing there staring at me instead of getting help, before she screamed and the grown-ups came for her, which is how they found me. Mum said she panicked, which is something stupid people do when they can't remember what to do in case of an accident or emergency. Once I was out of hospital, two weeks later, Lila tore her wrist open with a can, but I didn't panic, as I recognized that this was an accident or emergency, and I remembered what to do. I called the emergency services, even though I don't like speaking to strangers, and gave our address, and the ambulance arrived and took care of her quickly and she didn't even get much of a scar. I was told that I was very brave and got a Blue Peter badge for my quick thinking, which upset Lila, as she had always wanted a Blue Peter badge.

I saw a movie recently, about a schizophrenic maths professor who made up his best friend out of his own mind, and really believed that his friend was as real as he was. I think it would be nice to make your own friends out of your mind, creating them so well that they feel real; it would be a little like being God, who created Adam and Eve, possibly because he was lonely and wanted someone to talk to him and keep him busy (although it seems to me that God is derivative rather than creative in this respect, because he created Adam and Eve 'in his image', which means to look like him, rather than making them unique). I'm not imaginative or schizophrenic so I can't make up my own friends, but sometimes I have a dream that is so realistic it is just like real life; I dream that I am lying in bed watching the moonlight shadows move slowly across the ceiling, but then I realize that it is a dream, and that I can do anything I want to, and so I fly around my room, where everything is ordered and familiar to me, but I don't open the window and fly outside, where everything is disordered and strange.

I like this dream, as it is very neat and contained, and contains no irrelevancies; it is comforting, as it is like a tidy garden in my untidy mind. And with my sight slowly deteriorating, I like to be in tidy places, where I already know where everything is. Like our back garden, the dream is a safe place for me to be.

SOLUTIONS NOT PROBLEMS

Asif is worried, which isn't unusual, as it is his habitual resting state since childhood. He is worried about Lila, whom he hasn't heard from in over two weeks; she hasn't returned his phone calls, which isn't all that odd, as sometimes she goes through periods when she just doesn't. She has even criticized him in the past for his own diligent habit of returning calls promptly; he remembers her telling him once to try not returning any work-related calls at the office: 'You'll make yourself so much more important,' she said cynically. 'People will have to chase you instead of the other way around. Just make sure that when someone does get hold of you, you act very busy, surly and stressed out, and withhold anything useful. By making yourself unavailable and uncooperative, your value will shoot up; it's market dynamics, you'll be a rare commodity.' She had said it in that dry way of hers, so Asif wasn't sure if she was making fun of him, or just the place that he worked. The scary thing was that she was probably right; he knew that the people he feared at work weren't those who were necessarily superior to him in the office hierarchy, but those who didn't have the time of day for him and treated him with contempt, like Clodagh, Hector's flint-haired, fire-breathing PA.

Asif is also worried about Yasmin, as the first stage of filming is due to start just after her half-term break. Yasmin dislikes changes to her schedule, and he is unsure how she will cope with the film crew, who are meant to observe but will doubtless get in the way and cause a meltdown of unforeseen proportions which will get recorded for posterity. He's not sure about the wisdom of having the documentary filmed so close to Yasmin's A levels, but Yasmin has been oddly insistent that she wants the filming done as soon as possible.

Yasmin does not seem perturbed by the potential disruption, and has become unnervingly calm and even more self-absorbed of late; when he talks to her, she looks so blank and withdrawn, he has to suppress the urge to shout, to make sure he gets heard; it feels like she answers him from a long way away, and although she remembers to make eye contact, it is as though she is looking through, rather than at him. He wonders what his dead father, who only knew Yasmin when she was a screeching, head-banging toddler, would make of her now, the outwardly serene, unnaturally composed young woman she was becoming, who now remembered to say the correct thing for given situations, more often than not, but with as little feeling as a pre-programmed automaton.

After all their hard work on Yasmin's social skills, perhaps their dad wouldn't think that the difference was much of an improvement at all.

Asif is also worried, in a vague indefinable way, about the woman he interrupted breastfeeding; he has looked for her every day, dawdling in the corridor which leads to the never-used windowless meeting room, but he has not seen her again. When he asked the secretaries casually in the Corporate Recovery and Corporate Financial Services departments if they had seen a woman with a baby, they looked at him as though he was mad, and having Madonna and child delusions. He begins to wonder if he really could have imagined the whole thing; it seems unlikely that he'd have a hallucination, but people did, didn't they? People who seemed perfectly normal sometimes had hallucinations with perfectly normal medical explanations; perhaps there'd been a funny mushroom in his Thai take-away on the Sunday night, perhaps there is a rapidly expanding tumour in his brain that needs urgent treatment. Perhaps he is an undiagnosed schizophrenic, like that genius maths professor in the movie that he and Yasmin watched the other week. He knows that it is ridiculous to entertain the idea that he has made up a lactating mother with chuckling infant, but the beauty of the woman is what throws him; could she possibly have been too beautiful to be true?

As Asif sits at his desk, Terry, the spiky-haired assistant, drops the latest management memo into his heaving in-tray – Asif scans the document without really reading it; the jargon has long since lost the power to alarm or motivate him, although he secretly admires whoever cares enough to put this sort of blurb together. The text blurs into one indistinct phrase: Working Smarter not Harder Exceed Expectations Be Proactive not Inactive Seek Solutions not Problems Emotivate to Empower Accentuate the Positive Everything is Possible No 1 in Team Optimism in Opportunity . . .

Ravi from Corporate Financial Services walks by, reading his own copy of the memo; he scrunches it up, and throws it into Asif's bin with impressive accuracy; 'Thank God for the Holy Memo, eh, Murphy?' he says. 'Here was I planning to sit on my sweet butt all day, but now I've read that I'm going to dedicate the rest of the afternoon to building shareholder value and consistently delighting customers.'

Asif grins sheepishly and shrugs. 'Yeah, me too.' He doesn't dare to throw his own copy of the memo away, although he longs to mimic Ravi's dramatic gesture; Hector is a lot less easy-going than Ravi's boss in CFS. 'Coming down to the King's Head for lunch? Two for one on any meal, botulism comes free,' asks Ravi.

Asif shakes his head, even though most of the team are probably there already. 'Sorry, mate, too much shareholder value to build,' he points to his overflowing intray. 'I'll just grab a sandwich from downstairs.' He has a secret, embarrassed pride at being busy; the one thing Asif is good at is his work. Not at the politics or the office camaraderie or anything that would ever get him towards management or promoted any faster than the rest of his graduate intake, but at being a worker drone for the colony, he excels. His attention to detail is meticulous, his figures are accurately sourced, his spreadsheets are crisp and informative; he even excels at Excel.

Be Proactive not Inactive Seek Solutions not Problems, thinks Asif on the way to the lift; it is still in his head, those strategy types in Management are cleverer than he likes to admit. He can't do anything about the mystery of the woman who was or wasn't there without drawing further unwelcome attention to himself from the admin team, and he can't do anything about Yasmin's frozen calmness, and so, on his way down to the canteen, he tries Lila again. Her phone rings and he leaves another message. He tries the record shop to ask for her, but the posh, slightly doped-out owner just says, 'She's not around, mate.' The laconic way he says it, it could mean that she's popped out for a couple of minutes, or hasn't been around for days.

'It's her brother, is she all right?' asks Asif, hoping that Lila won't kill him for embarrassing her in front of her boss with his Big Brotherly concern. When he was fifteen, he had gone up to a couple of bigger boys in the playground and told them to leave his little sister alone; the act of bravery had practically caused him to kack his pants, but Lila had been furious with him; they hadn't been picking on her, they'd been chatting her up, and he had destroyed her street cred in one fell swoop. He had been a Stupid Boy yet again.

'She's fan-tas-tic; better red than dead, hey, mate,' says the owner obscurely, before hanging up. Asif leaves the lift at the ground floor, looking at his mobile phone as though it might understand better than he the cryptic clue he's been handed. Better red than dead? Maybe it was her hair; Lila was always changing her hair colour. But she normally did it to mark the end of a particular look or phase, which tended to change with her relationships. Had she broken up with Wesley? He considers calling him, and then thinks better of it; Lila has been less than tactful with her boyfriends in the past, and sometimes hasn't even told them that it was over, assuming they'd get the message when she didn't return their calls. Perhaps, just like office politics, this made her feel more important. It is entirely possible that she has broken up with Wesley and that he's not yet aware of it; which would be an awful shame, as he quite liked Wesley compared to her other boyfriends, as he didn't do drugs and had a proper job.

'Hello again,' says the Most Beautiful Woman in the World, walking past him into the lift.

'Er – hi!' says Asif, almost dropping his phone in shock, having to catch at it like a flapping fish in that undignified way that had so amused the Finchley commuters some days earlier, and then instinctively backs into the lift with her.

'Weren't you going to lunch?' asks the Most Beautiful Woman in the World.

'Yes, I was, I'm just popping back to my desk for something, for my . . . phone . . .' he sees the woman look quizzically at the phone in his hand, and then back at him, 'for my phone . . . charger . . .' he improvises. He realizes that he's alone with her, and is relieved when the lift stops at the first floor, and three Audit grads join them, noisily laughing at some shared joke.

The woman nods, and looks at her own phone, checking a message, when Asif says, without really intending to, 'I'm so glad to see you.'

'Really? Why?' the woman asks matter-of-factly, lifting her chin so her silk curtain of inky hair swishes across her cheekbones.

Asif blushes, as he obviously can't tell her the truth, that he is relieved that she turned out to be real. 'I was worried that I'd frightened you out of the office, barging in on you the other day,' he mumbles instead.

'Oh, I'm a big girl, takes more than that to scare me,' says the woman. 'I've just had to work from home for a bit, my childminder's been ill.' They both get out at the fifth floor. She starts to walk towards the CFS department, and then turns around. 'Sorry, where on earth are my manners? I'm Mei Lin Thompson.'

'Asif Murphy,' says Asif. 'Pleased to meet you.

I work here in Corporate Recovery, moved over from Audit last year. I guess you're in CFS?'

'Nope, further down the corridor. Internal Marcoms, Marketing and Communications, for my sins,' says Mei Lin, nodding at the memos that are already filling the recycling bins at the beginning of the CFS corridor. 'Just back from maternity leave, obviously.' She smiles and turns to leave, and Asif can't bear the thought of looking at her walking away from him, and so he says anything to make her stay; after all, she hasn't yet said goodbye.

'Mei Lin's a great name, are you part Chinese?'

'Half, my mum's Malay-Chinese,' she says. 'And you? Irish?'

'Half as well. Half Pakistani too. Half-half,' says Asif, laughing a bit to make it sound like he's made a joke, although he hasn't, and just wishes he could have thought of one.

'Right, well, bye then, see you around,' Mei Lin says, with that tilting smile to her bright eyes, and then strolls off.

Asif doesn't watch her walk away, but he does watch long enough to check that other people have noticed her. Just to make sure that other people can see her too, to make sure that she is real, and that he hasn't made her up. Damn, he should have asked how her baby was. He could have impressed her with his thoughtfulness; women always liked people who remembered to ask after their kids. He remembers the beauty in the baby's laugh, and the cheeky shaving-brush hair and bright gimlet eyes; the kid probably has a handsome high-achiever of a dad. The trouble with meeting the perfect woman, thinks Asif back at his desk, is that she's probably already met the perfect man. He is still worried about Lila and Yasmin, but he puts the worry into a little box in his head to take out later, when he is on his way home and can devote some more time to it. Terry is heading off to the King's Head, and so Asif asks if he'll pick him up a sandwich on his way back from the pub, trying not to plead or sound inappropriately grateful for the favour. Terry forgets, of course, and Asif is starving by the time the team have made it back to the office. He has a couple of packets of crisps from the machine for lunch instead, and tries very hard not to notice the fact that they are yellow.

WHEN SHE WAS BAD

It was a rainy Saturday morning, and Lila was stuck indoors with only Yasmin for company. Their mum was working downstairs with a colleague, and had asked Lila to watch over Yasmin until lunchtime. Asif was out, as he played football on Saturday mornings; he wasn't very good, Lila had seen him play, but he went anyway, probably just to escape. Lila wanted to watch the TV, but the only upstairs TV was in Yasmin's room, and Yasmin didn't seem to want it on. Lila opened Yasmin's door a crack, and saw her sitting in the middle of the floor, surrounded by evidence of her latest obsession, her *Big Book of British Flora and Fauna*, with alphabetized examples in matchboxes, dead insects pinned to cardboard loo rolls and live ones in plastic ice cream tubs in the corner. Yasmin was eight years old, but seemed to have no natural squeamishness when it came to creepy-crawlies; she liked the fact that they were small enough to collect and keep. 'Yuk,' said Lila, watching Yasmin pull something slimy out of a carton, and as Yasmin didn't respond, Lila said it again, louder, 'Yuk!' When Yasmin finally looked up, enquiring rather than annoyed, Lila asked, 'What are you doing with those gross things?'

'They're called slugs,' explained Yasmin patiently, as though Lila were too dumb to know. 'I'm feeding them. I'm giving them all red food today, to see what happens to them.'

'I know they're slugs, they're totally disgusting!' said Lila. 'They're meant to be in the garden, not in your room, what if they got out?'

'If they got out, they'd probably travel up the walls, because the walls are smooth. They wouldn't like the carpet very much, as the pile would scratch them, and they wouldn't get very far,' replied Yasmin, answering the question and missing the point, as usual.

'I meant that it wouldn't be very nice for the rest of us if we had slugs crawling all over the house,' said Lila. 'Look Yas, can I watch the telly please? I'm missing *Superhero Saturday* because Mum asked me to stay up here with you.' Lila didn't ask this with any great hope, because although Yasmin liked Superheros, she didn't like them on Saturdays.

'No thank you,' said Yasmin, turning her back on Lila, and continuing to feed the slugs.

'I said, can *I* watch the telly please?' repeated Lila. 'You don't have to watch it.'

'No, thank you, I said I don't want to watch it,' said Yasmin. 'Lila, could you shut the door? You're distracting me, and I'm busy.'

'You're always busy doing stupid things,' muttered Lila, but it wasn't a question, and so Yasmin didn't answer. Lila shut the door, and went back to her and Asif's room to sulk. 'I'm sooo bored,' she said to the pop-star-postered walls, to her sequinned sorority of Barbie Dolls, to Asif's Miniature Monster Trucks and Robots in Disguise. She wrote in her diary, 'Dear Diary, I will call you Princess Naomi Moonbeam Rainbows from now on, as Diary is a stupid name, and sooo boring. I am writing to say it is absolutely and totally unfair that Yasmin gets to keep yucky slugs in her room, and I'm not allowed to have a puppy, or kitten, or rabbit, or even a hamster that I could keep in a cage, or even a S-O-D-D-I-N-G goldfish in a bowl.' Lila wrote out sodding carefully, as it was something she'd heard at school, but wasn't sure exactly what it meant, or how it was spelt, or whether it was as bad as 'F-U-C-K-I-N-G', which was the most important swear word, as she was never allowed to say it. 'It is also totally unfair that Yasmin gets to have the TV in her room so she can watch her stupid videos for the hundredth time, and Asif and I don't have one, and we're older. It is even more unfair that Yasmin gets a room to herself, but I won't say this to Mum, as then Mum might make me share with Yasmin and give Asif a room to himself, because he's a boy and he's the oldest, and I don't want to share with Yasmin – I think that I would rather BE DEAD than share with Little Miss Spock and her disgusting yukky slug farm.'

Lila looked out of the window, into the little garden, and carried on writing. 'And it's not fair,

Princess Naomi, that I have to be sooo bored and stuck indoors, when other families do fun things on the weekends. Leah's family go swimming to a heated pool, which has squirty things and waves and a fountain, but we never go swimming because Little Miss Yasmin doesn't like it. We never even go out for pizza or burgers because whenever we've tried Little Miss Yasmin makes a fuss and Mum gets annoyed and then we all have to go home, sometimes before we even start. And we never have birthday parties, because Little Miss Yasmin gets upset at having new people in the house and having things moved around. And sometimes, Princess Naomi, although this is a very great secret and you mustn't tell it to ANYONE, not even Asif, I wish that Little Miss Yasmin would just B-U-G-G-E-R back off to her home planet and leave us all alone.' Lila felt satisfied with her day's entry, which wasn't that different from many of the other entries that she had made. She got her felt-tip pens and drew a picture on the opposite page, of Yasmin on a rocket going to a distant planet with rings around it, like Saturn, and of herself and Asif with a puppy, a kitten, a rabbit and a birthday cake with twelve candles to represent her next birthday, and in the bottom left corner she drew her and Mum swimming in a pool with a fountain. She scrupulously used every coloured pen in her drawing, and then added a pool of sticky glitter to represent the water. She accidentally smeared the glitter on her new denim skirt with pink cloth flowers, and in trying to rub it off only rubbed it in deeper; Lila looked at the careless stain with exasperation – this was exactly why Mum told her she couldn't have nice things. When her picture was dry, she locked her diary shut with the special key which she touchingly believed really worked; she didn't realize that anything inserted in the lock, like a paperclip or a nail file, would snap it back open again.

Lila looked at the clock; barely half an hour had elapsed since she looked in on Yasmin; she still had two hours to go until lunch. She heard a funny sputtering noise coming from Yasmin's room, and opened the door again, wondering if Yasmin had at last put the telly on. Instead, she saw Yasmin lying in a shivering, trembling heap on the floor, her eyes right back in her head so she could only see the whites.

'Yas,' said Lila, 'are you playing?' She knew that Yasmin wasn't playing, and she didn't know why she asked. She recognized what was happening, as it had happened before; Yasmin was having an epileptic fit, just like she had when she was three years old, and again a couple of years later. She had until recently been on anti-seizure medicine, but was now being slowly weaned from it. Lila was unable to say anything further, and felt frozen to the spot; she couldn't do anything but helplessly watch as Yasmin drowned and flailed before her on the pile carpet, as though a hole was opening in the floor and was sucking her in like quicksand.

Yasmin's eyes flickered around from the backs of her lids, and focused on Lila without really registering her. Lila could see nothing in Yasmin's eyes, not fear, not reproach, not anger. Lila felt a thought forming in the back of her head, a command; help, her mind prompted her, you need to shout for help, you need to call for Mum. But Lila just stood there, as another, more sickly compelling thought, preoccupied her completely; Yasmin might die. Yasmin might die, and go back to her home planet, just like she wanted. And then it would just be her and Asif and Mum, and they could be a normal family and do all the things she ever wanted. And Lila, instead of being ashamed of this thought, instead of thinking that she should have been more careful about what she wished for, all those times she shouted I-HATE-you-I-wish-you-were-DEAD, found herself feeling a very different emotion. She felt hope. She was an eleven-year-old girl, watching her sister struggle on the floor, daring to hope that she might die. She was a monster. Revolted by herself, Lila finally reacted; she didn't scream for Mum, she just screamed, over and over again, for herself rather than Yasmin, at the horror of what she had become.

Later, when Yasmin was in the hospital with Mum, and Asif and Lila were in the waiting room accompanied by Jilly, their neighbour's inattentive eighteen-year-old daughter, Lila whispered to Asif, 'It's all my fault.'

'No it isn't,' said Asif sensibly, still in his football kit, his legs looking ridiculously thin and gangly dangling out of his shorts; his bony knees almost embarrassed to be on show. 'It's the doctors' fault, they stopped the anti-seizure medicine too soon.' Asif fidgeted in the moulded plastic seating, and continued to rifle through a magazine for something promising to distract him, like a crossword or cartoons. He didn't seem to think that this trip to the hospital was very different from the countless other times they came, usually for Yasmin's routine tests. She'd had epileptic fits before, and she'd always been fine. Just like he'd had mild asthmatic attacks before, and had always been fine, although he constantly kept an inhaler to hand just in case.

'It's my fault,' insisted Lila. 'I killed her. I killed our little sister. I just stood there while she might have been dying.' Tears were rolling down her face with the admission, but she was otherwise pale and perfectly composed. Asif looked at her with surprise; she really seemed to believe what she was saying.

'Don't be soft,' he said briskly. 'You panicked, that's all. That's what Mum said, you panicked.'

Lila shook her head. 'I just stood there, Asif,' she repeated. 'And I thought how easy it would be if she wasn't around.' She turned to check that their neighbour's daughter wasn't listening, but Jilly was still plugged into her earphones, her head bobbing in time to the music. She saw tear-stained

114

Lila look at her, and gave the little girl a reassuring smile and a thumbs up. 'All right?' Jilly
mouthed perkily, and Lila nodded, and turned
away. She whispered urgently to Asif, 'All I could
think of was how much nicer it would be if she
wasn't around. I'm a bad, bad person, and I think
I might be going to hell.'

Asif watched his sister for a moment, and then
took her hand. 'Listen to me, Lila. It's not your
fault. It probably felt like you were standing there
a long time, but Mum said it couldn't have been
more than a minute or two.' He squeezed her palm
reassuringly. 'OK?'

Lila realized that Asif couldn't understand what
she had said, and that he never would. He was
too good himself to understand evil in others; he
didn't let evil enter his world. 'OK,' she promised,
mustering a brave smile. She didn't deserve to live
on the same planet as Asif; she felt as though she
might contaminate him. She didn't deserve to
live on the same planet as Yasmin, either; she had
betrayed her, she had wanted her gone. But Lila
knew that no one would believe her, much less
punish her; if she was going to make things right,
she would have to punish herself.

Asif was still flicking through the magazines, but
he was no longer paying attention as he shuffled
automatically from page to page. He was thinking
that Lila had finally dared to say something he
had been depressingly aware of since he was four
years old; that everything would be so much easier

for them if Yasmin wasn't around. He could never admit this out loud; he wasn't as brave or honest as Lila, he was a coward, a fraud. And when Lila slashed her wrist two weeks later on a jagged can lid, and was rushed to hospital after Yasmin's timely phone call to the emergency services, he knew that it wasn't really an accident, as they all pretended. He knew that it wasn't really a cry for help or attention, as the psychologist insisted. He knew exactly why she did it, and the guilt that knowledge brought tightened his asthmatic chest so much that he couldn't even breathe.

PYJAMAS IN PUBLIC

Lila is nursing a coffee and a hangover in her stone cold flat; she is wearing a pair of her father's stripy old pyjamas, which are far too big for her, the fabric so worn that it gapes into holes at her knees; her hair is dyed a delicious cranberry colour and chopped untidily into a tousled crop. She'd changed her hair on impulse after breaking up with Wes a couple of weeks previously; the sleek café-au-lait style no longer felt right, and she had got bored of having to blow-dry it straight; besides, she'd found the scorching heat of the hairdryer a little too tempting: she'd sometimes held it right against her scalp and the base of her neck until the skin was practically blistered, her insidious itching briefly numbed with the exquisite, ebbing pain. She marked her return to single status by indulging in another impulse, and had foolishly begun sleeping with Mikey. Although to say they were sleeping together was probably too grand a way to describe their sliver of a relationship, as they never actually slept, but simply shagged hurriedly in the back room of the record shop, and once in his cramped Mini

Cooper, an act which was memorable only for its extreme discomfort. She hadn't been interested enough in him to ask him home, and he had surprisingly returned the favour; which Lila realized was unflattering, but something of a relief. He had been a decent enough distraction to start off with, but she soon discovered, bending over the back office desk while he mechanically pounded in time to the music, that he was about as exciting as a masturbatory aid, and arguably less inventive. She became heartily hacked off with the prospect of having sex with him, and had quit her job yesterday evening. The tipping point had been when she heard Mikey boast to one of his cronies about her 'fantastic tits', when he thought she wasn't listening. She told him bluntly she was leaving, adding that their fuck-buddy days were over, and he had the gall to wince at her choice of words.

'Fuck-buddy? Man, that's crude. There's no need to put it like that,' he said reproachfully.

'Sorry, should I have said, "fuck-partner"?' suggested Lila sarcastically.

'You don't need to be like this. You're not just a casual shag, I *like* you, Lila,' Mikey said insincerely, looking at her figure rather than her face.

'Yeah, I heard. You think I'm fan-tas-tits,' she retorted, getting her coat. 'Just post me my cheque, Mikey.'

So here she is, unsurprisingly hungover after finishing two lonely bottles of wine herself in front

118

of the telly last night, boyfriendless, jobless and probably soon to be homeless, as she has no idea how she is going to cover next month's rent. 'Really smart, Lila,' she mutters to herself; she doesn't really regret breaking up with Wes, but she knows that it was downright idiotic to sleep with her boss. But some self-destructive urge had made her take the opportunity, just because it was there. 'I should be locked up for my own safety,' she tells herself. Bloody hell, she has to stop talking to herself like some deranged lunatic, or they really will lock her up.

She pours herself another cup from the cafetière, and notices that the coffee, brewed just a few minutes previously, is already lukewarm, and that her breath is misting in front of her; the flat is much, much colder than usual. She pulls on an oversized cable-knit jumper that hangs snugly to mid-thigh, and a pair of socks, and then checks the boiler; she realizes with a sigh that the heating has packed up again. Asif had advised her to get boiler breakdown insurance last year, and she had laughed, thinking that he'd made it up; the notion that you could get boiler breakdown insurance just seemed ludicrous to her, something that was invented for middle-class professionals who didn't have enough to worry about; like wine buffs insuring their tongues against scalds from hot beverages. It doesn't seem quite so funny now; sensible, solid Asif has been proved right yet again. She automatically goes to call the breakdown number stuck to the fridge, but stops as she remembers that she can no longer afford the usual call-out fee. Bugger, she thinks. And then decides to hell with being a lunatic, and shouts 'Bugger! Bugger! Crappy-Shit-Bugger!' out loud, which makes her feel foolish, but a little better.

She goes back to bed, but it is too cold to sleep, and the small electric fan heater that she has purchased for these emergencies seems to be using all its energy to generate a deathly rattle rather than any heat. And her phone keeps ringing. She unplugs it, but still feels uncomfortable when she thinks of the phone line worming its way into her flat, twanging with the tension of unanswered calls, of unheard, persistent voices. She needs to get out, but she doesn't know where. She looks out on to the grubby street for inspiration, and sees her banged-up old motor gleaming in the chilly sunshine; it occurs to her that the car would be warm if she put the engine on. Lila doesn't think she'd get to the car without being seen by someone; she is incapable of even answering the door to the postman without cosmetically smoothed skin, she's too discomfited by how she looks otherwise, and so she scrapes and scrubs the flaky patches from her face and neck as well as she can with the icy water, and rubs in emollient cream thickly until she has a greasy glow. She then makes up her face and neck sufficiently to show it to the outside world; she checks her reflection, satisfied that she looks like someone normal who has just got out of bed, who just happens to have a dewily perfect complexion. Having got that far, she briefly considers changing, but the flat is too cold to undress, and the thought of even removing her socks fills her with dread. So still in her jumper and pyjamas, she drags her duvet down the rickety communal stairs of her building, out of the heavy front door, across the gritty pavement, and into her car. She starts the engine, turns on the heating, and leans back to feel the magnified sunshine on her face, the wind-screen acting like greenhouse glass. In no time at all she is as warm as toast, and she wishes that she had remembered to bring some down with her to munch on. She fuzzily wonders why she bothers to rent a flat when she can always sleep in her car, and drifts off to a dreamless sleep.

Lila wakes to the sound of an urgent banging on her window. 'Stop, it's not worth it!' shouts a frantic voice, which isn't completely unfamiliar.

Lila looks up blurrily from her duvet, to see the blind researcher from Yasmin's documentary, Henry something or the other, muffled up in a scarf and his duffel coat, and raising his retractable stick with the unmistakable intention of smashing her window. She hurriedly swings open the car door, pushing him back roughly. 'What the fuck are you doing?' she demands. 'You almost broke my window.'

'Are you all right?' asks Henry, suddenly seeming confused, and putting his stick down.

'No, I'm not bloody all right. I'm trying to get some bloody sleep and some batty blind vandal comes along and tries to wreck my car.'

'Sleeping? In your car? With the engine on?' asks Henry.

'Yes, what did you think I was doing, trying to effing top myself?' demands Lila. Once she says this, and sees the look on Henry's face, she bursts into laughter, and feels more cheerful than she has in days. 'Oh my God! You thought that I was going to top myself! In my resident's parking space outside my flat! That's hilarious . . .'

'Sorry,' says Henry. 'I feel so stupid, I was just trying to help.'

'No, thanks, you've made my day,' says Lila, still laughing, even though it makes her head feel sore. 'I'm just here because my heating's gone off. Did you think I'd stuck a hosepipe to the exhaust . . .'

'Something like that,' admits Henry. He stands a bit awkwardly outside the car, and explains, 'I've been trying to call you to apologize about the other day; I couldn't get hold of you, and your boss said you left your job yesterday. I thought I'd try you at home, I hope you don't mind. I asked one of the neighbours where you were, and he pointed me to the car. I should have guessed there wasn't anything wrong, he didn't seem that concerned. But from what I could tell, you were just out cold.'

'Could you see me, then?' asks Lila with interest.

'Just your shape,' says Henry. 'So, I'm here to apologize . . .'

'Yeah, you've said that already. Night, night,' says Lila, and shuts the car door. She sighs, as Henry starts knocking on the window again.

'What?' she says irritably.

'I was just wondering, if you wanted to talk,' asks Henry. 'I know we didn't get off on the right foot. But I'm here now. We could go for a cup of tea or toast or something, somewhere warm. It's on me.'

Lila suddenly feels hungry again; food would sort out her throbbing head, and she can't bear the thought of trying to negotiate her freezing kitchen; even the rat footmen have probably abandoned it by now. She weighs up her state of inappropriate dress against her increasingly urgent desire for anything fried. 'OK,' she says, impetuously switching off the engine and sliding out from underneath her duvet. 'There's a greasy spoon café just down there.' She starts to stride down the street quickly, to avoid getting too cold, but then stops and waits with a bit of embarrassment. 'Um, do I take your arm, or something?' she asks.

'I'll take yours, if that's OK. I'm the batty blind one,' replies Henry, once he's caught up with her. 'Have you changed your hair colour, or something? It seems a bit brighter.'

Lila nods, and then realizes that he can't see her nod, by which time it seems a bit too late to reply, as they've already got to the pedestrian crossing at the end of the road.

★   ★   ★

In the café, Lila tucks her pyjama-bottomed legs under the plastic tablecloth, and drinks an enormous mug of tea with two sugars, slurping slightly as it is still too hot. She demolishes a slice of fried bread, and then starts wolfing her way boisterously through her scrambled eggs, baked beans, hash browns and fried mushrooms. Henry is just having tea and toast, and if he is annoyed at her table manners and her cheerful abuse of his offer, he doesn't show it. 'I guess you were hungry,' he says.

'Starving,' agrees Lila. 'I didn't really eat dinner last night, unless peanuts and tortilla chips count as dinner.' Lila is much more interested in her breakfast than in Henry, and doesn't even glance at him.

'I've been trying to track you down for weeks,' he starts. 'I didn't mean to be so horrible to you; when you ran off crying I just felt like such a shit. I don't normally behave like that.'

'Don't torture yourself about it,' says Lila dismissively. 'I've had much worse stuff said to me. And I've got much more serious problems to worry about than what some nerdy little researcher thinks of me, no offence.' Mopping up the sludgy remains of egg with her toast, she suddenly feels full-bellied and generous, and so she admits, 'You were probably right, anyway. Sometimes I'm not a very nice person; sometimes I can be an utter bitch.'

'But I don't think I was right,' says Henry earnestly, leaning forward. 'I wouldn't have gone

124

to all this effort to apologize if I was right. I was deliberately unkind, because I took it personally.'

'Took what personally?' asks Lila. 'The stuff I said about your precious documentary?'

'No, what you said about being stuck with Yasmin. You were being painfully honest about how it felt to have grown up with a sister like her, to be stuck with her until you die, to be pushed aside because her needs have always come first; and I'm afraid I didn't like it very much. I'm not used to such frankness.'

'Why would you take it personally?' asks Lila, realizing the answer almost before she has finished asking her question.

'Because in my family, I'm Yasmin,' says Henry.

Lila is unable to look Henry in the face, and finishes her breakfast with much less noise and fuss than when she started it. She sips her tea, and finally says, 'Apology accepted. Thanks for taking the trouble, I don't know many people who would have. And don't worry about the breakfast, I'll pay my way.'

'I won't hear of it,' says Henry, with a very proper firmness.

'Don't be daft . . .' Lila starts to say, but is interrupted by Henry.

'Really, it's a matter of honour,' he insists. 'I asked you, remember.'

'God, are you for real?' asks Lila with amusement. 'You speak in unusually full sentences, and you make a Full English breakfast a matter of honour. It's like you jumped out of a P.G. Wodehouse novel.'

'Yeah, my family takes the mickey out of me all the time about those sorts of things,' says Henry, suddenly sounding a lot less formal. 'I went to a different school to my sisters and brothers.' For a moment it seems that he wants to say more, but then he leans back instead, and asks conversationally, 'So, what about those problems you mentioned? Is there anything I can lend a hand with?'

'Why? You're not responsible,' says Lila. 'It's not your fault that I broke up with my boyfriend, lost my job and now I've lost my heating so I don't even have anywhere warm to mope.'

'You didn't lose your job, your boss said that you quit,' Henry reminds her.

'You're right, I did,' replies Lila, waving for another cup of tea from the burly, avuncular owner. 'But I didn't think that you media types would be that bothered about historical accuracy, when it comes to spinning emotional hard luck stories . . .'

'Why did you quit?' asks Henry, ignoring the jibe. 'Was it a bit too dull for you?'

'I'll say – the dullest part was shagging my boss,' says Lila, and then feels guilty as Henry sputters his remaining tea all down himself.

Her own mug of tea arrives, and she rewards the owner with a beaming smile; he has a wide, kind face, and asks with interest, 'Are you still wearing your PJs, love?'

'Yes, I am,' replies Lila, surprised by her lack of

embarrassment; she is almost proud of how little trouble she has taken over her clothes, of her impulsive decision to step out of the car and walk down the street; for the first time in years she has let herself be seen in public in what she normally wears in private.

'You'll catch your death,' the owner says. 'You should look after her, mate,' he adds seriously to Henry. 'She'll bleedin' catch her death going around like that.'

'You're still wearing your pyjamas?' asks Henry, seemingly lost between admiration and disapproval. 'Why didn't you say?'

'Oh, I'm afraid that the opportunity didn't arise,' says Lila, mimicking his meticulously correct voice perfectly, and he laughs despite himself.

'Well,' says Henry, after a moment, before adding regretfully, 'I guess I'd better get off to work. Thanks again for agreeing to see me, I feel so much better.'

'So do I,' says Lila. 'Better fed, I mean,' she justifies a bit too quickly. She asks curiously, 'Shouldn't you be at work already?'

'That's the great thing about having a bona fide disability. I get to work flexitime, so no one ever knows whether I'm meant to be in or not,' says Henry with a smile.

'You complete fraud! And there I was believing you were the last honest bloke in television,' laughs Lila. 'So, you're not going to try to talk me into contributing to the documentary?'

127

'No,' says Henry, 'I think you've made your views very clear on that point.' He goes to the till to pay, and then asks, 'So, what are you up to for the rest of the week?'

'Now that I'm jobless, nothing. I might see if I can get the heating fixed though. Can't sleep in my car all week, I don't think my council tax covers it,' says Lila, before adding provocatively, 'And I'd rather DIE than have to go home to Finchley, especially now that Yas is on half-term and is going to have your crew sniffing after her all day.'

Again, Henry doesn't rise to the bait, and just asks, 'I was wondering, would you like to meet up again some time, for tea or toast, or anything really?' He says it casually, without any obvious nervousness, but his grip on his stick is so tight that his knuckles are white. He's looking down and not trying to focus, so his eyes aren't screwed up, and Lila can see the fineness of his nut-brown lashes against his winter-pale skin.

'Why?' asks Lila suspiciously, reminding herself that he is a tweedy, nerdy researcher who wears duffel coats like Paddington Bear and is blind as a bat to boot.

'Because I think you might be the most interesting girl that I've ever met. Absolutely barking mad of course. Surprising choice of expletives, breakfast attire and sleeping location. And awful table manners. But definitely, really, quite interesting,' says Henry.

'Oh, when you put it like that,' says Lila, thinking she ought to be offended, but instead feeling ridiculously flattered. She adds sincerely, 'It's nice of you to say that, but I'm not that interesting really. I'm completely superficial – most of my personality's in my hair.'

'I don't think so,' says Henry. 'I don't get distracted by surfaces.' He pauses, and says, 'You haven't said yes.'

'I haven't said no, either,' says Lila, and she gets up, giving him her arm to take, so she can walk him to the door. As she does, the burly owner shouts after her with brusque concern, 'Hey pyjama girl, don't think you're going out like that! You look a right old state!' He rushes over with his own enormous coat, and puts it over her shoulders. 'Bring it back when you can, love. You want to be looking after her, mate,' he says critically to Henry. 'You can't let her go around in a knackered old pair of pyjamas with holes like a bloody Swiss cheese! She'll catch her death.'

'You see, you were right,' says Lila, as she walks Henry to the tube, snugly wrapped against the cold in the oversized coat. 'I do get by on my looks.'

BETWEEN THE LINES

My name is Yasmin Murphy, and although I understand the words that people say, I sometimes find it hard to understand what people really mean. It's called subtext. Or reading between the lines. These are the things that aren't explicitly spoken, and so have to be guessed, but which are still somehow obvious, because it seems that everyone else can hear them without a problem. I sometimes have to ask someone to explain for me, as though I am abroad, and need a translator. I have outgrown a lot of my more extreme autistic habits, like the public head-banging and the tantrums, but I think that when it comes to understanding the unspoken questions, I will always be a foreigner. Like 'L'Étranger' in the book we read by Camus, although 'L'Étranger' can also mean Outsider. I think of myself more as an Insider, as I live mainly inside my head, and everyone else as Outsiders, as they don't.

The way I make sense of subtext, or reading between the lines, is that they are things with a negative value; an absence that is like a presence. Or perhaps it would be better to describe them as something real, but just not apparent; like the invisible forces in a mechanical maths problem, the G force acting downwards and the N force acting up from the ground, and if these forces aren't taken into account, the result will be wrong. So when I am asked questions during the filming, I have to be able to understand the invisible questions that accompany them, or I won't give the right answer. The film makers told me that there are no right or wrong answers; they said this to reassure me, but instead the idea of this just made me panic and feel like I was swaying in a strong wind; I panicked, as if there are no right and wrong answers, then that would mean that NOTHING is right and wrong and nothing in the world would make sense. But I know that what they said was just an expression, like saying love at the end of an email or card, which you need to say even if you're not sure whether you mean it, or the recipient would get upset. Or saying 'one in a million', as the chances of something actually being precisely one in a million are unlikely, so it is just a misleading way of saying 'rare'. Or saying 'pull your socks up' to a child who isn't wearing socks, because you need them to finish doing something faster or better. I used to take expressions quite literally, and it is still my instinct to do so, but now I have learned to tell myself, 'It's just an expression,' and overcome my initial reaction. So I didn't believe what the film makers said, and I know that there are right and wrong answers, depending, of course, on the questions being asked.

I have been asked lots of questions during the documentary filming. I sit in a room in our house and have conversations with a psychologist, which I don't find too distressing, as I speak to my own psychologist regularly, and have practised filming myself and talking to a camera. But I find some of the questions quite difficult to answer, especially ones like:

What did it feel like when my mum died?

Who is my best friend?

Who was my first love?

Do I feel happy?

Do I feel hope for the future?

These are questions which would be very easy for an NT person to answer; it was explained to me that the subtext to all of these questions is to explore how a non-NT person might feel emotion in the way that an NT person can. They want to know if someone like me could be someone like them. So these were my answers:

I felt Loss when Mum died. Not a loss the way other people seem to feel, which involves lots of physical grief, like tears and shouting, but still a loss in my own way. It was a literal loss in my head of the memories that should have been made that day. Which is why I don't remember anything much about the day that she died.

My best friend is my brother Asif, because he does things with me, and explains the way people

132

should behave to me, and gives me advice which is usually right.

My first love was my mum, because she is the first person I said that I loved.

Yes, *of course* I am.

Yes, *of course* I do.

The psychologist wanted me to say more about the last two questions, but I didn't, as I had lied, and I didn't want her to know that I had lied; although perhaps by saying 'Of course', I had already given it away. In fact, I do not feel happy. I am not sure that I have ever felt really happy, in the way that people do in books and films, in the pure way that very young children or dogs appear to be happy, which they show by laughing or wagging their tails. There are things that I like doing, and in theory if I just kept doing things I like doing, like watching *The Simpsons*, washing up and re-reading books I enjoy, I should be happy, but I don't think that doing these things adds up to being happy, as happiness is a state rather than an activity. And I am possibly closer to being unhappy rather than happy, as I think that I might be slowly going blind, but I have not told anyone this. I do not feel a lot of hope for the future, as if I am going blind, like the polite researcher with the retractable stick who came and spoke to me before the filming, it will not be a hopeful situation, and plenty of the things that I enjoy doing will be less easy to do or impossible. And there are lots of things that I want to do, but haven't as yet, as I have been busy studying for my A levels.

The part of the documentary when I am speaking and answering questions is 'prompted', which means that it has been staged and wouldn't exist in normal life if the film makers hadn't organized it. The rest of the filming is meant to be 'spontaneous and non-intrusive', which means that they just follow me around doing the things that I normally do, and they don't intervene. But of course it is still intrusive, as I am not normally followed by a camera, and a director, and lighting technician and sound man. I try to ignore them, but it's not easy, as they are noisy and take up a lot of space, and so I have to try extra hard not to have a Meltdown and upset Asif, as he is very worried about me having a Meltdown on film, as he doesn't trust the film makers not to put it on national TV. I have promised that if I feel upset, I will go and sit somewhere quiet and private, like the staff bathroom, until I feel calm again. I didn't feel calm the whole first morning of the filming, and so I stayed in the staff bathroom, which smells of chemical vanilla and peaches, and has pink embossed loo paper which is much softer than the normal loo paper in the cloak-rooms, and missed Double Maths, and History and German. And then I got upset about missing all my lessons, and stayed in the bathroom catching up on most of what I missed through lunchtime. And by the time my first afternoon period had started, the school had called Asif and asked the film makers to leave as they were being disruptive. I went to class like normal in the afternoon, and when Asif arrived he couldn't see what the fuss was about, and he had got into trouble with his work for nothing. So the film makers decided to try to make the non-intrusive bit even less intrusive, by just putting a camera in each of my classrooms, which didn't bother me at all.

I am feeling uncomfortable that I lied to the film makers when I answered their questions, as lying is not something that I do often, and my world makes a little less sense.

Do I feel happy?

Do I feel hope for the future?

They want me to show them that I feel emotion just like other people, but I'm not sure that I do; I think that probably my emotions are chemical reactions linked to my logical processes; I think that my emotions are a function of my logic. When a newborn cries, it isn't because it is sad, but because it wants to remind people that it is there and needs feeding or burping or changing. When I feel lonely, it is because I know that it is better not to be alone, as I might need someone to help me. When I want to be held, it is because I want to be warm and protected; when I don't want to be touched, it is because I don't want to be harmed or injured. I feel that the documentary-makers would be disappointed in me if I told them this. When I think of their questions, about happiness and hope, I think of red with orange blotches, and I try to calm myself down by remembering my dream, when I am flying around my room, and feeling safe.

SOMEONE WHO CARES

Asif has given up calling Lila, and has gone round to her flat first thing on Saturday morning. He is annoyed with Lila for ignoring him, but he is incapable of ignoring her back, even though he risks Yasmin's wrath if he doesn't return before she gets back from her chess club. He rings the buzzer impatiently, thinking that once he's heard that Lila's all right, he might not even bother going upstairs to see her. However, Lila doesn't answer; he knows now that she has broken up with Wes, and left her job, and so he can't imagine that she is anywhere else but home this early in the day. He buzzes the ground-floor flat, and asks them to let him in, explaining that Lila's buzzer isn't working. It might even be true. He goes up the creaking wooden stairs to the second floor, and knocks on Lila's door. No answer. He knocks again. Still no answer. He knocks more urgently, trying not to feel any panic. 'Lila,' he calls out cautiously. Perhaps he should have come around sooner; perhaps Lila is lying injured on the floor in the outrageous squalor of her apartment, fending off rodents and cockroaches with a stained plastic spatula. He feels a sudden gut-wrenching fear for her, and shouts her name loudly, not caring about bothering the neighbours. He remembers what it was like to come home when he was twelve going on thirteen, and seeing the kitchen counter smeared with Lila's blood, when she had slashed her wrist with the jagged lid of a sweetcorn can. There was no one in the house to tell him what happened, but even before he saw the note on the fridge door, he knew that it was Lila's blood, he just knew; it couldn't have been Mum's or Yasmin's, because they were invulnerable, they couldn't bleed, they couldn't be hurt like he and Lila could. Mum and Yasmin were made of solid steel. 'Lila had accident. In hospital with her and Yas. Don't mind the mess. Call me on mobile. Love Mum.' He took the note from the fridge, and later, when Lila was stitched up and complaining at home, when Yasmin had received her Blue Peter badge for making her prompt call to the emergency services while their inattentive babysitter snogged her boyfriend in his car, and everything was back to normal, he would take out the note and, lying on his bed, would smooth it down gently against his pillow, and run his thumb over where Mum had written Love. He knew that it was just an expression, just a word, but it didn't seem to matter. He kept the note in a box with his birthday and Christmas cards, which were all Love Mum as well.

'Lila,' Asif practically screams, uselessly charging

against the door and hammering it with his fist, causing Lila's neighbours to open their own doors curiously and look down the banister. Asif charges against the door again, but this time he falls over the threshold and into the apartment when Lila opens it, wearing her bathrobe and with a towel wrapped loosely around her head.

'Did you practise that?' asks Lila with amusement. She shuts the door on her neighbours and helps him up from the floor.

'I rang you from downstairs. Why didn't you answer?' asks Asif, hiding his relief with irritation.

'Duh. Can't you guess?' asks Lila, removing the towel from her head and rubbing her short red crop briskly. 'I'm not going to get out of the bath for just anyone; it's way too early for casual callers, I thought it was just the postman or something.' She adds infuriatingly, 'You should have called first.'

'I HAVE been calling! I've called for two weeks,' protests Asif indignantly. 'You never called back.'

'I wasn't in the mood. I'd broken up with Wes, shagged Mikey on a disastrous rebound, and quit my job,' says Lila unrepentantly. 'I didn't want to have to listen to you saying, "I told you so," and shaking your head with sympathy, and giving me that pitying face because I've crapped up my life again.'

'Oh Lila,' says Asif, stung by her judgement of him; is he really the sort of big brother who says, 'I told you so'? He absorbs the confirmation of Lila's

139

newly single and unemployed status without comment, and looks rather more kindly towards her.

'That! That's the face I was talking about!' complains Lila. 'Stop feeling sorry for me, I'm fine.'

'I'm not feeling sorry for you,' argues Asif. 'Just, concerned. It's OK to be concerned, isn't it?'

'Oh, whatever,' mutters Lila. 'Do you want a coffee?'

'Please,' says Asif, and looks around the apartment for somewhere clear to sit. He eventually gives up, and sits on the floor, leaning against the sofa, and watches Lila rinse out the coffee cups in the sink. From the back, it is disconcertingly like watching Yasmin washing up the clean crockery; they share the same slightness of form, except that Yas has a brown ponytail, and Lila now has a berry-red, mussed-up crop. 'I like the new hair; it's really striking,' he says politely.

'Does that mean you hate it?' asks Lila shrewdly, setting the coffee in front of him on the pale, worn carpet.

'I think I preferred the last style,' admits Asif, before adding sincerely, 'But you know you always look nice.' He thanks her belatedly for the coffee. 'Cheers,' he says, sipping it gingerly; Lila always makes the coffee too strong. 'I didn't mean to make a scene outside just now. I was worried about you. I hadn't heard from you in days.'

'Suddenly I appear to have become an object of concern,' comments Lila. 'Someone else thought I was gassing myself in the car the other day.'

'Oh, I didn't mean anything like that,' says Asif. He adds with a glimmer of humour, 'I was thinking that the oven might be more your style. More poetic.'

'That's a little dark for you,' laughs Lila. 'You know, it's nice to have someone care. Whether I'm gassing myself or not, that is.'

They sit companionably catching up for a little while; once Asif has finished his coffee, he looks apologetically at his watch. 'Well, I guess I'd better head off. Yasmin's due back from . . .'

'. . . chess club,' finishes Lila in a bored voice, trying to hide her disappointment. She likes chatting to Asif; she likes him being in her flat away from Yasmin. It happens all too rarely; only, apparently, when he is concerned that she might have put her head in the oven. Like Mum before him, he belongs to Yasmin now.

'Why don't you come back with me, for lunch or something?' says Asif, equally sorry to leave her on her own.

'What, with you and . . .' Lila stops herself saying 'Sodding Raingirl?' and says, 'Yas?' instead. She is absurdly proud of her self-control; if she was American like Wes she'd be congratulating herself on her personal growth. 'Sod that for a lark. Anyway, I've sort of got a date.'

'So soon? After Wes? And that Mikey bloke?' says Asif with surprise. 'Do you think that's a good idea?'

'I said sort of, which means nothing serious.

And if I were you, I'd save your concern for your own love life. I don't think you've got laid since the last budget was announced; you should get out more,' says Lila.

'Yeah, I should,' agrees Asif. He's not been in a serious relationship since he left Cambridge; he'd been going out with Faith for almost a year, but she had ended it a few months after he'd gone back down to London, and he didn't really blame her; they'd barely been able to see each other. Since then, he'd had a few dates, but nothing promising enough to take much further, which would risk upsetting Yasmin's routine; the last time he'd had sex had been a singularly unpleasant one-night stand with one of the assistants from Audit during the Christmas party; they'd had a drunken shag under the table in one of the third-floor meeting rooms, which she had initiated, only to ignore him completely the next day. It turned out that she already had a boyfriend, and obviously didn't want anything further to do with him.

'And you work in a building with about six hundred people,' adds Lila. 'There must be some attractive girls there.'

Asif shrugs sheepishly. 'I guess,' he says. Suddenly, he can only think of one. He remembers Mei Lin's firm chin, narrow, smiling eyes and swish of hair across a smooth ivory cheek. An older, married woman with a baby. And so far out of his league that he doesn't even feel guilty thinking about her; it was like having a fantasy about a movie star. He kisses Lila goodbye, making her promise to ask him if she needs any help with her rent. It doesn't escape him that she hasn't asked how the documentary is going.

At home, Asif is back just before Yasmin, who seems even more introspective than usual. She goes straight to the kitchen without acknowledging him, and puts the kettle on, to make the usual cup of herbal tea that she has mid-morning at the weekends.

'How was chess?' Asif asks, following her in. He sees that she has put out two mugs; she does this out of habit, as Mum had taught her to make tea for the number of people who were in the house, but he still finds it touching to be included in her ritual, even though he actively dislikes Yasmin's camomile tea, which always reminds him of dilute cat pee.

'Fine,' says Yasmin briefly; she seems preoccupied rather than rude. She puts two teabags in the teapot, and watches the kettle intently, as it starts to rumble and fizz to life.

'Did you win all your games?' perseveres Asif, trying not to look at the photo of Mum on the fridge door.

'Yes, I won all my games. I almost lost one because someone's mobile phone started ringing, and it had a really distracting ring tone that went on for ages. I had to press on my ears, and shut my eyes, and hum, so that I could focus on my

143

next move; sometimes I find it easier to see the board if my eyes are shut,' she says.

'Right,' says Asif, trying not to feel mortified as he pictures Yasmin humming with her ears blocked and her eyes shut in the middle of the doubtless sniggering chess hall. 'Were the documentary team there?' he asks casually.

'Yes, I kept my back to them so they wouldn't distract me,' Yasmin explains. She counts as she pours the boiling water into one cup, stopping at three when it is full. She then shuts her eyes, and counts as she pours the boiling water into the second cup, stopping at three again. She opens her eyes, and seems displeased that the second cup is marginally less full than the first. 'I must have poured too slowly,' she tells Asif, without giving any explanation for this odd deviation from her usual routine. Asif makes a mental note to call the director of the documentary, to check that the footage from the chess club won't make Yas look stupid, and takes his own cup of cat-pee tea to the table.

'I've decided I'm going to stop going to chess club on Saturday mornings,' says Yas abruptly.

'Really, why?' asks Asif in surprise; normally Yasmin hates changing her routines.

'Because I can play chess with my eyes shut,' she replies simply, and Asif is unsure whether she means she finds it easy, or that she can literally play with her eyes shut, and doesn't have to go and seek out a match which she could play in her

144

head. 'I'd like to play something else on Saturday mornings instead. Something I haven't done before, like tennis. Will you help me find a place to play?'

'Sure,' says Asif, amazed at the request. 'You can play at the courts in the park if you have a partner, or you can join a tennis club, and they'll pair you up with another beginner.'

'Great, thanks,' says Yasmin automatically. 'I'm writing a list of some other things I want to do, around my A levels. It's like a project. Will you help me with them?' She looks him in the eye, Mississippi One, Mississippi Two, although it seems to take her a lot of effort, and her focus slides through him before she drops her gaze back to her tea.

'Of course,' starts Asif, but Yasmin has forgotten to wait for his answer, and has already turned away to go back up to her bedroom.

TEENAGE BIOLOGY

Asif was sitting in the school playground among a loosely formed group of his classmates; he liked being one of the crowd, it was where he felt safe. They had just sat their Biology GCSE, and were doing the usual post-mortem of the paper. 'What did you put for that one, mate?' asked Owen anxiously, having gone through yet another question in tedious detail.

'Ventricle,' replied Asif.

'Aaw shite. I put aorta,' grumbled Owen, pushing the hair out of his eyes. 'I knew I should have spent more time on the effin' heart.' He looked through his notes, 'What did you get for the bones of the middle ear?'

'Hammer, anvil, stirrup,' replied Asif reluctantly, trying to hide his embarrassment.

'I didn't even have that down in my revision cards. Christ, you're a swot, Asif,' said Owen.

'I didn't say that I knew they were right,' argued Asif.

'Liar,' said Bob, a wiry kid with glasses and slightly greasy hair. 'You're always right. That's why you're a swot.'

'Rather be a swot than a trekkie,' said Asif boldly.

'Rather be a trekkie than a geek,' replied Bob.

'Hello four eyes, a trekkie IS a geek,' interjected Owen. 'OK, what about the question on DNA?'

'Owen mate, you're being boring,' yawned Bob. 'Only two more exams to do, and we're out of this dump! I'm going to burn my school uniform and scatter the ashes.'

'You may as well keep the shirts,' said Asif. 'You'll need white shirts for sixth form.'

'Buggered if I'm going to sixth form,' said Bob. 'Don't let the glasses fool you, I'm actually thick as shit.'

'Not as thick as me,' said Owen. 'Effin' ventricle! How could I have screwed up on that?'

'It's only worth about a point,' said Asif reassuringly.

'Yeah, I know,' said Owen. 'Isn't that your sister over there?' Asif looked across the school yard, where a couple of the bigger boys from his year were picking on a younger girl. He realized that it was Lila, and jumped up from the step instinctively; he felt fear freeze his guts as he strode over, but he didn't have a choice; Lila was in trouble, he had to be brave. He kept his pace up as he walked, knowing that if he hesitated he might give in to his cowardly panic.

'Hey, leave my little sister alone!' he said with what he hoped was a forceful demeanour, hoping no one else would notice how reedy and high his voice had suddenly become. He saw too late,

147

as Lila turned to face him, that she had actually been laughing with the boys, and that one of them had his arm casually around her.

'Asif,' hissed Lila, completely mortified. 'Bugger off!'

'Oh, sorry . . .' he started to say, relieved that he had completely misread the situation, when he was pushed away with casual violence by Fergus, the bigger of the two boys.

'Yeah, bugger off, Arse-if,' said Fergus, lingering over Asif's name with humiliating precision.

'Don't speak to him like that,' retorted Lila.

'Who are you, his fag-hag?' laughed Fergus, squeezing her waist. He turned around to Asif, 'I thought we told you to bugger off.'

'I said don't speak to him like that,' said Lila, shrugging him off her. 'Bugger off yourself.'

'Shame,' said Fergus, looking Lila up and down. 'And I thought you were cool. Guess you're just a silly little fourth year, after all.' Lila stormed off, taking Asif with her. She didn't stop until they got to the steps leading up to the library, where she sat down.

'Thanks a lot, Asif,' she muttered furiously. 'I've fancied Fergus all year.'

'Sorry,' said Asif. 'I didn't mean to get in the way, I just saw you and got worried.'

'Yeah, I know,' said Lila, still cross, but annoyingly touched by his concern. She sighed and glanced to where her brother was standing, just a couple of steps down from her; it was impossible

148

to stay mad at Asif when he was always so bloody well-intentioned. 'I'll never get to snog him now,' she complained regretfully. 'It's the end of term in two weeks.'

'You could do better,' comments Asif. 'He's thick as shit and thinks with his fists and is always getting into trouble.'

'Yeah I know, but he's fit as you like,' said Lila dreamily, looking back over to where Fergus stood, despite herself. Asif saw Fergus had been watching her too, but then he hastily turned away, as though to pretend he hadn't been.

Asif said nothing; he supposed that Lila was fourteen years old now, and didn't need him around defending her honour. He'd be going down the road to the sixth form college to do his A levels in the autumn. Yasmin would be leaving the school too, she was in the last year of juniors, but had received a scholarship to go to a prestigious private establishment for senior school. He wondered how Lila felt about this; perhaps jealous, perhaps just relieved that she wouldn't have to take Yasmin to and from school any more. He couldn't see Yasmin anywhere in the playground; she normally sat there alone with a book. She was probably in the school library or computer room instead.

Lila spoke up suddenly. 'Did you ever hear the story about the girl who thought she was blind? It turned out that her hat was just too large. And the girl who thought she was deaf? It turned out that she'd forgotten to take the cotton wool out of her ears. And the girl who . . .'

'I don't get it,' interrupted Asif.

'Have you ever thought that there's nothing wrong with Yasmin at all? That she might just be wearing too large a hat and have her ears stuffed with cotton,' said Lila.

'I still don't get it,' said Asif, although he thought that perhaps he did.

'Everyone's told Yasmin ever since she was six years old that there was something different about her. And she's been treated differently because of it. She doesn't get told off for having a tantrum, she doesn't get told off for not wanting to take the bus or eat her dinner. It all becomes part of her condition. But what if there was nothing wrong with her in the first place? What if they just got it wrong? What if she's just a highly strung, bad-tempered, tantrum-throwing little cow who's been indulged more than is healthy? It's like putting a sane person in an asylum, you leave them long enough and they'll start acting mad.'

'She's been diagnosed,' said Asif wearily. 'That's just the way it is.'

'Did you know that Asperger's Syndrome wasn't recognized before 1994? Before that, Yasmin wouldn't have been diagnosed at all.'

'They'd probably have called it high-performing autism,' said Asif. 'She'd still have been diagnosed.'

'They're just words, Asif,' cried out Lila in frustration. 'Asperger, autism, they're just words.

I've thought for a long time that there's nothing really wrong with Yas – she's just lucky that she has that phenomenal memory. There are probably science nerds all over the world who are as particular and neurotic as she is . . .'

Asif wished he could agree with Lila. 'I know that you don't want her to be different,' he starts to say.

'I think you do!' contradicts Lila. 'I think you want her to be bloody different, because then nothing's her fault. You can blame it all on Yasmin's "condition". Then no one has to admit that we've got a bloody great controlling jerk for a little sister.'

A small, monotonous voice came out behind them, 'Are you talking about me, again?' said Yasmin.

'Hi Yas, I thought you were in the library,' said Asif, looking warningly at Lila, who had the grace to look a bit abashed.

'I was, but the windows are open, and I got distracted because you were talking so loudly. Were you talking about me? I heard you say my name.'

'Yes, we bloody were,' said Lila defiantly. She looked like she wanted to say a lot more, but Yasmin had no further interest in what Lila might have to say beyond the confirmation of her question. Yasmin looked at her feet, and began speaking quickly in her dull monotone, the words tripping over themselves as she let them out as fast as she could, like someone was twisting open a tap to full flow.

'You use too many swears when you talk, Lila. You say the really bad words that begin with F quite often, and you use bloody all the time. Although bloody isn't as bad a swear as people think, because it doesn't refer to the blood of Lord Jesus Christ or to the Virgin Mary as a corruption of "By our Lady". Instead it refers to being like a "Blood" which is an old term for someone who belonged to the aristocracy, that is someone of good blood, and Bloods were not known for being nice, hence the term "bloody-minded" and they drank too much, hence "drunk like a lord".' Yasmin stopped abruptly, and turned to go back to the library.

'That's interesting, Yas,' said Asif. 'Where did you read about that?'

'I didn't read it, I saw it on *Countdown* on Channel 4, nineteen days ago at 3.37 p.m., they spoke about it on the Dictionary Corner,' said Yasmin, without turning around.

Asif turned back to Lila. 'Eleven years old and she comes out with all that. And you just think she's being deliberately annoying.'

'And you think she isn't?' retorted Lila. She looked up with interest as Fergus's friend approached her, and looked so threateningly at Asif that he involuntarily backed away. 'See you later, Asif,' Lila said definitely, nodding to him that it was OK to leave.

As Asif walked off, he heard Fergus's henchman mutter, 'All right Lila. We're sorry about what happened just now. Just wanted to say, like, that my mate fancies you.'

'Result!' said Lila with delight. 'Tell your mate to meet me at the chip shop after school today. He's pulled.'

UNDER HER SKIN

Lila is desperate to know about the filming that Yasmin has been doing, but doesn't want Asif to guess this; when he was over at her flat she intended to feign studied indifference if he mentioned the documentary, but infuriatingly, he didn't. Henry, her sort of date, is proving just as infuriating; Henry talks a lot, possibly more than any man that she has ever met before, in conspicuously long sentences; he speaks so much that he needs punctuation. He uses words like 'peripatetic' in casual conversation with a surprising lack of affectation, as though he really thinks that she would already know what it means. But he doesn't talk about his work, and Lila doesn't want to have to ask him. And so they talk about everything else instead. She finds his loquaciousness infectious, and finds herself responding in kind with a fluency that she hadn't realized she possessed, as she is so used to making terse, clever put-downs and brittle asides instead. Henry, for all his chatter, is a generous conversationalist; he listens at least as much as he speaks, and listens intently. Lila isn't quite sure what to make of all this talk; it seems odd and slightly unflattering that someone wants to speak so much to her, and know so much from her, before he has so much as touched her hand.

'So, who was your first love?' asks Henry, as they come out of the National Film Theatre on the South Bank, having just been to *Romeo and Juliet* during the Zeffirelli season. Lila is not absolutely sure why she keeps meeting up with him; she has now seen him three times in the last two weeks. She supposes that it must be pity, although she finds the efficient way he calls her up with the proposal for what they might do and where they might go curiously compelling; he is so well organized that it just seems easier to agree to fall in with his well-laid plans than to say no. And it isn't as though she has anything else to do; she has continued to paint, but in an uninspired, treading-water sort of way, just keeping her hands busy until she can occupy them with a new idea, and her latest job waitressing at the greasy spoon café at the end of her road is pleasantly undemanding.

'That's easy, Brad Pitt,' says Lila. 'Wasn't he everyone's?'

'I meant your real first love,' says Henry. 'Is here OK?' he asks, tapping an empty seat at the NFT café.

'I guess,' shrugs Lila, and they order a couple of coffees and sit down. 'You know, you don't normally ask about people's first loves . . .'

'When you say "you don't", do you mean that I don't, or that one doesn't generally?' asks Henry for clarification.

'Christ, you sound like Yasmin,' says Lila. 'I mean that *One Doesn't*,' she pronounces the words with exaggerated care. '*One* normally asks about the last relationship someone's just had, not the first one.'

'Sorry, didn't realize that I'd committed some awful dating faux pas,' apologizes Henry without a trace of sarcasm. He seems so sincere that Lila feels she ought to apologize herself for something, just to even things out.

'Don't be sorry,' she says briskly. 'It seemed a slightly odd question, that was all. If you must know, my first love was Fergus Stewart, when I was fourteen going on fifteen. He was in the year above me at school. I fancied him rotten for months, and we finally got together two weeks before he left to go to sixth form.'

'Why did he have to leave to go to sixth form?' asks Henry with interest.

'Oh, our school was rubbish,' says Lila lightly. 'Really rubbish. It was on the telly for being one of the failing schools in the area; the only time I've ever been on TV was when the BBC News 24 crew came to do the filming outside the gates. It probably just wasn't worth having a sixth form, because the school was too full of thickos who'd drop out at fifth year anyway.'

'So you were two teenagers, madly in love,

together for just two weeks, and then he had to leave. That's a sad story, like *Romeo and Juliet* without the poison and subplots,' he says with a slight smile that he quickly represses.

'No need to be sarcastic. It was more like two days, actually. We had a few fantastic snogging sessions, but then he said something hurtful, and I didn't want to see him again.' Lila is quiet at the memory, although she's not sure why it should still bother her. It was almost ten years ago.

'I wasn't being sarcastic,' says Henry, seeming a little aggrieved at the suggestion.

'Then why were you smirking?' counters Lila.

'Because you didn't contradict me when I implied that we were on a date,' he says, and this time he positively beams. 'I'm flattered.' His smile is so choirboy pure, so suddenly luminous that it practically lights up his pale skin and slightly sharp cheekbones from within. Lila finds herself staring at him, momentarily disarmed, before she catches herself and realizes what he's just said.

'I'm not sure that's what we're doing here,' she replies bluntly, and then feels bad again, as the glow evaporates from Henry's face. 'Don't look at me in that tone of voice,' she says, half-joking, thinking she might make him smile again. 'I just meant, that . . . well, you've already got one bitch at home. You don't need to get cosy with another one.'

Henry winces, 'I wish you'd stop referring to yourself that way, it's so unnecessary.'

Lila shrugs again. 'Just because something isn't necessary, doesn't mean we shouldn't do it. Swearing isn't necessary. But neither are tattoos, coloured socks or nose-rings . . .'

'You've not really sold me on the value of un-necessary items with your choice of examples,' says Henry. 'How about oysters, beers and lazy afternoons on the beach?'

Lila laughs. 'Put all those together and you've got a fantastic date.'

'Which gets me back to what I wanted to say,' says Henry. 'If that isn't what we're doing here, what are we doing?'

'I don't know,' says Lila. 'Just making conversation, I guess.'

'Oh,' says Henry, and because he seems to find it impossible to say so little, adds, 'Ironically, that was rather a conversation killer, wasn't it?'

'Well, I'd better be going anyway,' says Lila, refusing to feel guilty again. It would be far worse to lead Henry on, as she was sure she didn't find him in the least attractive; he wore awful clothes, and always had three days of stubble on his chin, and his hair was too fine, and his eyelashes too straight, and he was so pale and English that he'd need a tan before he could be described as white.

'Right, OK then,' says Henry, a bit sadly. Lila is touched, he really does seem to like her. 'But I wanted to ask something, if it's not too personal. What did Fergus say to make you not want to see him again?'

'Oh nothing, just something stupid,' mutters Lila. Henry appears to be regarding her intently, with that screwed-up eye look that he sometimes has, and she adds again, 'And I said to stop looking at me . . .'

'. . . in that tone of voice,' finishes Henry. 'It was funnier the first time.' He adds, 'You don't have to tell me if you don't want to.'

'Duh, of course I don't have to,' says Lila. It occurs to her, at this moment, that she will very likely not see Henry again. She has pretty much said that she has no interest in him, and has given him no further reason or encouragement to call her. The documentary filming will soon be completed, and then there would be nothing that would bring him into any of their lives again. She feels absurdly nostalgic, as though she has lost a friend she never had. Perhaps it was nicer to have someone to speak to than she liked to admit; perhaps she was lonelier than she liked to admit. She decides that she may as well take the opportunity to tell Henry what Fergus said, because she is certain that no one else will ever be interested in this. 'He just said, when we were snogging, that the skin on my arms felt like sandpaper. He said that he probably had softer arms than mine.' She feels so stupid, that this tiny, inconsequential comment could have affected her so much; she adds in a small voice, 'He didn't even mean it in a horrible way. It was just a fact. It was true.'

She looks at Henry, half expecting him to laugh or shake his head, but he just smiles at her again, that artless luminous smile which makes him unexpectedly appealing; he seems so radiant that Lila has to stop herself leaning unthinkingly forward, as though she might stretch out and warm herself on him. Apart from taking her arm on occasion to guide him, he has never touched her, never even tried to hold her hand, but now he leans forward himself, and places his warm palm over her upturned forearm. 'What matters is underneath, Lila,' he says, brushing the skin at her wrist very slightly with his thumb. 'Everything that is wonderful about you is underneath your skin. You might not have known that at fourteen, but you should know it now.'

Lila is stunned by the sudden intimacy of touch, and with his unexpected gesture feels a wave of something she can't place go through her. She is aware that his thumb is just above her childhood scar, where she slashed at her wrist with the lid of a can; feeling the blood pulse through to her hand against his thumb, she sees his face, and guesses that he has felt the scar too. But he doesn't say anything, and withdraws his hand as gently as he offered it. At least he has nice hands, Lila grudgingly admits. She gets up from her seat, and says, carelessly, 'Well, thanks for a nice evening.' Her mother would be proud, her mother had always taught them to say 'Thank you for having me' to their friends when they left their houses, a phrase which was to take on a whole new meaning when Lila grew up and visited boyfriends instead.

'It's a pleasure,' replies Henry, standing up politely himself. 'Don't mention it.'

'Goodbye,' says Lila, wondering if she should peck him on the cheek, as it will probably be the last time she'll see him. She doesn't, but as she picks up her handbag, finds herself saying instead, 'You know, if you wanted to get together again some time. Just for more conversation. That would be nice.'

'Really?' says Henry, stepping towards her. 'I was thinking about getting out of London next weekend, and maybe going to the beach. Somewhere with beers and oysters. Would you like to join me?'

'Well,' says Lila, taken aback by his sudden enthusiasm, 'I can't let you do all that alone. You'd just look daft.'

'Great, it's a date,' says Henry unthinkingly, and then he pauses, and waits for Lila to correct him. But she doesn't, just to see his smile.

MAKING UP NUMBERS

Asif is staying late in the office, stuffing envelopes with Terry. He has to send a notice to the several hundred creditors for one of his receivership cases; the reason that Asif is stuffing the envelopes with Terry, rather than the trainees or the secretarial staff, is because the firm can charge a much higher hourly rate for Asif's time. Even his boss and Hector the partner did a ceremonial dozen envelopes each, just so they could put half an hour of their exorbitantly priced time against the job; mindful of the annual bonuses issued to the senior staff members, the Corporate Recovery Services department missed no opportunity to pad their bottom line.

Asif knows he should feel humiliated about stuffing the envelopes, but he is secretly glad to have an excuse not to go home. He called Yasmin to explain about being late at the office, and she was remarkably calm about it; she said she was working on her post-documentary project, and stoically advised that she would have frozen pizza for dinner. The project seemed to be her latest obsession; one in a long line of seemingly random things that occupied her interest so intensely that it was practically unwholesome. It had been *Teletubbies* when she was very young, then Flora and Fauna, then Greek and Roman Mythology, then Photography, and so on. As far as Asif could tell, the project was just a To Do list; something about the documentary seemed to have made Yasmin feel that she didn't have enough life experiences.

Asif knows that it is a bit pathetic, but he actually quite likes the physical act of envelope-stuffing, the neat folding of the papers to be delivered, smoothing the sticky address labels on to the envelopes, pressing down the gummed edge of the envelopes to seal them; he likes the soothing repetition and keeping his hands busy. He supposes that this is why some people knit. And he likes the calm of the office after hours, when the chattering masses have gone home, and the Corporate Recovery and Corporate Finance departments, linked by a corridor lined with sunless meeting rooms and their shared support staff, become banks of shiny, empty desks, peopled only by framed photos of smiling loved ones, and occasionally blinking desktop computers. Terry, however, is not taking the envelope-stuffing quite so philosophically; he is younger than Asif, still not fully qualified, and having not yet been ground down by the crushing monotony of the office, still has some ambition, and enough energy to be indignant.

'Four A levels and a BA degree,' he complains as he peels an address label from the printed sheet and slaps it untidily on an envelope, a bit too high, slightly lopsided, and with a wrinkle in the top right corner from where he held it. 'And so far, two years of Accountancy training, with Conversion and Intermediate exams, and where has it got me . . . ?'

'Not stuffing fast enough,' replies Asif, whose own pile of envelopes is nearly double the size of Terry's. He doesn't mention the untidiness, as he doesn't want to seem too anally picky, but Terry's non-centred, drunken-looking labels are really bothering him.

'I think you're missing the point, mate,' says Terry over-familiarly. 'No one wants us to work quickly. The whole point of this exercise is to charge as many hours as possible for our precious, over-qualified time. So that Hector the Projector can factor up his estimate of client revenue for the second quarter, and get a nice fat cheque.'

'Shush,' says Asif anxiously, looking over his shoulder.

'Oh, what?' says Terry irritably. 'You don't think that the great man's going to slither in between his last meeting and his first martini? He's never here after five thirty.'

'Who's never here after five thirty?' booms Hector, his voice echoing down the hallway as he strides impressively towards them.

Both Asif and Terry stiffen instinctively and nod with insincere smiles in his direction as they struggle to come up with an appropriate response. Terry recovers first. 'The printer guy,' he improvises smoothly, losing Hector's interest instantly; Hector barely acknowledges the existence of support staff, or any other 'little' people.

'No one else in?' Hector comments, looking around. 'We're doing drinks in the sixth-floor board-room for the new grads, and need some bodies to make up the numbers. The CFS people are still stuck over in INSEAD, some balls-up with the flights from Paris, and it's like a bloody morgue up there.' He considers and dismisses Terry, looking with disapproval at his loose tie and spiky boy-band hair, and then nods towards Asif, 'All right Arse-if,' he says, carefully over-pronouncing Asif's name in the way that Asif always finds embarrassing, 'you'd better come with me. Terry can finish that off.'

Asif nods and gets up; 'Sure . . .' He pauses as he is suddenly unsure what to call Hector face to face. Sir seems too crawlingly formal, Hector might be too career-threateningly cosy. '. . . Boss,' he finishes uncertainly. It is the perfect thing to have said, as Hector booms with laughter.

'Boss!' he guffaws. 'I like your feudal spirit, lad, but better call me the Big H in front of the grads, we don't want them to be scared of me now, do we!' He strides off towards the lifts as importantly as he arrived, and Asif rushes to keep up with him. He glances back at glowering Terry; Asif gives a helpless wave and mouths an apology. Rather than feeling reprieved, he is genuinely reluctant to entrust his tidy stack of envelopes to Terry's slip-shod workmanship. I can't even delegate a bloody

165

mail-out, thinks Asif, suddenly annoyed with himself; this was exactly the sort of thing which made it painfully apparent that he'd never make it into management, no matter how crisp his spreadsheets were. He gets into the lift with Hector, and as he feels awkward with the silence, he asks politely, 'So is there an agenda for the graduate induction today?'

'No, they'll do all that rubbish later,' says Hector. 'These are the ones who've been offered places for September. Most are still at college. We just have to get them nicely soaked now, so they feel all warm and fuzzy about coming to join us. Then we throw them to the sharks . . .' Hector laughs again. Asif doesn't think he's exchanged this many words with Hector since his own graduate drinks reception three years previously; back then, he thought that Hector was the most impressive man he had ever met. The sort of man that Asif could himself become if he worked hard enough; back then, he thought that the firm would be the answer to his prayers, if only it could give him the sense of inflated self-esteem that Hector possessed.

Asif follows Hector into the meeting room, and is relieved to see that there are probably enough people in the room for him not to have to do anything. He really is there just as another body, to add a bit of background noise and bustle, but otherwise unimportant. He grabs a drink and finds himself next to Ravi from CFS; 'So, they got you too?' he asks Ravi.

'Looks like it,' says Ravi, adding drily, 'Hector Protector strode into town, and I didn't make it to the gents fast enough, so he saw me.' He clinks his wine glass to Asif's beer. 'Well, here's to free booze at least.'

'Is this everyone?' asks Asif, looking around. He sees the six graduates, the boys looking a bit gauche in their suits, and in ties they had either been given for Christmas or borrowed from their dads, the girls rather appealing with shiny hair and new heels, although one is ostentatiously blowing her nose, one has a haughty blonde regard, and the other is laughing too loudly; with them are the three ladies from Personnel, and the managers that the grads will be working for, and Hector, holding court with a newly snipped cigar and a champagne glass.

'No, we're just waiting for Matt and Lynn from Marketing,' says Ravi. Asif nods; he doesn't know who Lynn is, but he rather likes Matt, the excessively cheerful Director of Internal Communications; he is one of Ravi's best friends, and always takes over these sorts of situations by making inane group conversation, making people stand in a circle and demanding things of them like, 'So tell us – what was the first record you ever bought? And what's your favourite movie? And what team do you support – and for God's sake why?'

A corporate recovery manager wanders over to them. 'What do you think of the new talent?' he says, nodding towards the girls in a manner which Asif thinks is rather inappropriate. He notices that the manager's eyes are slightly glassy, and decides that he must already have got himself half-cut with the effort of making conversation.

'Sneezy, freezy, breezy,' says Ravi promptly, his analysis so well-put that Asif can't help but giggle.

'Still, you would, wouldn't you?' the manager leers slightly; he is possibly double the age of the girl graduates, and Asif feels a little bit sick.

'I wouldn't. I'm married, Percy, remember?' Ravi taps his wedding ring proudly. Asif is wondering how he can get away from Percy, and downs his drink quickly, thinking that he could go to the drinks trolley as an excuse; he takes a final long swig, and sees Mei Lin walk into the room through the bottom of his beer glass, accompanied by Matt from Marketing.

'Hello Lynn,' Percy calls out eagerly, and Mei Lin turns, and gives him a nod that might even be described as curt. She takes a glass of Chardonnay from the trolley, and goes straight over to the little circle where Personnel are still chatting to the grads. She smiles as she introduces herself, and her narrow eyes twinkle as they reflect the buttery glow of the wine.

'Toffee-nosed cow. I don't know who she thinks she is,' hiccups Percy. 'And she's not nearly as good-looking as she thinks, either.' Asif hides a smile; Mei Lin has clearly not succumbed to Percy's low level harassment.

'I think she's rather attractive,' says Ravi, 'in a low maintenance sort of way. She should wear a little make-up. A bit of lipstick and powder on her nose would work wonders.'

Asif looks at Ravi in astonishment; how can he not see what Asif sees, that Mei Lin is the most beautiful woman in the world, with her silken hair and her ivory skin and the warmth of her deep, brown eyes? He feels brave with his second drink, and goes and stands beside her. 'Hi Mei Lin, how's Melody?' he asks, pleased that he has remembered to ask after her daughter and even remembered the baby's name.

'Hi . . .' says Mei Lin, looking apologetically at him. 'I'm really sorry, I don't remember . . .'

'Asif,' says Asif promptly, before she can finish her question; saying his name is like pulling off a plaster, something unpleasant but necessary, and best done quickly to minimize the pain. 'Asif Murphy. Don't worry, it happens all the time. It's not an easy name to remember.'

'Mine neither,' says Mei Lin. 'It used to feel like I spent half my working day spelling my name to people on the phone; I've been called everything from Mailing as in You've Got Mail to Mauling as in Big Scary Animal. It's easier just to let everyone call me Lynn. And Melody's fine, thanks for asking. She's not crawling yet but rolls around everywhere – she went right under the sofa the other day and came out covered in fluff.'

'Was that scary?' asks Asif with interest; he has

always thought of babies as fragile things to be kept wrapped in sterile coverings.

'More funny than scary, I should think, but I wasn't there, so I don't really know. The child-minder told me about it.' Asif looks at her briefly, as he isn't sure if he caught an edge to her voice. She gives him her capable smile, and he decides he must have imagined it.

'And how's work?' asks Asif, determined to attempt a conversation before he melts back into the wallpaper. He has only the sketchiest idea of what Internal Marcoms entails; he thinks it might be the same thing as marketing, which he knows just slightly more about, based on his first-year Conversion examinations. Wracking his brains, he can only remember two specific things: Maslow's hierarchy of needs, where you start with food and shelter, and eventually build up to comedy ties and leg waxing; and the theory of group formation. Forming, Storming, Norming, Performing and possibly Mourning, although the last one didn't seem to quite fit. Neither seems appropriate for small talk, so he is glad when Mei Lin finally stops fiddling with her watch and replies.

'Oh, fine. Can't complain. Seems that Matt hired some steering group to come in while I was on maternity leave, and undid all the work I had done on our corporate identity. Replaced all my nice simple statements with hyper-intelligent, convoluted ones to justify their fees. And now I have to work all next weekend to implement their

170

brainless schemes across the company. You know the sort of thing, vox pops to be played in the lunch queues, notepads and novelty toys for all staff with the new mission statement . . .'

'Be Proactive not Inactive Seek Solutions not Problems . . .' says Asif.

'My God? You actually read the memo!' laughs Mei Lin. 'I think you might be the only one who has!' She pats his arm in solidarity, and then groans audibly as Matt approaches.

'My dears, we're being far too cosy aren't we?' he rebukes them. 'The point is to *mingle*, dears, mingle!' He sighs as he sees the new grads are formed in a closed group and chatting amongst themselves. 'Well, looks like Uncle Matt's going to have to take things in hand.' He taps his wine glass with his cufflinked sleeve, and once he has got everyone's attention, he calls out, 'Right, everyone in a circle; starting with YOU.' He points to a reluctant Ravi. 'So what was the first record you ever bought?' Ravi laughs despite himself, familiar with the drill, naming something obscure but acceptable by a Brit Pop band, and Asif is left desperately thinking what he can say that might leave him with an ounce of office credibility. He can't remember what he might have said last time he was asked this, and there is no way that he could tell the truth; the first record he bought was 'Teletubbies say Eh-Oh' as a present for his youngest sister.

Almost two hours later, made bearable only by extreme amounts of imported beer, Hector finally leaves, which means that everyone else can too. 'Thank God,' mutters Mei Lin. 'I'm paying Melody's sitter golden time while she's just sat on the sofa watching *Supernanny*.'

'Have a good evening, Mei Lin,' says Asif a touch wistfully. 'Well, what's left of it, anyway.'

Mei Lin stops outside the door, and asks Asif, 'Why don't you call me Lynn, like everyone else does?'

Asif feels caught out in some way, and answers uncertainly, 'Because it's not your name. Your name's Mei Lin, and with you, it just doesn't seem right to abbreviate it, somehow.' He adds apologetically, 'I'm sorry if I've been annoying you, by calling you Mei Lin all evening. Do you not like it?' He is appalled by how exquisite he finds her collarbones, which he can see in the open neck of the shirt she is wearing.

Mei Lin gives him a small, delicate smile, and looks up at him frankly as she shrugs her suit jacket on. 'I do like it,' she says, before she walks off towards the lift.

SHADOW ANIMALS

My name is Yasmin Murphy and I don't like Change, as it makes me feel unhappy and itchy, the way that bright sunlight used to make me feel when I was on anti-seizure medication, and even though I haven't been on anti-seizure medication for years, the memory is so strong that I still feel uncomfortable when I go out in the sun. I know that the unhappy, itching sensation is just caused by electrical impulses in my head triggered by thoughts, rather than triggered by sensors in my skin, but I can't ignore it, and so I always wear dark glasses and a hat and long sleeves in bright sunlight. This is a sensible thing to do anyway, and it reduces the chances of skin cancers and life-threatening melanomas.

I used to be scared of the sunshine, and so my mum taught me how to make lots of different shadow animals, so that I could play with the light and shadows, and see it as something fun rather than something horrible. My favourite shadow animals were the bunnies, because the bunnies were easy to make, and you could do one with each hand and make their noses twitch with the

173

tip of your thumb, and they were always the same shape, although my mum would change the ear position to make it into a happy bunny (perky ears pointing up), sad bunny (droopy ears pointing down), cheeky bunny (one ear up, one ear down).

I know that it is illogical to dislike change, as change is something that is inevitable; just like day turning to night turning to day is inevitable, except on the rare occasions of solar eclipses, and there won't be another one of those in the UK in my lifetime. The way that my mum taught me to deal with change was to prepare for it. When I was a little girl, I prepared for the night by putting my pyjamas on, and drinking warm milk before bedtime. When I was eleven, I prepared for puberty, going with Mum and Lila to the shops when they bought bras and sanitary towels.

And now I have two changes to prepare for. I have to prepare for the fact that in a few months, there will be a documentary about me on the TV, and people might recognize me, and ask me questions to do with my AS. And that also, I might be going quite blind. I have looked up my condition on the internet, and I have Stargardt's disease, which is a degenerative disease that presents in adolescents and is without a cure. Once I am substantially blind there will be lots of things that I won't be able to do, so I am going to do them now while I still can. I don't like the uncertainty of not knowing the exact amount of time I have, and so I have given myself four months, so that

I can organize my plans. I hope that my sight lasts at least this long, as I don't like having to rearrange my plans once I've made them.

Here are some of the things that I want to do: Learn to play Tennis like Mum did See all the *Simpsons* Episodes See every film with a Superhero including fake Superheros like Batman and Even the Badly Reviewed Ones which were Commercial Flops Learn to play Golf like Dad Go to a Fairground See the Sea and Collect Sea Shells See the Desert See the Mountains Reach the final level of *Doom* Make Candyfloss Use a Potter's Wheel Bake Bread Ride the Big Red Sightseeing Bus Around London Draw St Paul's Cathedral and the Houses of Parliament Go to France Go to Germany Go on an Aeroplane Go on a Boat Go on a Helicopter Wear A Wig Look After a Baby Save a Life . . . There are lots more, and this isn't a linear list, they spin haphazardly around me like electrons around a neutron, some getting closer and more important, some getting further away, and some colliding with others to knock them out of the way, or joining and becoming something new. It's like I am at the centre of a set of concentric circles, and these items are dotted around the circumferences at different points, and then the circle folds open to become a sphere, and then folds open again to become something with four dimensions and no surface area, and this new shape is a little like the landscape of my mind.

Asif has promised to help me to do all these

things, although he doesn't know why, as I haven't told him; my deteriorating sight is Mostly or Wholly Irrelevant to him. I'm not worried about what will happen once I am blind. I have a plan for that too.

I do not think that this is the same as lying, as lying makes me feel uncomfortable, and I don't feel uncomfortable about not telling Asif about going blind. At most, it's a lie by omission, which means not saying something that you know to someone else. Lies by omission are also called secrets, and everyone has secrets. My whole mental landscape is a secret, as if I tried to explain it to someone it would take for ever and would be exhausting. Even Mum had a secret, and she was very keen on honesty, and used to tell us all that we should never have to lie, except on occasions where safety was compromised, as keeping safe was more important than being honest. She also said it was OK to lie to a teacher if they said something like 'Do you think I'm stupid?' to me, as once a classroom assistant called Miss Mellon did, and I told her the truth and got into trouble, but Mum said that most good teachers wouldn't say things like that anyway, and once I went to my private school for seniors, no one did.

Mum's secret was that she used to cry in the bathroom at night when she thought that Asif and Lila and I were asleep and not listening, but I always slept very badly because of all the chattering in my head, and when I heard Mum move at night,

I would go and watch her through the crack in the door, as I didn't like the door shut all the way at night. And once, Mum saw me in the shadow when she was coming out of the bathroom, and she stopped and stared at me for a moment, and looked like she was going to start crying again, as her mouth started to shake a bit, and she was wearing her red silky pyjamas with the frayed buttonhole two up from the bottom, but she didn't cry. She stood up straight, and said, 'Sleepy time, Yasmin.' She came to take me by the hand, but I pulled away, as her face was all wet and messy and salty. So she went back into the bathroom, where I heard her wash her face. And then she looked nice and dry, and smelt of lavender soap, and I let her take me by the hand, and put me back to bed, and she sang, 'Yasmin's off to sleepy land, on her feather boat. Yasmin's off to sleepy land, her dreams keep her afloat.'

When I was older I realized that it wasn't that usual to cry alone at night, but she was dead then and I couldn't ask her about it. But it was probably OK as she did it in the bathroom, and you can do lots of things in bathrooms that you can't do in public, like pooing and peeing and farting and banging your head and having sex which is called 'cottaging' if you're gay and cutting yourself and even throwing up on purpose. It's all right as long as other people can't see what you're doing. As long as they can't see, they can't get upset. That's why bathrooms have locks.

CREATING CLOUDS

Lila is standing naked in front of her mirror, smearing her freshly scrubbed skin with glutinous handfuls of thick, unscented petroleum-based emollient. The cream leaves white traces across her calves and belly, and she rubs them in, leaving her glowing palely in the poor light of her damp bathroom. The room is windowless, and so she has painted the ceiling and each wall different shades of sky blue, with billowing cloud formations so accurate that they might have been photographic projections; when she lies in the bath, she looks up at her hand-crafted clouds through lidded eyes, and imagines them moving across the room like real clouds, merging and dispersing with the wind to create fantastic creatures. It is wrong, she knows, to indulge herself with fake clouds rather than real ones, and sometimes she is tempted to paint out the fraudulent images with whitewash, and bathe in a clean, white box, like a lunatic's padded cell. But she hasn't painted the room white, as she knows that the blankness would give her nothing to focus on apart from her slippery self. She stares at herself now, looking critically and even assessingly, as though she were a piece of meat for sale, hanging from a hook; her skin is a little better now that the weather has turned, the dry chilly air and brittle sunshine finally promising the approach of spring, and her unmade-up face seems less raw than usual, the thick layer of cream causing her to gleam with a slick semblance of health. Her breasts are still high, and she wonders how much longer it will be before her youthfulness slides away – she supposes that a pop star her age would be described as relatively young, rather than just young. Her inner thighs aren't bleeding or bandaged; she had picked up her scalpel, and with some mixed-up regret and relief, put it back down again. For some reason she can't cut herself on a day when she is going to meet Henry, as even though he can't see her, she feels as though he would know. Perhaps it is because he can't see her that he would know, as he has the disconcerting habit of seeing through her instead.

'Who shall I be today?' Lila asks the unwrapped lump of meat in the mirror. That was the difficulty with Henry; he couldn't appreciate what she wore on the surface, and so there was no particular costume to wear with him, no particular image to try on with a set of clothes. She doesn't have to be a high-heeled exec, a tempestuous goth or a flower-wielding hippy. She doesn't have to be anyone. She is suddenly unsure who she really is; she suspects the truth is that she is just someone who wears torn pyjamas and ice-cream-stained T-shirts and grey

179

frayed underwear when she is alone, but she couldn't go out like that – perhaps as far as her car, but certainly not all the way to the picturesque Kent coastline. After some hesitation, she pulls out a pair of her painting jeans, smattered with splashes of astonishingly clashing colour, and an ancient faded T-shirt bought from Chinatown that bears the legend *Intevnational Love All Around The Wovld*, with two typos that were hard to spot because of the curling violet font, but which still caused Yasmin to shrink in horror whenever she saw them. She pulls on a pair of expensive, sinfully comfortable boots that she bought during her preppy catalogue model time with Wesley, and notices that there is a dark, gungy splodge of something unidentifiable on the heel and side; it could be anything, paint, tar or even dry dog turd. Mum was right, she thinks, I can't keep nice things, and she pulls them off and tosses them aside, replacing them with a pair of well-worn trainers. She looks at herself again in the mirror – she is no longer certain who this woman is, dressed like anyone in jeans and a T-shirt, and topped off with ludicrous cranberry hair. It is possible that, for today at least, she is no one but herself.

After having carefully made up her face with a matt foundation that tones down the emollient glow, and with just a slick of lip gloss, Lila gets in her car and drives to the Finchley house, where Asif is waiting for her.

'What's up,' she asks, after kissing him hello.

'I can't stay long, I'm due down at Whitstable for lunchtime.'

'Whit-where?' asks Asif, whose knowledge of the UK outside the M25 is sketchy.

'Does it matter?' replies Lila, a bit testily, not wanting to talk about it.

'I guess not,' says Asif, and she is suddenly unreasonably disappointed that he doesn't want to know where she is going, who she is seeing. She wants him to be concerned about her, the way he was the other week, the way he is concerned over Yasmin. She wants someone in the world to be a little interested in what she does, a little curious at least. 'You look different,' Asif says, standing back and looking at her properly.

'Is that bad? Normally you say I look nice,' says Lila pertly.

'You know you always look nice. It's just that T-shirt – you haven't worn it for years. You used to wear it before . . .' Asif doesn't know how to finish the sentence, it seems inappropriate to say that she used to wear clothes like that before Mum died. Before she left school and started to try on other lives with different costumes. He takes refuge in saying something even more inappropriate instead, '. . . you had boobs,' he jokes weakly.

Lila looks at him. 'Before you had boobs, you mean,' she says, unkindly poking his pectoral muscle with her finger.

'Ouch,' says Asif, backing away. 'Not fair, it's

181

impossible to stay fit when I sit on my butt in an office all day. Anyway, I've started going to the gym at lunchtimes. And I might start playing tennis too.'

'Why tennis?' asks Lila suspiciously. Their mum used to play tennis; she used to play with their dad, and when he died, carried on playing at a local club.

'It's why I asked you round; I wanted to show you something. It's a surprise,' says Asif mysteriously. 'Can we take your car? Mine's started making funny noises when I change up to third.'

'Sure. But isn't Yas due back from chess soon?' asks Lila. She follows Asif out of the front door, and unlocks her car.

'That's the surprise,' says Asif cheerfully, belting himself in. 'Do you remember the way to Mum's old tennis club?'

In the tennis club, Asif and Lila sit in the balcony section overlooking the courts, and see Yasmin walking in a circle with three other beginners, bouncing a ball on her racquet. They are divided into pairs, and start banging balls at each other on half the court, with the instructor shooting out instructions to correct the forehand. 'I don't think I've ever seen Yas do a sport. Voluntarily, I mean,' says Lila. She watches Yasmin miss a ball, and then, without skipping a beat, just take one from the basket next to her, and serve one back to her partner instead. No panic, no fit, no moody refusal to move, no melt-down.

'This is her second week. She told me that she wanted to do this instead of chess,' says Asif. 'I organized the lessons,' he adds unnecessarily; he is conscious of being slightly too proud of this. 'She's even said that she wants to do a day trip to France, on a boat or plane, just not on the train, for some reason. She's never wanted to travel before. Something's changed,' he adds.

'She hates change,' says Lila, as though she has misheard Asif. 'Wasn't she worried about starting something new, so close to her A levels?'

Asif shrugs. 'I don't think she's worried about her A levels. It's just revision stages now, and she remembers everything anyway. She'll probably ace them without having to do much more work at all.' He realizes that this is insensitive, remembering how Lila had managed to plough her exams at the eleventh hour following Mum's death, and stammers apologetically, 'Not meaning, you know, about . . .'

Lila interrupts him. 'So what does this mean? Tennis and bloody day trips to Calais? That she's getting better? Is that the big surprise?' She is amazed how furious she feels, with Yasmin, with Asif, with herself. It is as though she is watching herself down on the court in Yasmin's place, missing the balls, but not dealing with it nearly as calmly as Yasmin.

'Well, yeah,' mumbles Asif, wondering whether he has missed something sinister and obvious in this new development. Wasn't it a good thing that

Yasmin had started to do something different, that she might be overcoming some of her behavioural idiosyncrasies?

'She can't get better,' Lila practically spits. 'I always told you that there was nothing bloody wrong with her in the first place.' She stalks out, and calls back over her shoulder, 'I've got to go, you can get the bus back with Yas, right?'

'Don't go,' says Asif, running after her, sure that he has done something indefinably wrong that he needs to make right. Lila in her *Intevnational Love* T-shirt looks just like the teenager to whom he broke the news of Mum's death, the tearful, blotchy-faced girl who shouted and shook Yasmin until she was a humming heap in the corner, with her fingers in her ears.

'I'm late anyway,' says Lila, not quite apologetically.

'Oh, OK then,' says Asif, despondently. 'Who are you seeing?'

'Just a friend,' says Lila, and having made enough of a scene, finally leaves. She sits in the car knowing that she has behaved badly, yet again. She has got something wrong. She has failed where Asif and Yasmin have succeeded, because they were brave enough to endure. She has lived so long with Yasmin, blaming her for everything that has gone wrong in her life, for the theft of their mum, for the stress-related eczema, for the string of failed relationships and unappealing jobs; what would happen if she couldn't blame Yasmin any more? She has another brief fantasy, in the not-too-distant future, of Yasmin as a Languages graduate of King's College, London, living in a minutely ordered flat while she does technical translations for a pleasingly anonymous multi-national; a successful, independent Yasmin, who plays tennis at weekends, and is so outwardly normal that only Lila can see that her smile is simply a socially conditioned response, and isn't the slightest bit sincere. While Lila grows old in her hovel, waiting tables and sleeping in her car when the heating goes off, crying in the early hours for the generous, loving, better person she might have been, if Yasmin had never existed. She wipes away her tears with the back of her hand, turns the ignition, and drives off, biting her lip to stop her mouth trembling.

On the courts, Yasmin is concentrating so closely on the balls heading in her direction that she doesn't even notice Asif and Lila enter the balcony, or Lila's swift departure. She misses more balls than she should, as her left eye has a cloudy section that makes it difficult to focus, and her sense of perspective is compromised even more than usual, so that everything appears to be somehow flat-tened. She runs for the airborne balls awkwardly, as she is unused to running for anything, and the sensory feedback up from the arches and heels and toes of her feet is overwhelming, making the rest of her body feel so light that she thinks she might bounce off into the air herself. Tennis, she ticks off her mental list. Learn to play Tennis like Mum did See all the *Simpsons* Episodes See every film with a Superhero including fake Superheros like Batman and Even the Badly Reviewed Ones which were Commercial Flops Learn to play Golf like Dad Go to a Fairground See the Sea and Collect Sea Shells See the Desert See the Mountains Reach the final level of *Doom* Make Candyfloss Use a Potter's Wheel Bake Bread Ride the Big Red Sightseeing Bus Around London Draw St Paul's Cathedral and the Houses of Parliament Go to France Go to Germany Go on an Aeroplane Go on a Boat Go on a Helicopter Wear A Wig Look After a Baby Save a Life . . .

Tonight she will bake bread. And next weekend she will go to France with Asif, and on the way they will see the sea, and collect shells. A ball approaches Yasmin so perfectly positioned for her forehand that it appears to move in slow motion, and she swings and finally makes a good return, her arm following through all the way to her shoulder, but a celebratory whoop from the upstairs balcony breaks through her concentration. She looks up, annoyed by the distraction, to see Asif, waving and smiling, his face glowing with cheap, shining hope. Yasmin does not recognize the hope, she has been told that for her faces are only decipherable at their simplest states, like those of infants and animals, happy, sad, neutral, but she imitates him the best she can, and waves and smiles back. He is too far to make eye contact with, so she simply looks in his direction for a count of Mississippi One and Mississippi Two, before returning her attention to the court.

BODIES IN THE SAND

When Lila pulls up along the pebbled beachfront at Whitstable, she is still unreasonably angry and sorry for herself. She tried to call and cancel the date with Henry, but couldn't get through, and she knew that texting him would be too cowardly, not to mention insensitive. Did he have to ask other people, strangers who happen to pass by, to read out his text messages, or did he have some clever device that read them out to him? 'You can't park here, love,' says an ancient old man in a fisherman's jumper, with a black beanie hat pulled snugly over his ears. 'There's a car park over there, right on the beach.'

'Right, cheers,' says Lila, utterly disappointed by the old man's friendliness, by the still, chill beauty of the beach, by the glimmering sea in the bright bone-white sunshine. She knows it's wrong to feel miserable on such a glorious day, in such picturesque surroundings. She feels suddenly nostalgic for her rubbish-tip flat and the rubbish-strewn, grey streets of mildly neglected, grumbling Finchley, where she can snipe and cavil and slum without standing out. 'Don't suppose you know where the

Royal Native Oyster Store is, I'm meeting a friend there?'

'Of course I know it. Everyone knows it. The oysters used to be my living. Had to give it up in my seventies, my wife told me I'd catch my death. Finest oysters in Kent.' He winks at her cheerily.

'Right,' replies Lila, not wanting to be rude, but not managing to be polite. 'So where is it?'

'Right by the car park, love, like I said,' says the old man, and with a hearty 'Cheerio, then', carries on his way.

Lila gets back in her car, finds the car park on the beach, and goes across to the Royal Native Oyster Store. She sees Henry sitting out front in the sunshine on a rough wooden bench, facing the sea with almost a full glass of beer in front of him. 'All right,' she says. She slouches next to him, wrapping her coat around her, and sticks her legs straight out, watching a dog frolicking around the water's edge. 'I know I'm late,' she says, sounding unreasonably fractious rather than apologetic, as though the lateness is somehow his fault rather than hers. She is vaguely aware that she is behaving like a teenager. 'Took longer than I thought to get here. Middle of bloody nowhere, this place.'

'What's wrong?' asks Henry.

'Nothing,' says Lila shortly. The disbelieving silence hangs between them for a moment, and then Lila adds, 'To be honest I didn't want to come, but I couldn't get hold of you. I shouldn't be here. I'm just not in the mood to hang out on a postcard pretty beach and enjoy the bloody scenery today . . .'

She is interrupted by Henry, who says without the slightest glimmer of self-pity, 'No, I'm not much of a one for enjoying the scenery either . . .' Lila looks at Henry's profile, his straight nose, his high, sharp cheekbones and the fine eyelashes fanned over his cheek, as his eyes are momentarily shut even though he is facing straight ahead. He would have had to travel all the way from Putney to Victoria, and then take the train down here, and then have a treacherous walk from the station to the beach; it must have taken him hours. She wants him to yell at her, to make her feel bad for ruining the day out. It would make her feel better, because then she could yell back, and go to her car, and drive home, and make little cuts on her leg, like notches on a headboard marking a new fall from grace.

'. . . To be honest, it's the company that I came for,' he finally says, opening his eyes and turning to face her. Lila stares at him, at his luminous smile in the pale sunlight, and feels all her anger melting away. She has an absurd urge to press her face against his awful duffel coat and cry hot, grateful tears of relief. Instead she just edges closer to him on the bench, so that the sides of their arms are touching, and tilts her head so it rests slightly, and barely perceptibly, on his shoulder. Henry reaches for her hand across the bench, and takes it in his, palm across palm, his thumb lightly brushing her scarred wrist. Lila cannot remember the last time she sat quietly with someone, holding one, holding their hand; she has never felt so calm and protected in her life.

'This is definitely a date, if I get to hold your hand,' says Henry.

'You're an idiot,' says Lila, hoping that brusqueness will cover up the warmth in her voice. 'For liking me, I mean. I'm obviously far too much trouble. I turn up here, late and whining like a complete bitch, and then you go and say something nice to me. It's all wrong.'

'I said to stop calling yourself a bitch,' says Henry. 'It's possibly the only thing that I dislike about you.' He stands up from the bench, and pulls Lila up with him. 'If you like, I'll introduce you to a real one.' He walks a few feet forward, still holding Lila firmly by the hand, and gives a low whistle. 'Daisy!' he calls out. The dog that has been gambolling in the surf, a golden Labrador with a glistening coat, comes racing over and starts jumping up and licking their hands. 'Sorry, she's a bit over-friendly,' says Henry apologetically, 'and she's far too excited at being off-duty on the beach, after working all morning to get us here.'

'So this is the mystery blonde you share your life with,' says Lila caustically, and then gets practically knocked over by Daisy's enthusiastic scrabbling. 'Great, now I smell of wet dog,' she mutters, as Daisy starts licking her again, and tickling her with her wet muzzle. 'Stop it! Halt! Heel!' she tries

191

ineffectively, unable to stem the dog's winsome and unsolicited affection. 'OK, she's lovely,' Lila admits, standing up, and patting her coat. As though this is the validation Daisy needed, she woofs and whoops merrily back to the shoreline.

'Well, I think so. But I would anyway, because she's mine,' says Henry. 'Do you want to go for a walk?'

'Sure,' says Lila, coming forward to join him. 'What about your drink?'

'Oh, we can get a beer together later, if you like. I didn't really want this one, I hate drinking alone, I find it vaguely depressing, but some bizarrely friendly local bloke insisted I try it. Apparently it's the Finest Brew in Kent.' Lila stifles a laugh, and as they walk along the beach, finds that her hand has naturally slipped into Henry's once more, without her even noticing.

Hours later, Henry and Lila are sitting on the beach, with half pints of beer in plastic cups, and sharing oysters on a paper plate. 'I love the beach,' says Henry. 'I grew up in Southwark, in a crowded council house with my two brothers and two sisters, and we never got to go to the seaside. There were just too many of us for my mum to manage, and my dad was always working. He's a plumber, like my brothers are, and with so many of us to support, he never turned down any jobs. I didn't come until I started to go blind; I wanted to see the sea before it happened.'

'You knew you were going blind then, it didn't just happen?' asks Lila.

Henry shrugs his shoulders. 'I had lots of time to prepare. I was diagnosed when I was eleven. I had a grant and went to a fantastic school, with much better facilities than my brothers and sisters got. I was spoilt rotten, to be honest, and I wasn't even properly blind then, some of my depth, colour and central vision were compromised, but I could still see quite a lot, and get around myself, I could even play sports. My brothers and sisters were completely pushed to the side; they must have hated my guts, they even claimed that there was nothing wrong with me, and accused me of making it up just to get attention, although I'm sure they wouldn't admit that now. It's almost as though they couldn't wait for me to go blind, just to justify all the unfair, preferential treatment, so they could stop feeling angry with me and start feeling sorry for me, start liking me again, even.' Henry picks up an oyster shell, realizes that it is empty, and puts it aside. 'You probably think that sounds really paranoid.'

'Not really,' says Lila matter-of-factly, not bothering to explain herself. She passes him another oyster, and swallows one herself, shivering a little with the salty, wet kick on her tongue. 'So how long did they have to wait, to start liking you again?'

'Oh, only about five years,' says Henry drily. 'It happened so gradually, it was like drowning by inches. One day I went to our corner shop, and I realized that I wouldn't be able to get home without help; it was odd having to admit it, it was almost a relief.'

'Five years,' muses Lila. 'So you must have been able to do all the things you wanted to, over those five years, things you couldn't do later.'

'Not everything. I really, really wanted to drive. I bought all the daft auto magazines and learned the highway code and everything. But by the time I was old enough to take lessons it was too late; the only things I was allowed to drive were dodgems. And sometimes my brothers let me change gear for them, when we drove places. All boys like cars, I guess,' says Henry wistfully.

'Still, there's lots of other stuff you must have done. Learn Braille, get laid, that sort of thing.'

Henry chokes on his oyster in shock. 'Get laid? At sixteen?'

'Well, yeah,' says Lila, not thinking she's said anything controversial. 'Most sixteen-year-old boys would hump their hairy forty-year-old gym mistresses given half the chance.'

'Well, not me. I've never slept with anyone I didn't love,' says Henry defiantly. At Lila's silence he feels the need to explain. 'I know that came out sounding a lot more pompous than it should have. I'm not being judgemental, but it's just the way I am. My brothers thought I was a complete freak of nature. Still do, probably.'

There is a silence, which Lila breaks pertly. 'Sorry, was that my cue to disagree with them?'

Henry laughs, unoffended. 'If it was, you missed it.'

Lila lies back on the pebbles, her hands behind her head. 'I'm not sure I like the beach that much, on stunning days like this when everything sparkles. The light's so bright that it's blinding, it hides as much as it reveals. There's something sinister about it. It makes me think of bodies hidden in the sand.'

'You're the kind of person who sees something dark everywhere,' comments Henry, 'even on the brightest day. You'd probably say that roses are sinister, because they've got closed petals and sharp little thorns.'

'But they are!' agrees Lila, amazed that he has guessed this about her. 'I've always thought that.'

'Well, they're not the friendliest flower,' admits Henry. 'Whenever I buy roses I always manage to injure myself on them. But I buy them anyway, not because they're beautiful, because that's not something I can properly appreciate, but because they smell so amazing, even with their thorny stems.' He adds, with a hint of embarrassment, 'This is going to sound stupidly romantic, but they remind me that even wonderful things can have their flaws. But that's no reason to reject them altogether.'

'Are you talking about me, or you?' asks Lila, amused.

'Someone thinks a lot of herself,' retorts Henry. 'I was just talking about roses.'

Lila rolls over, and picks up another oyster. 'The last two are yours; I've been eating faster than you. Because you've been talking too much, as usual.' She swallows it, and says offhandedly, 'I suppose I should give you and Daisy a lift home. Rather than letting you battle it out on the train. I should have offered earlier, to bring you down here; it didn't occur to me before. I'm a bit clueless about etiquette.'

'No thank you,' says Henry, politely but rather curtly. 'I'm not eight years old, I don't need to be delivered and collected by a grown-up for my play-dates.' He pushes himself up from the pebbles where he has been lying. 'Sorry, I don't mean to be ungracious. But I like the fact that you don't feel you have to make exceptions for me, that you don't have to help me.'

'Why would *I* need to help *you*?' asks Lila in genuine surprise. 'You're the white-collar worker with the higher education and the good job.'

'Big deal,' shrugs Henry. 'I most likely wouldn't have got either if I hadn't gone blind, and bene-fited from positive discrimination on both counts. I'd have just become a plumber like everyone else in my family – I had to go and work in an office, because I wasn't fit to work with my hands.' He adds wryly, 'You could say I got lucky.'

Lila looks at him a bit sharply, wondering if he is expecting her sympathy. 'In fact, you probably only hang around me because *you* get to feel superior,' she says provocatively. 'Because you think someone else needs you for a change.'

'Oh, you don't need anyone,' replies Henry flatly.

'You're probably the most independent person I know. You'd sleep on the street before you admitted needing help. But don't you ever think that it would be nice to have someone there for you, whether you needed them or not?'

'I'm not sure what you're getting at,' says Lila, shutting her eyes as she feels a little bit drunk and hazy with the sunshine, even with the cold, knobbly pebbles beneath her.

'I guess I'm asking when I get to call you my girlfriend,' says Henry.

'What?' laughs Lila, but Henry looks completely serious. 'Why would you want to do that?'

'Because then I can tell my family all about this wonderful girl I've been seeing.' He smiles, and corrects himself, 'Well, not seeing, so much. In the literal sense. But you get what I mean.' He adds, 'And then I could kiss you with complete confidence.'

'You mean you wait until someone's been formally pronounced as your girlfriend before you kiss them?' asks Lila with amusement.

'Well, in my situation it's best to err on the side of caution,' shrugs Henry. 'I don't have the benefit of visual cues, so it's very easy to misread the signs.' He lies back down next to Lila; he is close enough for Lila to sense his breath, his chest rising and falling beside her, but they do not touch.

'I'm flattered,' says Lila, blinking up at the clouds streaking the blue sky, 'but the truth is that I'm not a very nice person, and I'm not a very happy one either. It's highly unlikely that you'd want to spend much more time with me, if you knew what I was really like. And it's even more unlikely that I'd become a nicer or a happier person just to avoid disappointing you.'

'I think I said to you once before,' says Henry, turning towards Lila, 'that just because something is very unlikely, doesn't mean it's impossible.' He lifts his hand, and hesitating a moment, asks, 'May I?' before smoothing the side of her face lightly with his palm. His fingers whisper across the tip of her nose and along her eyebrow, tracing around her eyes and from her cheekbone to her jaw. 'I suspect,' he says cautiously, 'that you are far too pretty for your own good.' His hand still rests against her cheek, and Lila has to resist the urge to turn her face into it, to breathe in against his palm. 'I suspect that you think you're only special on the surface.' He continues, 'If that's what you think, Lila, you're wrong. I know I don't know you very well, but sometimes I have this ridiculous feeling that I'm the only person who can see who you really are, underneath. There's almost nothing I couldn't like about you . . .'

'Apart from?' asks Lila, pulling away from him.

'Apart from when you don't appear to like yourself,' finishes Henry, putting his hand down with a touch of embarrassment.

Lila lets a puff of laughter escape, and then finds that she is unable to stop. 'You're priceless,' she says. 'You're so achingly sincere that it hurts.'

'It's one of my flaws,' agrees Henry with wry self-deprecation. 'And now you're laughing at me.' He shakes his head. 'God, this is humiliating. You can see why it's better that I err on the side of caution, in relationships.'

'Oh, sod caution,' says Lila, 'just shut up for once,' and she turns back towards him impulsively, her own hands warm against the side of his face, feeling his angular cheekbones, the slightly rough stubble. She suppresses a sigh, and lies back down, her cheek against his. Henry finally understands, and puts his arms around her, just holding her, saying nothing. Lila feels that eerie wave of intimate calm she sensed the first time he touched her, the first time he held her hand, and she finally feels protected against the sinister beauty of the day, against her own twisted, obdurate nature. 'Get your coat, Henry,' she whispers, saying the words so close to him that she can feel her lips brush his face as she speaks. 'You've pulled.' And when they finally move together and kiss, lips chapped by the wind, mouths warm and swollen with salt, it happens as naturally as a flower turning towards the sun.

UNLOCKED DOORS

Asif is sitting in the anteroom outside the company's inhouse gym, pretending to read one of the Men's Health titles stacked on the coffee table next to the water cooler. He had arrived at the gym as soon as his lunch break began, already dressed in trackie bottoms and T-shirt so he wouldn't have to change with the other blokes in the communal changing area, but despite his apparent keenness he wasn't terribly disappointed to find that the gym was shut. Sometimes the cleaning staff left it locked by mistake. After having left a message with Facilities, he had flicked through the selection of glossy sporty magazines, looking in vain for a sudoku or a promising crossword; the magazines were all brawn and no brain. 'All right, Murphy?' says Rupert, one of Asif's senior colleagues from his previous year spent in Audit. Rupert had been a rowing blue at Oxford, and strolls in looking very tanned and sporty; like Asif, he has already changed, and is wearing shorts that showed off his lean, muscular legs, and a branded top made from some unnatural, professional-looking material, probably designed for exploring rugged Arctic wastelands. He has a towel slung around his neck, and a bottle of water in his hand. 'Aren't you worried that you'll look a bit gay reading stuff like that?'

Asif puts the magazine down sheepishly; the model on the cover is grinning with manly smugness while he lifts his T-shirt and displays his perfect six-pack. 'No chance, mate. I'm not fit or well groomed enough to be gay.' He looks at Rupert, and feels a bit envious of his healthy glow. He makes a mental note of the brand of Rupert's top, and decides that he needs to start bringing a bottle of water to the gym; it makes Rupert look so much more serious, as though he actually intends to sweat. Asif, on the other hand, intends only to worship, but his goddess has not yet arrived. 'I've called Facilities, they'll be along to open up in a minute,' he adds, feeling disappointed that he has to share the gym with someone who'll show him up. The matronly lady from Facilities arrives, tutting apologetically, and Rupert follows her into the gym as she unlocks the doors and switches on the lights. Asif can hear the hoovering whoosh of the rowing machine start almost immediately; he pours himself a glass from the water cooler, and feels a jolt of familiar pleasure when he hears a friendly voice behind him.

'Hello again, Asif. Are you stalking me?' asks Mei Lin, still in her office suit, with her gym bag over her shoulder.

'No,' lies Asif, as that is probably exactly what

he is doing, coming to the gym on days when he has spotted Mei Lin doing the same. When he was a kid, before he went to university, he used to hang around the newsagents where Jilly Cox, their neighbour's teenage daughter, worked, for much the same reason. He'd go religiously every day, just to be able to share her space and a few words of conversation with her, to have the unbearable intimacy of passing her change warm from his hand, and receiving his pack of salt and vinegar crisps and can of Coke by return. He has an unrequited crush on Mei Lin that is even more painful, as it is untempered by the adolescent hormones that might excuse his behaviour; his admiration is so pure that it verges on an obsession. He doesn't feel comfortable until he is able to assert that Mei Lin has entered the building; he feels unreasonably bereft every evening when she leaves exactly at 5.30 p.m., always in a slight rush, as she has to relieve her childminder, and if she is a moment late or early when she walks in or out of the fifth-floor lifts, he feels the blood pulsing at his temple, because he wants to know why. He glances at Mei Lin discreetly as she passes in the corridor at lunchtimes, and stares openly at her back if there is no one to see him, and thinks that he would do anything, absolutely anything, if she were to turn and look at him kindly, if she would just call out his name. He thinks that he is in real danger of making a fool of himself. He protected Yasmin from herself, when her behaviour veered towards the antisocial, and even chaperoned her on occasions when it was deemed necessary; but there is no one to protect him in the same way, nobody provides care for the carer. He jokes to conceal any obvious discomfort. 'I got here first. I thought you were the one stalking me?'

'Well, I do like younger men,' says Mei Lin good-naturedly, without an ounce of flirtation, as she walks into the ladies' changing room.

Asif goes into the gym, an uninspiring, base-ment room with grey strip-lighting and no windows, with viciously cold air con that is somehow ineffective against the slightly damp smell that always seems to linger. The TV at the end of the room is permanently set to BBC News 24. It wasn't surprising that the gym wasn't that popular, even though it was free. Most people preferred to pay for the posh fitness centre that was ten minutes down the road, with its shiny banks of plasma screens, heated swimming pool and sauna; it was only time-starved parents, like Mei Lin, who couldn't go after work, or work-obsessives like Rupert, who used this gym, as they could do a session in half an hour of their lunch break, and be back at their desk within five minutes if they were needed. Asif takes the cycling machine that is two along from the one that Mei Lin normally uses, and starts on a warm-up programme while he is waiting for her to arrive. When she does, wearing a white sleeveless vest

203

over a loose pair of yoga trousers, her inky hair scraped back with a careless scrunchie, her magnificently unmade-up skin glowing in the unflattering light, he has to catch his breath. Her bare arms and the fluid fabric covering make him think of the statues of Greek deities that litter the Victoria & Albert Museum; she seems so perfect she might be carved from marble herself. I'd do anything, he thinks hopelessly to himself, but he makes sure that he says nothing. He smiles and nods in her direction, but she just squeals, 'Rupe!' and trots over to where Rupert is showing off his prowess on the rower.

'Lynn, sweetheart! How are you? Long time no see, where have you been?' says Rupert, drawing to a whooshing halt. He gets up and gives her a bear hug, kissing her chastely on the cheek.

'Making babies, remember?' says Mei Lin. 'I've got a lovely little girl, Melody. I've been back in the office for a few weeks now.'

'I was on an endless job in South Africa, working out of the Cape Town office. Just got back on Monday,' says Rupert.

'So that explains the tan, you look really well,' says Mei Lin. 'How's that gorgeous girl you were dating before Christmas? Patricia, wasn't it?'

'Oh, she's great, or so I hear,' says Rupert guardedly, shrugging his shoulders, dismissing Patricia as a past irrelevance. 'How's Stephen?' he asks. He doesn't notice the cloud that passes over Mei Lin's face with his question, as he carries on with oblivious good cheer, 'I should really call the old bugger up for squash.'

'He's also great, or so I hear,' says Mei Lin, equally guardedly. 'You really didn't know? We separated almost three months ago.'

Rupert shakes his head with sudden discomfort, and looks relieved when his phone starts vibrating on the floor next to the rowing machine. 'Bugger,' he says, glancing at the message, 'my meeting's been moved up, better hit the showers.' But he doesn't sound the slightest bit sorry; it would be tempting to think that he might even be lying, if it wasn't for his obvious pleasure in being so busy and important. 'Lunch, soon,' he insists firmly and insincerely to Mei Lin, kissing her goodbye so abruptly that he might as well be kissing her off.

'Great,' says Mei Lin tonelessly, to the air he has left in his efficient wake, his brown legs disappearing through the changing room doors. She gets on her usual cycling machine, and starts pedalling viciously. 'Absolute git!' she mutters to Asif, who can't pretend that he hasn't been listening, as he has forgotten to plug himself into his i-Pod.

'Pardon?' asks Asif politely, trying not to be thrilled by Rupert's swift fall from grace, however nice his Table Mountain tan and professional-looking togs, trying not to be grateful that Mei Lin has singled him out from the empty room to speak to.

'Rupe, he's an absolute git! The moment he hears that Stephen and I aren't together, he can't get away quickly enough. He doesn't know why we broke up, and he doesn't care. He just knows that he's on Stephen's side. Guys are all the bloody same.' She gets off the machine with a yelp of frustrated annoyance, and kicks it with the back of her foot.

'Not all guys,' says Asif, dismayed as he watches Mei Lin fall from grace herself, a fall as sudden as it is absolute. She isn't an untouchable goddess any more, she isn't a happily married woman wrapped in the protective bubble wrap of domestic bliss. She's an ordinary person, upset and in need of a bit of sympathy. Asif feels ashamed of himself, for having elevated her to somewhere where he couldn't see her problems, her own flaws and fragility; he had assumed that she was made of stone and steel, like his mother had been, but now he can see that she is just flesh and blood and tangled nerves like anyone else. He realizes that he can help, and he should at least offer, as some poor penance for having mistreated her, for having objectified her in an unflattering way she will never realize. After all, one thing he does know is how to provide comfort; it's very familiar territory for him. 'I didn't realize you were separated. I'm sorry – it can't be easy for you with Melody,' he says kindly.

Mei Lin kicks the machine again. 'Melody I can cope with. She's the only good thing to have come out of that bloody relationship. It was a quick marriage, and it'll be a quick divorce, and good

206

bloody riddance. It's the politics I can't stand, the who's-saying-what-to-who, and the who-did-what-to-who-and-why, and the divvying up all our friends. Well, we're not even divvying them up. Stephen gets them all. The guys are all slapping him on the back, and the girls are all fixing him up with their girlfriends or angling for him themselves.' She gives another short shriek of frustration, and this time punches the machine. 'Ouch,' she says inadequately, sucking her bruised knuckles.

'Look, would you like to get a coffee upstairs, in the cafeteria?' says Asif. She looks like she's going to hit the machine again, and adds cautiously, with a glimmer of humour, 'Maybe something decaf?'

Mei Lin smiles, and almost laughs. 'OK, a drink might calm me down.' She picks up her bag, and asks, 'Are you sure, I don't want to disturb your session?'

'It's all right. I don't really like being alone down here, anyway. There's something about basements; I'm always worried that someone will quietly lock the door on me at the top of the stairs, and leave me here for ever,' says Asif, wondering why he's telling her this.

'I'm guessing that your parents have a lot to answer for,' says Mei Lin, strolling out of the gym, already in a better mood.

They don't go to the cafeteria, as when they walk in Mei Lin sees Rupert sprawled at a table at the front, still in his gym gear and plugged wirelessly into his mobile; he gesticulates importantly while he speaks with unnecessary loudness. 'I knew the bugger didn't have a meeting,' she mutters. 'Look, let's just go to the juice bar around the corner.' She doesn't wait for Asif's reply, and she walks off with the confidence of someone used to being followed; Asif is so used to being told what to do in the office that he doesn't even take offence, and trails after her apologetically, as though it's him rather than Rupert who has let her down.

'Git,' Mei Lin says again, unnecessarily, as they take their curvy plastic seats in the bubble-gum-coloured juice bar. The décor is self-consciously groovy, and the place is full of girls from the office; Asif hadn't even known it existed – the guys on his team just go to the pub, or to the sandwich shop. Mei Lin is inspecting the menu of organic juices and healthy salads and soups. 'Sorry for dragging you here,' she says. 'It's the one place I can be sure not to bump into Stephen's rugger-bugger cronies.'

'That's OK,' says Asif, 'although Rupert should be the one hiding from you, not the other way around. He's the one who lied.'

'Yes, and it's OK for me to know he lied, but if he saw me, he'd know that I'd know that he lied, and that would be worse. For me I mean. It's humiliating enough as it is.'

'Oh, I see,' says Asif, who plainly doesn't. 'What's good here?' he asks conversationally, inspecting the brightly coloured menu himself, with juices promising everything from slimming properties to heightened sexual prowess. It was an organic minefield; which weakness did he want to confess to by ordering?

'I don't know, I always spend ages looking at the menu, and order exactly the same thing. The one with peppermint and ginger to keep me awake through the graveyard shift,' says Mei Lin.

'Sounds great, I'll need keeping awake,' says Asif, and then realizes what he's said. 'Through the graveyard shift, I mean. Not lunch. Not that we're having lunch, unless you want to.'

'No thanks, I brought in a sandwich from home this morning,' says Mei Lin distractedly, still too self-absorbed to register Asif's discomfort. 'Git,' she says again, abruptly.

Asif sighs, and orders the drinks. 'Does your ex work in the office or something?' he asks.

'He pretends to, just swans in to deposit his briefcase before flitting off around the world for another unnecessary, carbon-guzzling meeting with the States or Asia Pacific or the back of bloody beyond. Stephen's a partner in Audit.'

'You mean Stephen Baden-Ross? You're married to Stephen Baden-Ross?' asks Asif in astonishment. Baden-Ross was practically famous; he was the photogenic face of the firm that was always chosen to appear to comment on financial newsworthy matters on Breakfast TV; he was on the board and so important that Asif had never even seen him during his time in Audit, although

Stephen admittedly headed a different division to the one Asif had trained in. Mei Lin being married to Stephen Baden-Ross was the Accountants' Anonymous equivalent of being married to George Clooney. Asif stares at Mei Lin's perfectly smooth and symmetrical face, at her carved cheekbones, and is in mortal danger of propelling her back to the dizzy heights of her untouchable pedestal, when she suddenly looks so upset that her face crumples into that specific sort of plainness unique to those who are truly unhappy.

'Why does everyone react like that? He's not a bloody god, he's just another bloody accountant, when all's said and done. The world's full of them.'

'I'm sorry,' says Asif, 'I didn't mean to . . . imply . . . I don't even know what I didn't mean to imply. I'm sorry,' he says again, sure that this is the only word that can make things better. He's mucked things up again; he was meant to listen, and instead he's interfered. Worse than interfered, he's judged. He realizes that he doesn't deserve a kind word from Mei Lin; he doesn't deserve anything from her.

'Oh, stop apologizing,' says Mei Lin, 'I'm irritated with myself, not you. I should have calmed down by now.' Their drinks arrive, and Mei Lin drains half of hers with one long gulp. 'I should have got the Calming Concoction, not the Get Up and Go,' she realizes belatedly. 'It's just that everyone seems to think that I should have been so bloody happy with Stephen. Stephen's so handsome, Stephen's so clever, Stephen's so important, Stephen bloody walks on water and turns it into wine and is so much better than me in every way, so why can't I shut up and be a grateful home counties haus-frau . . .'

'I guess it's hard,' says Asif slowly, 'to be in a relationship with someone like that. Especially with a baby. If they've always got work priorities, and they're never around . . .'

'Exactly!' interrupts Mei Lin, looking with amazement that someone as unpromising as Asif, a mild-mannered Corporate Recovery junior executive, has actually understood. 'The funny thing, is that he doesn't even seem to think that we've broken up. How do you break up if you're never together in the first place? He wasn't even a weekend dad for Melody, he was an every other weekend dad, at best. She didn't know who the hell he was whenever he finally turned up.' She finishes the rest of her juice, and starts looking at the menu to order another. 'He still thinks that we'll sort it all out the next time he makes time for us in his schedule, as though me getting childcare and going back to work is just something incidental, trying to prove a point. He keeps advising me that I'm not going to get anyone better than him; it's infuriating that he really seems to believe it.'

Asif nods without thinking, as part of him believes it too; and then he shakes his head, as he remembers that Mei Lin is the most beautiful woman in the world, and can have anyone she

211

shines her gaze upon. He finds it very easy to listen to Mei Lin, especially to listen to her complain about her husband, and thinks that he could bask in her presence for ever.

'And you know what?' says Mei Lin, as though reading his mind, 'He might be right. I might never get anyone better than him. But that's not the point. I don't want someone better. I don't want someone extraordinary. I just want someone ordinary, someone who cares enough to put me and the baby before their career. Someone who doesn't think that the notion of me carrying on with my own career is some sort of feminist insult to them.' She pauses, and repeats flatly, 'Not someone better. Just someone different, I guess.'

Asif realizes that he can't remain silent for much longer, and asks, 'Maybe he could change, if he knew that's what you wanted?' It seems obvious to him; if he was married to someone like Mei Lin he'd move heaven and earth to make her happy.

Mei Lin snorts a short, bitter laugh. 'He didn't try. He didn't even offer to try. I guess at thirty-eight he's too set in his ways.'

'He's only thirty-eight?' repeats Asif in wonder. It was odd to think of someone like Stephen having an age, he was one of those immortal management types who had been around for ever. 'Still, he's quite a bit older than you,' he adds.

'Is that a roundabout way of asking my age?' asks Mei Lin drily. 'He's not that much older than me, I'm twenty-nine.'

212

'I'll be twenty-four in September,' replies Asif so quickly that it sounds almost competitive; all he was trying to say was that he wouldn't be twenty-three for ever. That he would grow up too, even if he would never be a Stephen Baden-Ross, although he was not so sure that he wanted to be; if Stephen Baden-Ross was able to let go of Mei Lin, he was probably the stupidest man who had ever existed. He finds himself mulling over the incontrovertible fact that Mei Lin is six years older than him, six years separate them; they would have listened to different bands growing up, watched different programmes; she would have started going to school before he was even born. He realizes with a pang of hopeless nostalgia that she is exactly the same age as Jilly Cox from next door.

'Well, thanks for coming out with me,' says Mei Lin, apparently deciding against another juice, as she puts the menu back down on the table. 'Sorry for dumping so much crap on you.'

'It's OK,' says Asif. 'Any time. I'm used to it, I've got two sisters.'

'I know,' says Mei Lin, surprising him. 'The documentary team asked our permission to use some shots of the office, to intersperse with your interview about your youngest sister.'

'Oh,' says Asif inadequately, not sure if he is happy or relieved that his depressing home reality has been revealed so unceremoniously to Mei Lin. He'd wanted her to think that he was a normal bloke, who went to the pub and drank pints and played darts and went to football at the weekends and dated. Not someone who stayed at home and looked after his little sister all day.

'Of course we said yes,' says Mei Lin reassuringly, misreading his apprehension. 'It's great PR for the company. I think it's amazing that you've cared for your sister since your mum passed away. No wonder you're so mature for your age.' Asif sits and waits dumbly for the final sentence, the damning indictment that always falls at this point in the conversation, the part where he is condemned for being such A Good Boy. 'I should take tips from you. You've been a parent for far longer than I have,' says Mei Lin, and she says it with admiration.

'Thanks, I think,' says Asif, with mixed-up relief. He is unsure what to make of this assessment of him; it is possible that it is true, but so obvious it has never occurred to him, even when Lila spat at him, 'Who died and made you Mum?' He sips his forgotten juice, as his throat suddenly feels dry, and in this new intimacy finds he can broach the one question that he has wanted to ask during their whole miraculous interview, where he has had nowhere to look but into the depths of Mei Lin's narrow, expressive eyes, sometimes solemn and still, sometimes merry with dancing lights. 'Mei Lin,' he asks seriously, amazed by his bravery, 'I hope you don't mind me asking, but did you love Stephen?'

'Of course I did,' she says, 'I wouldn't have

214

married him otherwise. And I think he loved me, in his way. But not enough.' She pushes her hands back through her hair, realizes that she is still wearing her absurd scrunchie, and pulls it out, letting her inky bob fall back into place around her cheekbones, as naturally as water forming a pool. 'It was the little things that gave it away. It's always the little things, isn't it? It's when he couldn't be bothered to say my full name, and abbreviated it to Lin. And I don't think he meant to anglicize it, but all at once the whole office was following his lead, and before I knew it I was Lynn to everyone. And I let it happen, without even realizing, wondering how I'd suddenly become someone I wasn't. Lynn from Internal Marcoms.'

'I've never called you Lynn,' says Asif, a bit defensively, not sure what he is going to prove by reminding her. It's absurd to think that this small point might favour him above everybody else, but it still gives him a feeling of hope out of proportion with its significance; like a plain girl who has manicured her nails for a party, as though a decent nail job would be enough to make her pretty.

'I know,' replies Mei Lin simply. She looks at him for a moment too long, as though suddenly seeing him clearly for the first time. It no longer seems such a trivial point. 'You know, this was nice,' she says, picking up her things, and getting out her credit card. 'I'm sorry, I'd better run. I have to get changed before my next meeting. The drinks are on me.' Asif doesn't have a chance to

215

protest, as she has already walked over to the till, where her card is swiped and handed back efficiently. 'I guess I'll see you at the gym on Thursday.'

'Yeah, Thursday,' repeats Asif casually, trying not to make it sound more than it is, wishing it was something miraculous, like a date, or a promise, or a secret. He imagines a braver, different him saying something like, 'We could grab another juice afterwards, if you've got time. Seeing as I owe you one,' and is shocked when the words actually tumble out, unbidden, a little bit mumbled, but otherwise perfectly intelligible.

'Why not?' says Mei Lin. 'And you should make sure you get something to eat,' she adds. 'I've seen how often you skip lunch, staying at your desk while your team abandons you. I do the same thing when I'm with Melody all weekend. It happens when you care for someone else all the time, you forget to care for yourself.'

'Oh, I don't need looking after,' lies Asif lightly, touched that she has noticed this about him. 'But I'll get a sandwich, or something.' She walks out of the door, and Asif tries hard not to stare at her, at her shoulder blades, at the curve of her elegant back, at her rubbing the gooseflesh on her bare arms in the cold, sunny street. He tries less hard to suppress his foolishly happy grin as it sinks in that 'Why' and 'not', two such unpromising little words when taken apart, actually meant 'Yes', when put together. He realizes that Mei Lin is even more amazing to him now that she is no longer a

216

goddess, now that she is someone who can feel pain and bleed, someone whom he can look at without turning into stone for the blasphemy; he realizes that he would still do anything, absolutely anything, if she were to turn and look at him kindly, if she would just call out his name. As if answering a prayer, Mei Lin turns back and waves to him, through the window of the juice bar. 'See you, Asif,' she says.

Asif waves back, still smiling as he looks down to inspect the dregs of his drink. Could it be possible that Mei Lin really just sees him as an ordinary bloke, rather than a messed-up ball of nerves ruled by routine, who panics in private, where no one can hear him scream, and who hides it all with smugness and with the aping of domestic competence? Could it be possible that deep down, he really is just an ordinary bloke, like any other? She had called out and named him, and Asif finds that he has finally discovered something to like about his name. When she says it, it is As If anything in the world were suddenly possible.

GAME NIGHT

'What's the matter?' Asif asked Lila, walking in the front door; he was later home than usual, as he had stayed at school and worked in the library. It was easier than working at home, where Yas's music upstairs would noisily compete with Lila's TV programmes downstairs, or vice versa. He knew something was the matter, as Lila's face was a black cloud of fury, Yas's music was even louder than usual, and there was no reassuring scent of dinner cooking from the kitchen, which is what normally signalled Mum's presence in the house.

'What do you think's the matter?' hissed Lila, sitting on the bottom step in the hallway with the phone on her lap. 'What's always the matter? It's sodding little Miss Sunshine upstairs, she's what's the matter.'

Asif tried to suppress a yawn; he'd had a long day at school, and he was tired. He was terrified that his weakness in Mechanical Maths would bugger up his predicted A level results and compromise his Cambridge application, and so had been working non-stop in preparation for the lower sixth exams.

He wondered where Lila found the energy to be so prickly and angry about Yasmin all the time; he found it was just easier to accept her odd behaviour, to let it wash over him, like a wave over sand. It wasn't like being angry ever changed anything; if anything, with Yasmin it just made things worse.

'Well, I'm sorry that it's all so bloody boring to you,' said Lila, who hadn't missed the yawn. 'You're not the one who's had to deal with it. Where've you been anyway, mooning over Jilly at the newsagent's or snogging Carrie-Slutty-Slater behind the bike sheds?' She dialled a number on the phone, stabbing the buttons impatiently as though she'd had to do it several times before, listened to an unresponsive tone, and banged it down in annoyance.

'Neither!' said Asif indignantly, cross at the injustice of Lila's accusation after a dull afternoon of working out the forces of theoretical ladders propped against imaginary walls, and the angles and weights which would prevent them toppling. 'I've been working. And you still haven't told me what's the matter,' he points out. 'Specifically,' he adds, before Lila can make another snide comment.

'Bloody Raingirl up there took more than two hours to come home from school. Mum got into a panic, thought she'd got lost again, even though she's not got lost since the first month she started at the new place, and went out to look for her. Yasmin's back now, and is sitting in the middle of her room humming with her fingers stuck in her

219

bloody ears, and Mum's still not back, and I can't get hold of her on her mobile.'

'She's probably on the tube, looking for Yasmin,' said Asif. When Yasmin had started her new senior school, Mum had gone with her the first few weeks, leaving ridiculously early to avoid the commuter crowds, and so Mum could get to work on time after dropping her off. Eventually, Mum had let Yasmin's healthcare specialists persuade her that it would be better for Yasmin's independence to let her travel by herself. When Yasmin had inevitably got lost, Mum had taken the tube, and got out at every single station which Yasmin would have had to travel through, eventually finding her sitting on the floor at the northbound platform at Archway. The train had terminated there unexpectedly, and it simply did not occur to Yasmin to get on another one.

'Well, duh,' said Lila, muttering, 'Stupid, stupid *boy*,' unnecessarily.

'Well, what took Yasmin so long?' asked Asif reasonably.

'Buggered if I know. I just asked her, saying that Mum had been worried sick and gone out to find her, and she started bloody howling at me,' said Lila. 'So I told her that she's going to get sent off to the bloody loony bin if she doesn't sort herself out, and then she went up to her room in a fit and slammed the door on me.' Lila was painfully aware as she reported this that she might have handled the situation a bit better.

'Nice,' said Asif crossly. 'She's only twelve. Anything could have happened to her, and you've just had a go at her. Really nice work, Lila.'

'Shut up, it's not my fault,' said Lila, as she tried ringing Mum again. She slammed down the receiver once more, and was shocked to find it ringing back immediately. 'Hello? Yeah Mum, she's here. I don't know why she was late, she hasn't said yet. Yes, she looked fine. She's in her room. Playing some music. What music? Well I don't bloody know! Sorry, Mum. But I really don't know. Some opera, I think.'

'It's Tchaikovsky, *The Queen of Spades*,' said Asif helpfully.

'Tchaikovsky, *The Queen of Spades*,' repeated Lila. 'OK, see you in half an hour then.' She hung up, and looked at Asif accusingly. 'Bloody Know-it-All.'

Asif went through to the kitchen. 'What are we going to do for dinner?' he asked practically. 'Shall I order us a takeaway?'

'Mum was going to make us gnocchi,' said Lila. Gnocchi was one of her favourite things, and she loved it when Mum made it, as she felt sure that she made it just for her. Of course it helped that Yasmin liked it too.

'She won't have time, it's game night tonight. We'll have to start as soon as she gets home,' said Asif.

'As if, Asif! No one's going to be in the mood for game night. Yas is still sulking in her room, you don't really think that she'll be ready to come down and play Monopoly and Ludo in thirty minutes' time?' said Lila.

'You know she will,' said Asif. 'She hates to take something out of her schedule once it's in. It doesn't matter what's happened earlier, at 7 p.m. on Thursdays we have game night. It's what we do.'

'Yeah, well, I'll pass,' muttered Lila rebelliously. Asif looked at her reproachfully, and then she huffed, 'Oh all right then! Just stop looking at me in that tone of voice. But you better go up and tell Yasmin that Mum's coming home, I don't think she'd let me in the door.'

Asif nodded, and walked up the stairs. Yasmin's door was firmly shut, and he knocked gently on it, just loud enough to be heard over the speakers. 'Hi, Yas. Can I come in, please?'

There was a pause, and he heard Yasmin lower the volume. She took a long time to reply, but Asif resisted the urge to fill the silence by repeating the question or rephrasing it, as that would just delay Yasmin's response even more. She sometimes took so long to answer questions that more than one teacher at her primary school had suggested that she had hearing difficulties; but in fact there was nothing wrong with her hearing, sometimes she just needed time to process what people said and work out that a reply might be required of her; her special-ists were working on her communication skills, and they were optimistic that by adulthood she would be able to have ordinary conversations. After a while, Asif's patience was rewarded, as Yasmin's flat, high voice replied without a flicker of emotion, 'You know that you *can* come in. But you *may* not.'

The niceties of grammar were lost on Asif, who was better at sciences, and he gently pushed the door open. 'Hi there, just to say that Mum's on her way back. Lila didn't mean what she said, she was just worried about you. We all are.'

'I said you *may* not,' repeated Yasmin, as though Asif hadn't heard her properly the first time. After a few moments she registered what he'd said, and asked with what seemed to be genuine curiosity, 'If Lila didn't mean what she said, why did she say it?' It made no sense to Yasmin that Lila would lie because she was cross; Yasmin never lied herself, she lacked the instinct for self-interest it required; people lied to make other people feel better so the liar would feel better themselves, or very occasionally to make other people feel bad, so the liar would feel an unworthy satisfaction. Asif looked into the bedroom, and saw Yasmin sitting crosslegged in the centre, with playing-card towers built high around her in a square fortress, almost reaching level with her shoulders, protected by walls so fragile and precarious that no one would dare touch them. 'Wow, that must have taken you ages,' he said, privately wondering how they were ever going to get her out of the room without disturbing the towers.

'It took me fifty-four minutes. I left a gap at the back so I can get out,' she added. 'So I don't have to build it all again later.'

'Are you ready for game night?' asked Asif.

Yasmin nodded, and looked at her watch, 'Yes, in twenty-six minutes, at 7 p.m.,' she said.

Asif nodded back, and smiled at Yasmin, wishing that she would sometimes smile back at him. She almost never smiled, except occasionally at wholly inappropriate things, like someone bumping into something and hurting themselves in the street. Once she and Asif had been walking by a pub on a Saturday lunchtime, and she had laughed out loud at an aggressive drunk falling over outside. The drunk had yelled out, 'Do you think I'm fucking funny or something?' and Yasmin stood stock still while she considered this question, and then nodded, and had just begun to explain exactly why she thought he was funny, when Asif dragged her hurriedly off, putting up with her complaining and crying about being touched, just to avoid the drunk lashing out at them. He had reported this seriously to Mum, who had explained to Yasmin that sometimes it was better to lie, if safety was in doubt. He wasn't sure how much of this Yasmin had really understood.

'Yas, why were you so late home?' he asked simply.

There was a longer pause than usual, but this time when Yasmin spoke she didn't stop, and let the words flow in a burbling monotonous stream. 'Because when I had to get off the Circle line, there was a dog poo on the platform, and I didn't want to get off and walk over it, so I stayed on the train and missed the stop. And I don't like going backwards,

224

so I didn't try to get off at the next stop and get a train back; instead I just stayed on the train until it went all the way round the Circle line and came back to the right station. That's why I like the Circle line, it doesn't start or finish anywhere, it just goes round and round in a big loop all day. And by then the poo was gone, so I got off the train, and changed lines, and then I came home.'

'OK,' said Asif, feeling vastly relieved and vastly sorry at the same time. She hadn't been picked on, or bullied, or pushed aside by the swell of commuters; she hadn't even got lost. But if Yasmin couldn't even walk across a dog turd, how would she ever cope with all the rest of the crap that the big, wide world would throw at her? He felt comforted, and very unworthy for being comforted, that in a couple of years he'd be at university, and it wouldn't be his problem any more.

About twenty-six minutes later, Mum and Asif and Lila and Yasmin were sitting around the Monopoly board, along with the pizzas that Asif had helpfully ordered for dinner. Yasmin was the iron, as always, and she played with the fierce concentration that only children seem to have, the all-encompassing greedy concentration of a cat regarding a mouse. She looked so solemn, with her brown ponytail bobbing as she rolled the dice, that she looked almost winsome. Mum was smiling, and Lila was laughing as she pulled at the pizza with her perfect teeth, the stringy cheese stretching all the way from the slice in her hands to her mouth. Asif couldn't help thinking that a stranger looking in the bay window to their front room would think that they looked like a perfectly normal, perfectly happy family.

Later that night, Lila went downstairs to get the spiky brush from Mum's handbag she secretly used when her itching was unbearable; her nails were kept so short that they weren't that effective for scratching. She didn't switch on any lights, as she didn't want to have to explain to Mum what she was doing; if Mum found her, she'd say that she just wanted a glass of water. She took the brush from the bag that was slung over the chair in the kitchen, and poured herself a glass of water to be on the safe side. On her way back up the stairs, she heard a funny, moaning sound from the bathroom. Lila realized that Mum was crying again, like she did after Dad died. Lila stayed where she was, she didn't want Mum to see her, but she saw that she wasn't the only one who was awake. Yasmin had appeared at her doorway, barely visible as her door was only open a couple of inches, and something about the reflected light from the bathroom gave her a slightly creepy air, especially when combined with her unsmiling childishness. She might have been the ghost of a mistreated Victorian orphan, come to wreak her revenge, were it not for her cheerful Teletubbies pyjamas, which she still insisted on wearing even though they were far too small and frayed at the cuffs. Mum came out of the bathroom, beautiful and loose-haired in her scarlet silk pyjamas, even with her tear-streaked face, and stopped in shock when she saw the sliver of Yasmin's form at her bedroom door, pale in the poor light. Neither of them saw Lila. And suddenly, Lila saw something on Mum's face that she'd never seen before; not beaming proficiency, not wistful pride or controlled reproach; instead, she saw fear. Mum looked terrified. It was only for an instant, so quick that it might have been a trick of the light or of Lila's overactive imagination, and before she knew it, Mum's features had smoothed back into their habitual expression of omnipotent maternal competence, of Buddha-like serenity; an expression that seemed to claim that in their house, Mum was God, and that without her, there would be no house, there would be no wider world. And she went to take Yasmin back to bed with a cheerful announcement of 'Sleepy-time', as though Yasmin was still three years old.

'Mum, your face is all wet and salty,' said Yasmin, refusing Mum's hand and backing away a step. And Lila saw that expression again on Mum's face, that fearful expression, and she knew that she hadn't imagined it the first time; it was as though Mum's face had been split open, and revealed the real Mum writhing and scrabbling for air underneath the smooth, still surface. Lila waited on the stairs, her arms burning with the red hot agony of itching, but not daring to make a sound or move an inch; she dug her blunt nails in her palms, to distract herself with pain, while Mum washed her face and took Yasmin back to bed, singing her the same night-night song that she had sung to Lila and Asif when they were infants.

It was nothing, Lila told herself, when she was back in her bed, scratching her arms furiously with her mother's brush; her arms were even worse than they had been when she had gone down to the kitchen, it felt like the skin wanted to crawl right off them. It was nothing, she repeated, not believing it one little bit. All these years she had resented Mum for loving Yasmin more than her; but now she realized the truth; Mum didn't love Yasmin more, she was scared for her, or scared of her; it didn't matter which, as they both amounted to the same thing; so much so that she sobbed in the bathroom where she thought no one would see. Lila was appalled at how much she hated Yasmin at that moment, more than she thought was possible; she was aware of having seen something she wasn't meant to, and that she shouldn't tell anyone, especially not Asif, in case he reacted just as she did. She would have to keep her mum's secret for Yasmin's sake; she would keep it for ever, and let it prickle away under her skin like just another eczemic itch. She dug Mum's brush so deeply and sharply into her skin that it felt as though she might draw blood, and biting her lip instead, put the brush down with great effort. She would keep the secret, and if it all got too hard for her, she would find another way of taking control.

HAPHAZARD CIRCLES

Lila hangs up her apron as she finishes her shift at the café, and waves goodbye to the owner's wife. 'Don't forget your tips,' says Maria, running over to the door with a teacup filled with coins, which she shakes into a plastic bag for Lila. 'I never knew a girl who got so many tips for doing so little,' she jokes boisterously. She hands over a wrapped paper package as well. 'The scones,' she explains, 'they'll only go to waste otherwise.'

Lila isn't sure whether to find Maria's matronly attempts to feed her up charming, or annoying. Still, she accepts the little gift with a smile, and strolls down the short distance to her flat, relieved to be free from the overbearingly friendly hustle and bustle of the café, relieved that she will soon be alone in her squalid sanctuary, with just her paints and an enormous inward-looking canvas for company.

She heaves open the front door to the communal hallway, and stops short as she sees Henry there, sitting on the bottom step of the staircase, his long legs sprawled out in front. He's listening to something on his earpiece, and for a callous instant she wonders if she can simply back out and shut the door again, without him noticing. She doesn't get the chance to act on her ignoble instinct, as Henry calls out, 'Lila!' and stands up.

Sighing, Lila steps into the hallway. 'Henry, what are you doing here?' she asks, trying to sound cross, but only sounding tired.

'I was worried about you. I haven't heard from you in weeks. We had the most glorious afternoon ever, and then you don't answer my calls, or reply to my texts. I came over a few days ago, and rang your doorbell, and I was sure you were in, and you didn't even answer.' He pauses, and asks a bit foolishly, 'What's going on?'

Lila walks past him and goes up the stairs. 'How refreshing, another bloke who whines about all the messages he's left without getting the message himself,' she mutters, as much to herself as him.

Henry follows her up, astounded by her rudeness. 'Aren't you even going to pretend to make up an excuse? To say that you were busy, or something?'

Lila fiddles with her keys, ignoring him. 'I wasn't planning to say anything at all. But if it makes you happy, I was busy, or something,' she says eventually, and opens her door. She doesn't ask him in, but somehow doesn't quite have the nerve to shut it in his face. 'Bye, Henry,' she says, looking straight at him. He seems tired too; his fine brown hair is falling in his eyes, and she suppresses the urge to brush it away, as one might a child's.

As she starts to shut the door, he holds it open, with a gentle gesture and surprising strength, given the spareness of his frame.

'Lila, may I talk to you, just for a little while? I'm sorry to have intruded, but would you mind letting me in?' he asks. Lila hesitates, disarmed by the complete lack of reproach or righteous indignation in his voice, by his acknowledgement to have no rights over her time. She finds it impossible to be rude in the face of such respectful behaviour.

'Just for a bit, then. I'm working on something,' she says, and stalks off to her kitchen. She pours herself a glass of wine, and takes it over to her canvas, considering it in the early evening light. As Henry eventually stumbles in from the hallway, narrowly avoiding falling over the clutter, she remembers her manners, and calls out, 'There's a sofa in front of you, if you want to sit down. Would you like something to drink?'

'No, thank you,' says Henry, who doesn't sit, but leans against the wall near the entrance to the room. 'So this is where you live.'

'Don't you mean, "So this is how I live",' says Lila caustically, as she is used to this reaction about her flat, and even Henry couldn't fail to sense the mess, the teetering towers of dispossessed disorder, the floor so littered that it is barely visible, as though a small, determined tornado has whisked around the rooms.

'I like it,' he says. 'My place is just like a clean

231

white cell. There's nothing there at all. This place is like you.' He pauses, and says with a glimmer of a smile, 'It's busy too.' He walks in a few steps, finds the sofa, and leans forward with his hands on the back of it. 'What's that over there?' he asks, indicating to where Lila's canvas is stretched across the whole wall facing a window.

'It's something I'm working on,' says Lila. 'I'm not sure I'm going to let anyone see it, it's a bit vain.' The canvas is covered with hundreds of identical printed images of her, in an enormous graphic rectangle, and each image is painted with different shades of hair and clothes and and skin tone, so that from a distance, the effect of all her different selves is like that of a colour spectrum, shifting from dark and negro and gothic at one side, to so pale and washed out at the other that she is almost effaced; she has quite literally painted herself out.

'What's it about?' asks Henry.

'Just the effects of light and dark on surfaces, what they reveal, what they conceal,' says Lila simply.

When it is obvious that she's not going to say any more, Henry says, 'You said something about that at Whitstable. You said that light can be blinding, that sometimes it hides more than it reveals.' At the mention of Whitstable, Lila gives him a warning look, that he is about to cross the boundaries of what is acceptable, but Henry, of course, doesn't notice. 'It feels like I dreamed the other day. I can't remember when I've ever been so perfectly happy . . .'

'Right, so you've come in for a bit, just like I agreed. And now I think it's time you left,' interrupts Lila firmly.

'You said you were perfectly happy too,' Henry reminds her. 'You kissed me like I was the last bloke on earth.'

'Yeah, well, thanks for the memories. I said I think it's time you left.' Henry looks like he's about to argue, but then says nothing at all. 'Look,' Lila adds impatiently at the hurt uncertainty in his face, 'I don't want to be cruel, but it's not like I'm dumping you, because we were never really together in the first place. We've never even slept together. And believe me, you don't want to get together with me. It must be obvious by now that I'm a total bitch, and I'm really not good news. I could end up breaking your heart.'

'I don't think I've ever met someone who thinks so much of themselves, and so little, all at the same time,' says Henry, recovering himself. 'You don't need to protect me; I'm perfectly capable of looking after myself.'

'How have you not worked out that I haven't got a selfless bone in my body?' spits out Lila. 'I'm not protecting you, I'm protecting myself.'

'From what? Being cared for? Getting close to someone? You're too late, it's happened already,' argues Henry, his own voice rising.

'Oh for fuck's sake,' cries Lila in frustration, and she throws her wine glass at the brick wall above her fireplace, where it shatters, and the liquid and fragments spray out to merge seamlessly with the rest of the mess on the floor. 'What are you really here for, Henry?' she shouts furiously. 'You must have known before you came here that I didn't want to see you again. Yes, we had a lovely afternoon. And yes, we kissed a little. And yes, for a while I felt happy and safe. And then I came home, Henry, and guess what? I was still me. Miserable, toxic little me. I told you that I wasn't going to turn into a nice person just for you.' Breathing heavily to avoid crying, she stoops and starts to pick up the shattered glass, and cuts herself deeply on a shard. 'Oh fuck, fuck, fuck!' she snaps, as bright red blood drips on the carpet along with the red wine; she sucks at her sliced hand, and then goes and washes it in the icy cold water at the sink.

'Are you OK?' asks Henry with concern, crossing the room precariously, and standing near her.

'Still here, then?' says Lila sharply. 'So what *are* you really here for? Are you just after a farewell fuck for closure? Because believe me, if it'll get you out of the door, I'm happy to get it over with.'

'I don't want closure, Lila,' says Henry, 'I just want you. And I don't want you to be anything but who you are. I care for you, and I don't believe in leaving people I care for. Especially when they're bleeding at the kitchen sink.' He takes her cold, numb hand carefully in his, and kisses it tenderly. Lila feels numb herself now, all over, as she leans against the cupboards. She doesn't try and draw her hand back, and watches his face carefully, the angles of his cheekbones, the straight line of his nose, the curve of his tired eyes, as he dries and wraps her cut with his crisp, white handkerchief.

'You're an idiot,' she says eventually. She'd tried everything she knew to push him away, but he is still there, holding her hand.

'I know, you've mentioned that before,' says Henry. He leans towards her, his arm reaching around her waist, and is about to kiss her when she pushes him away, so resolutely that he's forced to take a few steps back.

'Would you like to go for a drive?' Lila asks, before he can say anything. 'If you're not busy tonight.'

'Where are we going?' asks Henry again, after Lila has negotiated the North Circular and headed into the south London suburbs.

'You'll have to wait and see,' says Lila, infuriatingly.

'That sounds ominous,' says Henry. 'You're not going to drive us off a bridge, or a cliff or something, are you?'

'I'm not quite that dark and dramatic,' retorts Lila, changing gear noisily. 'But thanks for the compliment.'

'You mean confidence,' says Henry.

'You heard what I said,' replies Lila. She carries on driving and after a little while, just as the sun starts to set, she pulls up outside a high wire gate, and starts tapping a security code into a box on the side. The door slides open, and she gets back in the car, and drives them both in. Henry gets out and looks around in wonder at the enormous, deserted arena in the failing light, screwing up his eyes with the effort to focus. 'Is this place what I think it is?'

Lila shakes her head. 'Not quite. It's a go-kart track, not a real racing track. One of my friends at college was really into it; he dropped out too, and he works here now.'

'But why are we here?' asks Henry.

She replies with a grin, 'Duh, I thought you'd have guessed? All boys like cars, don't they?' She throws her car keys towards him, and he catches at them after they collide in a sharp jumble at his chest.

'Ouch,' he complains, weighing the keys in his hands; he understands her meaning a split second later. 'You're joking, right?' he asks in awed disbelief. 'We couldn't, could we? My God, you really think we could?' At Lila's eloquent silence, that luminous smile lights his face. 'You are just amazing! I can't believe you even remembered.' He steps forward impulsively to hold her, but she just pushes him away again.

'We better get going quickly before it gets too dark,' says Lila. 'I can get in and out of here, but I can't work the floodlights.' She gets in the passenger seat. 'What are you waiting for, Henry? The handle at the side adjusts the seat, the clutch is on the left, then it's the brake and accelerator. Let's go.'

Henry gets in, fiddles with the gears until he is sure which is which, and then turns the key. 'God, I feel like a little kid,' he says, as the engine fires into life, and then protests with a roar as he presses too enthusiastically on the gas. He gingerly lifts his foot off the clutch, and the car inches off in first gear, and as he gains confidence speeds into second and third and fourth.

'Steer left!' Lila half-laughs and shrieks. 'I said LEFT!' She falls about in hysterics as he screeches around the bend, and they go round and round the track in crazy, haphazard circles until the sun goes down.

Lying on the hood of Lila's car by the track, his hands behind his head, his face turned up towards the stars, Henry says, 'And you told me that you didn't have a selfless bone in your body.'

'That wasn't me being selfless, that was bloody good fun,' says Lila, sitting beside him, chewing the remains of Maria's now-stale scones. 'I haven't laughed so much in ages.'

'It was possibly the sweetest thing someone's ever done for me,' says Henry. 'Thank you, Lila.'

'You don't need to thank me,' says Lila. 'I suppose it was my way of apologizing. I have a feeling that you're going to spend a lot of time forgiving me for things.'

'I like you so much that I suspect I'm going to

be quite annoying, so sometimes, you're going to need to forgive me for things, too,' says Henry.

He thinks about what they've just said, and sits up beside Lila. 'Does that mean I get to call you my girlfriend after all?' he asks.

Lila doesn't reply, and looks up towards the night sky. 'Do you know what I love about the moonlight?' she asks. 'It makes everything black and white and grey. There are shrubs planted over there by the entrance, and all the colour and complexity are gone. They're just dark outlines against a wall. I've tried painting by moonlight, but it's just not possible in Finchley; too much light pollution with all the sodium street lighting.'

'Why did you drop out of art college?' asks Henry. 'It seems mad when you love painting as much as you do.'

'I don't know,' shrugs Lila. 'It happened a bit suddenly, I had a set-to with one of my tutors, basically because I couldn't stand her criticism, and walked out. And I didn't feel that I was good enough to walk back in. I guess I wasn't ever sure that I deserved my place.'

'I don't know anything much about the visual arts, but every piece you've ever described to me sounds amazing. Maybe it's time to stop burning and hiding them. I'm sure that working in the café is all well and good, and it pays the rent, but if you're happiest painting, why not go back to college?'

'Because I might not be any good,' snaps Lila,

surprising herself with her frankness. 'And then I've got nothing.'

'So what?' says Henry. 'I play guitar a little – I might never be Johnny Marr, but that's not going to stop me doing something I enjoy. So what if you don't get glowing critiques; that shouldn't change what you feel about your work.'

'You don't understand,' says Lila flatly. 'And I'm not sure who the hell you think you are, to tell me what I should be doing with my life, trotting out bloody careers advice. I told you before, I don't need you to help me, and I certainly don't need you to save me.'

'God you're infuriating,' retorts Henry. 'I'm not trying to save you. And I know I'm not creative like you, but I do understand this much; life's just too short not to at least *try* pursuing what you love. Even if you haven't a clue whether or not you'll succeed. Why do you think I waited on your steps this evening, and followed you up to your door?'

'Because you're bloody annoying,' complains Lila. Her voice softens as she adds, 'But I'll forgive you, if you like.'

Henry puts his warm, dry hand lightly on the back of her neck, gently stroking it. 'So, if I try and kiss you, are you going to push me away again? Or is it a case of third time lucky?'

'You'll have to wait and see,' says Lila, reaching over and brushing the hair out of his eyes.

'That still sounds ominous,' says Henry. 'But I'm willing to take the risk.' And they move together and kiss in the damp night air, warmed only by each other, sliding closer until she is circled by his arms, her hands reaching inside his jacket to feel the reassuring solidity of his chest. 'Thank you, Lila,' whispers Henry again between kisses, his lips brushing hers as he speaks, 'for letting me be annoying. For letting me in.'

HOPE IN A BOX

My name is Yasmin Murphy, and when I am distressed by something like Change, even an expected change that I have prepared for, I find comfort in repetition. My name is Yasmin Murphy, and when I am distressed by something like Change, even an expected change that I have prepared for, I find comfort in repetition. Because repetition is the opposite of change. I even like the sound of the word, Repp-Ett-Tish-Shun, and repeating it calms me down when I feel anxious, just like some people who double numbers in their heads, or say their prayers on a rosary or mat.

Since I have done the documentary, everyone says that I'm not as bad as I used to be. The specialists even say that I am much better than I used to be, which technically means the same thing, but is more positive because it does not use a negative in the sentence. They say that it is a sign that I am outgrowing my autism, because I started doing different things that were not part of my routine. I started playing tennis. I tried to play golf but didn't actually manage to play as at the practice range I couldn't even hit three balls out of fifty, as my coordination wasn't good enough, and I didn't like the teacher trying to correct my posture, and so I stiffened away from him when he touched me, although I didn't say or do anything that would be considered anti-social, like scream or throw my club at him. I asked Lila to show me how to use a potter's wheel, as she had done ceramics in college; she hired one, but I couldn't use it in Lila's flat, as it is so untidy that it makes my head hurt, so we took it to our kitchen instead. I liked the spinning motion of the surface but I didn't like the sensation of the squelching clay and the way it sprayed and splattered everywhere, and although I managed to make a small pot, it was mostly with Lila's help, as I had to keep my eyes closed because of the icky feeling and the mess I was making in the kitchen. Lila wasn't pleased as I went to have a shower straight away afterwards, even though it wasn't my normal time for a shower, and she had to clean up the kitchen herself, and I hid the pot in a cupboard where I wouldn't have to look at it. I even went all the way to France with Asif on a day-trip, although the point of the trip was to speak to French people in French, but in fact the only person I spoke to during the trip was the waitress at the café on the ferry, and she was English.

I liked crossing the Channel, because in the middle all I could see was the sea, which was big and grey and bland, like a flat, wet sky, and I had never seen the sea before, except in films. The sea was so big that it made me realize that my attempt to see everything before I go blind was useless, as however many things I see, there would still be so many others that I won't be able to see, that the sum of experiences would still be just slightly bigger than nothing. And that's not just for me, but even for someone who has perfect sight and lives for a hundred years; that particular someone would still not see much more than slightly more than nothing compared to the infinity of visual experiences that exist, but their more than nothing would obviously have a greater value than my more than nothing, but still not be enough to be significant. If all the experiences in the world were summed up by the area of a circle, my experiences would be about the size of a line drawn from the centre of the circle to the circumference; and the experiences of the other person wouldn't be more than a hair-width bigger. My experiences would be about as significant as a grain of sand floating in the sea. And that realization was a vast relief, as it meant that I didn't have to put myself through all this Change any more, because the fact is that I found doing things that weren't part of my routine very stressful – apart from tennis which wasn't so bad as it just replaced chess on Saturday mornings – and I'd see red with orange blotches whether my eyes were open or shut, and when Asif was out I'd bang my head quietly and constantly in the bathroom until I'd dulled all the new sensory experiences away with pain, and the bruise on my head became so tender that it hurt when I pulled my hair up into my ponytail, but no one could see as it was under my hairline.

The specialists also said that I've got better, as I was so calm about taking my A levels. But I had no need to panic about taking my A levels, as the exams had been in my schedule for a long time, so I knew exactly when and where they would take place, and because I knew that the results wouldn't be of any significance either, although of course I would like to get the A level grades that I was predicted, which are three As and a B. But I don't think that getting these results would make me particularly happy; I just think that they would simply make sense, like a jigsaw piece fitting in place, or putting the numbers in a sudoku grid.
   While I was trying to do all the things that I thought it would be good to do before I went blind, I thought about the questions that the documentary maker's psychologist asked me. The psychologist was a woman with light brown hair, and a thin nose and a thin upper lip, and she had a silvery scar about two centimetres long on her right temple, and she wore dark blue jeans and a burgundy jumper with a mark below the left breast, and a floaty brown scarf, and her jumper smelt of rose petals, as though she might have

kept rose petal sachets in her jumper drawer. She wasn't pretty but she had a kind face, and a soft voice that asked questions as though they were statements, because her tone didn't rise at the end of the sentence. She wanted me to answer these questions:

Do I feel happy?

Do I feel hope for the future?

I have already told you that I didn't answer these questions properly before. I told her Yes, of course I do, to both, but this was a lie, and the memory of that lie makes me uncomfortable under my clothes, just as though I were sitting in the sun. The truth is that I would like to feel happy, but I'm not sure it's possible. I like keeping to my routines, having everything minutely ordered, right to the times when I cut my fingernails and toenails (at 9 p.m. in the evening on the third day of each month), and these keep me comfortable and stop me from getting upset, but being comfortable isn't the same as being happy. And my life is complicated by paradoxes, which is when things don't make sense, and these make me feel very uncomfortable and confused. A paradox is when someone says something like 'Can't live with him, can't live without him,' about their husband, or 'I'm damned if I do and damned if I don't,' about something they might or might not do. A paradox is when my French teacher asks the class, 'Who'll pair up with Yasmin?' and no one volunteers, and I feel sad that no one wants to work with me, but I also feel relieved, as I would rather work alone. A paradox is when I want to be held and be close to someone, but I don't want to be touched by anyone or be too near to them. A paradox is when I want to experience love, a physical, romantic love like I see in the movies, but when the thought of being loved is scary and claustrophobic. This is a long way to answer a short question, and the honest answer is No. I am not happy.

The second question was about hope for the future. Hope is something that I have difficulty understanding, as it is an abstract concept, and I have been told that I have difficulty in comprehending abstract concepts, just as I do in comprehending other people's minds. Hope, as far as I see it, is when you cannot be certain of a favourable outcome, but you still expect the outcome to be favourable anyway. It doesn't make a lot of sense to me, as expecting something good to happen doesn't help shift the odds in your favour. There are two stories that I know about hope from my *Encyclopedia of Greek and Roman Mythology*, and these are stories that I re-read on the day of Mum's funeral when Lila was in a mood and I didn't think that she would let me play Tetris or watch *The Simpsons*. I read N-P that day, and the bits about hope occurred under 'P' for Pandora. In the first story, Zeus was angry with Prometheus for giving men the use of fire, so he commanded Hephaestus to create the first woman as a punishment for mankind, and all the gods and goddesses gave her gifts like beauty and skill, but made her treacherous and unreliable. Her name was Pandora, which means 'The gift of all' or 'Every gift'. They gave her a box containing all the evils of the world, but in the bottom was Elpis, who was the personification of Hope. Pandora was given to Prometheus's brother, Epimetheus, as a gift, and she was curious about the contents of her box, and opened the lid. All the evils of the world flew out that have burdened man ever since, and Pandora was so terrified that she shut the lid, trapping in Elpis, or Hope, which might have helped to make things better for everyone.

In the second story, Pandora was still the first woman created for man by the gods, but she wasn't treacherous or unreliable, and the box from the gods wasn't full of awful things. Instead, it was full of every good thing, including Elpis at the bottom, but when she opened the lid, all the good things escaped and were lost for ever, apart from Elpis, which remained in when she slammed the lid shut again. So hope is the only thing that humans have left in their box of gifts, which helps them put up with all the horrible things in the world.

The thing is, because I'm not happy, and I don't understand hope, when I think about these questions, it is as though I have opened my own box, and all the tidy, ordered routines that I use to make

247

myself comfortable have flown away and been compromised. It feels as though I have got lost in my wilderness mind, with everything whirling around me like during a tornado, and I am in the middle and shouting stop. It is like a bad version of my dream, where I'm not safe in my room, and where I am falling rather than flying. It is like an absence that takes up so much space, it is like a presence, a black hole that gets bigger and bigger and eats up everything around it. It is as though I am watching my world shrinking, and I can't do anything about it, even with the most minutely ordered routines, even if I accounted for every single minute of every single day for the rest of my natural life.

So I have decided to take control, and stop my world shrinking around me, by stopping it altogether. That's why it doesn't matter what my A level results are. That's why it's Mostly or Wholly Irrelevant to Asif that I'm going blind. He won't have to take care of me as I won't be around any more, except possibly in a decorative jar with a thimbleful of my dust, like Mum on the mantelpiece. I need to wait until the documentary airs though, as it will help people understand what it is to be someone like me, and be nicer to other people who aren't neurotypical who are carrying on with their lives. And if I organize it carefully, I can try and do one last thing on my list at the same time, which is the only thing that wasn't to do with a sensory experience for myself: I could save a life. In fact, I could save several, if I manage to end my life in a way that means my organs can be effectively harvested for donation. It makes logical sense; they could save lots of lives if they organized a lottery once in a while where one person who was dying gave their organs to everyone else before the organs got ruined by whatever disease was killing them, but I suppose the families would object. The thought doesn't bother me, but I'm just realistic that I'm dying anyway. Everyone is. It's just a matter of more or less time. And no one person is more significant than another, no more than a grain of sand in the sea.

Most people associate suicide with depression, but I'm not depressed, not like Lila was after Mum died, when she wouldn't even eat. I have my breakfast at exactly the same time each morning, and I always eat exactly the same amount of cereal, although I vary whether I have scrambled eggs or banana or toast depending on what they look like. For example, if the banana's too underipe or overripe I won't have it, because I don't like green or brown fruit.

There's an exception to what I said before, about hope, as I said that expecting something good to happen doesn't help shift the odds in your favour. In fact, with depression, it does; it's been medically proven that giving depressed people placebos in tests is more effective than genuine medication, because their expectation that they will get better actually gets them better, as it helps them to manufacture their own dopamine. Lila didn't take her depression medication after Mum died, or placebos, but she went on long walks when she was gone for ages, sometimes the whole day, because she said she didn't want to be in the house. Asif was worried about her, but I told him that walking or other moderate exercise has an equal or better effect on depression than drugs, reducing symptoms by up to fifty per cent, which explains why doctors used to tell depressed people to stop moaning and get a bit of fresh air and exercise.

Now that I've started to make my plans, I feel better than I have in ages, and the colours in my head are no longer red with orange blotches, but a misty grey and blue, like the swelling of the sea.

THE PLACE HE USED TO LIVE

'Didn't May used to be warm?' Asif asked Faith as they walked swiftly through the Cambridge streets towards the train station, his college scarf wrapped firmly round his neck against the nippy breeze, a necessity rather than the usual badge of pride. Why did he always find himself wearing his college scarf on his monthly visits home? He suspected that it was to remind him, and remind them, that he had escaped; that he belonged to another world now, a world miles away from grey and cluttered Finchley. A world of ornate architecture and quadrangles, a world of trimmed oval lawns, of noisy, good-natured bars where the dark stone walls would drip with condensation in the early hours when dancing bodies filled the space with hot breath, sticky lager and sweat, of boats being punted silently under bridges by inept young men trying to impress their new lovers, of cluttered, ancient libraries where students fell asleep among their books, where it seemed as though the books themselves snored in dreamless content until they were taken off the shelf.

'It is warm. Or at least it's not cold,' replied Faith, adjusting the clip in her long, brown hair, before slipping her hand into his. Asif glanced down at her slim fingers, intertwined with his own, as they hurried along; he felt grateful for her hand, for the easy and confident way in which she offered it. He loved the fact that if he ever reached out his own hand to her, he knew that she would take it. Faith's gentle grip was something that held him to this world, the world to which he had aspired to belong all through his school years, all the time during sixth form which he had spent studying and ignoring social events and sports and hobbies, just so he could prove himself worthy of entry. He breathed a sigh of relief: he had been here almost a year, he had handed in acceptable papers, he had performed sufficiently in exams; the first part of his tripos was almost under his belt. No one could pull the rug from under his feet now; he knew that he would stay.

'Stop!' he said abruptly to Faith, breaking his stride and bringing himself to such a sudden halt that she swung ahead of him, still holding his hand. He pulled her towards him, and looked carefully at her open, freckled face, the sweetness of expression around her eyes. They stood there for a moment, and then kissed each other on the mouth, warmly, almost chastely, as though sharing a secret. Faith was wearing sparkly pink lipgloss, which made her taste of sugar almonds. Asif zipped up her sports top protectively and bent his head to kiss her again, but she tugged at his hand.

'Your train, remember? You don't want to miss it?' she said, and they started walking again.

'Maybe I do,' said Asif. 'I've got loads of work to do this week, it's a pain having to go home. I'd rather be here, to be honest.'

'So why do you go?' asked Faith.

Asif shrugged. 'Guilt, I guess. My dad was a Catholic, I must have inherited it. I only go back once a month, just for a couple of days; my mum and Lila have to be there the whole time, looking out for Yasmin. I guess it's the least I can do.'

They arrived at the station just a couple of minutes before the train came in, Asif rather more out of breath than Faith, who played first-team lacrosse for the college. 'Next time I'll listen to you and take the bus,' he said. 'Thanks for coming down with me.'

'Stop!' commanded Faith as the train came in, pulling him back towards her, and she gave Asif another chaste, sugar almond kiss. 'I'll see you the day after tomorrow, on Saturday. Remember it's the Pyjama Party.'

'See you,' said Asif, as he got on the train. He held her hand for a moment through the window, and waved at the small, slim figure until she was out of sight. Lila had disparagingly described Faith as 'cute as a button', and Faith, in turn, had described Lila as 'hippy horrific'. Faith was Asif's second girlfriend, and his first lover. He was her first lover too, and although he knew that Faith liked him, he did not presume to think that he would be her last; they were too young for permanency, they had been brought together by circumstance, she from Liverpool and him from London, they studied the same course at the same college, and one day, he supposed, circumstance would pull them apart. Still, he felt satisfied, almost smug with his life at Cambridge. He wondered what the other people on the train thought of him, shuffled behind their papers; perhaps they had seen him kissing Faith on the platform, perhaps they recognized his stripy college scarf; perhaps they thought that he was one of those Cambridge students who might one day rule the world.

Asif, despite this, felt his heart sink as the train approached London, and tried to remember why it was a good thing that he was going home. He would see Lila, and listen to her gossip about her latest crush and complain about her A level revision, and watch her pretend not to be impressed while he told her about all the parties he'd been going to, all the twee Varsity things he'd started to do: rowing (in the third team, admittedly), punting along the scenic waterways, croquet on the college lawn, hiring the black tie outfit for the May Ball, like something out of a Merchant Ivory film. He would see Mum, and perhaps she would have made her famous chocolate cake for him, the one she knew that he loved, which she split horizontally into three layers, and filled generously with fudge icing and vanilla-scented cream, so it was moist all the way through. He would see Yasmin, and . . . he scratched his head. Of course there were good times with Yasmin, there had to be, he just found them hard to remember among the sulks and the tantrums and the way that they were always forced to go along with her routines, and not do the things that they liked and she hated, like swimming or eating out. Because of Yasmin, Asif had never been to a real restaurant before he went to college; the first time he went to one, just a casual pasta place with friends, he'd had to resist the urge to clear and stack the plates like he did at home. Mum's argument was always that if Yasmin didn't like something, it wouldn't be much fun for the rest of the family. Mum's argument made sense, but it didn't help, not really.

Asif loosened his scarf, and unbuttoned his corduroy jacket that he had bought from a Cambridge market stall on Faith's insistence. Faith was right, it wasn't cold, especially now that he was out of the persistent breeze. He leaned his head against the window, watching the country-side go by, and the animals grazing in the fields like unconvincing props, Sheep, Sheep, Cow. Or as Lila used to say when they were children, in the rare event that the family had to take a train trip, Lunch, Lunch, Dinner. With a child's capacity for being practical and cruel all at once; Lila hadn't changed that much, really. Perhaps he hadn't either; he was almost nineteen years old, but he still felt so bitter about his childhood that he couldn't even summon up a happy memory to do with his little sister. This seemed something of a failure to him; it showed a lack of growth, a lack of maturity. Think, he urged himself, Think, Think, Think.

Asif couldn't think. He couldn't even think of when to start. He supposed that he had better start at the beginning, and suddenly, a memory strolled into his head so clear and present, it was as though he had just that moment made it up, or been shaken awake from dreaming it. He was four years old, dressing himself because his father was busying himself with Lila, who wanted to wear an inappropriate party frock with white tights, and had to be coaxed into a normal dress and knee socks. Asif pulled on his khaki trousers with six pockets, and a stripy green and white top he had worn the day before. Dad was trying to brush Lila's tangled hair, but she made such a noise about him doing it rather than Mum, shouting furiously, 'Ouch, that hurted me!' as soon as the brush touched her, that eventually he gave up and just fastened her wild strands back with two sparkly butterfly clips. Dad took Lila to the car first, strapping her efficiently in her car seat, and then came for Asif, who sat sagely on his booster seat while Lila complained that Asif had a window seat and that she was stuck in the middle. Normally they both had window seats, and the central seat was empty, but today, there was a strange plastic apparatus strapped into the other window seat, with a handle and a hood. 'For the baboo,' Asif explained to Lila.

Dad drove them to the hospital, where he fussed over getting change for the car parking ticket, and swore to himself about the price. Asif and Lila looked at each other knowledgeably; Dad never swore like that if Mum was around, she wouldn't let him. He unstrapped them, and as Lila started running off straight away, giggling furiously and banging the parked cars with her fists, he picked her up, and took Asif firmly by the hand, although Asif was happy to follow, and didn't really need holding on to. They went into the building, which smelt both sweet and acrid, a chemical smell that wasn't unpleasant once he got used to it, and went up in a lift. Lila needed to go to the loo when they were upstairs, so Dad took them both to the toilets, and washed their hands with extra care, rubbing soap all over them before rinsing them with warm water. 'It's to stop germs getting on the baby,' he explained.

They went with Dad down a long corridor, and then through a swinging door, which led to a room with four beds surrounded by curtains, and sitting on one of the beds with the curtains pulled back was Mum, still wearing her dressing-gown. She put down her magazine and waved to them excitedly, holding out her arms. Asif ran to Mum, and hugged her; he'd missed her, she'd left last night before they went to bed, and hadn't been at home that morning when they woke up. Lila struggled out of Dad's arms to do the same. And Mum, holding them both, one on each side, as she sat with her legs dangling over the edge of the bed, showed them a clear plastic box on wheels next to her, where a sleeping, wrinkly little doll was all wrapped up in blankets, with a fluff of dark hair. 'She's only six hours old,' said Mum. 'She's very, very tired because she was up all night getting born. She finally arrived early this morning when you two were still in sleepy-land. Daddy hasn't slept all night either, because he was here with Mummy after you two went to bed, and then he went back to get you up. Mrs Cox from next door sat in with you overnight, and you didn't even know it.'

'What is that?' asked Lila, pointing at the doll, which opened its mouth, yawned, and settled back down with its face turned aside.

'It's the baboo,' said Asif authoritatively, trying to look at the baby, but he couldn't see it properly as the box was too deep.

'She's your baby sister,' Mum explained. 'She's called Yasmin.'

'Do you want a closer look, champ?' asked Dad, and he lifted Asif right over the curved plastic box, so that Asif could reach in and touch the little creature on the face. 'She's your baby sister, Yasmin,' repeated Dad. 'You're her big brother, so you have to look after her now, just like you do with Lila.'

'Baboo,' said Asif, his hand very gently stroking the baby's pink cheek. He had never seen anything so perfect and so pure.

Once Asif started remembering, all the other memories that had been suppressed through anger or bitterness suddenly flowed out. The first time he had been entrusted with giving Yasmin a spoonful of mashed banana, and how she had not spat it out like she had everything else, but swallowed it greedily and even licked the spoon. How he had rocked her back to peaceful sleep after she woke screeching, the night that Mum stayed downstairs crying in the kitchen, after she had opened the door to the two respectful officers who told her that Dad was gone. The painful fear in his gut when Yasmin got lost in the supermarket when she was five years old, and the spasm of giddy relief when he was the one who finally found her, standing inappropriately close to a pretty young lady who was handing out leaflets at the entrance. The tense and nervous moment when he handed her the 'Teletubbies Say Eh-Oh' record, which he had bought with his own pocket money, and the enormous smile she gave to herself on realizing what it was, a smile that was still on her face when she raised her head up and looked at him; it was the first time he was aware that he had made her happy, it was the first time she managed to look him in the eye and say thank you.

'Baboo,' said Asif dreamily to himself, still

looking out of the window. He was cheerful when he got off the train, and when he got home, he found that Mum had indeed made him his favourite chocolate cake. It was game night, and they played Scrabble, which Yasmin won because she knew all the sneaky two-letter words that earned lots of points, like ZO and JA and XI and XU and KA. It was, against all expectation, a really good evening; someone looking in the bay window would have seen that they really were a perfectly happy, perfectly normal family.

But Asif never made it back to Cambridge for the college Pyjama Party that weekend. He never rowed or punted or played croquet again, because the following day, without warning, when Yasmin and Lila were at school, Mum died. And everything changed for ever; and everything stayed the same.

SHALLOW WATER

Lila wakes to find herself nestled against Henry's chest; his slightly freckled arm is tucked around her, the skin inside his elbow is soft and pale as a baby's. She looks at his profile; he is solemn in sleep, and although he's not good-looking in any classic sense, he somehow has the serenity of a statue, with his fine carved lips, straight nose and lidded eyes. She is deliciously warm and cosy, and Henry's still mouth suddenly seems irresistible. 'Mmm,' she says, unable to stop the tiny articulation of pleasure escaping, as she kisses him lightly, before she rolls away from him decisively. The early morning light is filtering through Henry's blinds and casting narrow shadows on the walls of his Spartan apartment; in sharp contrast to Lila's cluttered hovel, Henry's place is just as he described, so tidy that it is prac-tically empty. Still drowsy, she almost falls off the bed, as Henry's bed is much narrower than her own, and swings her legs over the edge instead.

'Mmm yourself,' replies Henry sleepily, pulling her back towards him. 'Where are you going? It's really, really early.' He buries his face heavily between her neck and shoulder, before kissing her skin softly. 'You smell heavenly,' he says, lying back down with his arm around her. 'God, this is nice. I wish you'd stay over more. It's just a lovely way to wake up.'

'I'll smell a lot more heavenly once I've had a bath,' says Lila, wriggling out from his embrace. 'I didn't mean to wake you, you can stay in bed.' She sits on the edge of the bed, and picks up her T-shirt from the floor, pulling it over her head. 'I'll just be a couple of hours.'

'Lila, it's six a.m. on a Sunday,' says Henry, checking the time on his bedside clock with an outstretched palm. 'Give yourself a break, and stay in bed. I really don't mind if your skin's a bit dry.' He strokes her back gently while he says this, but Lila, aware of the roughness of skin towards the base of the spine, practically slaps his hand away.

'Well, I do,' she says shortly, annoyed that the moment of perfect peace she had on waking has evaporated so quickly. It was all his fault, why couldn't he have stayed asleep? None of her other lovers had woken up with her when she went to the bathroom to scrub and cream first thing in the morning; she hated the risk of being seen to be so scabby and flaky and vulnerable. It was why she normally avoided staying over. 'Besides, we're seeing your family today and I need to have enough time to sort myself out.' She gets up and stalks to the bathroom.

'They'll adore you,' says Henry, still sleepy, as

he rolls clumsily out of bed himself. 'They'll definitely say that you're too good-looking, and that
you're wasting your time with me. They're funny
like that. Funny ha ha, I mean. They're always
finding hilarious ways to put me down.' He pulls
on a dressing-gown, and stops at the bathroom
door. 'Do you want a coffee, or something?' he
asks.

'No thanks,' says Lila. 'And what are you doing
up? I thought I told you that I don't mind if you
stay in bed while I have a bath.'

'Well, I do,' says Henry just as shortly as she
had done. 'And there's no need to be so bossy.'
He yawns, and wanders off in the direction of the
kitchen. 'I'm making you that coffee,' he calls out.

'So who's being bossy now?' mutters Lila, as she
drops the T-shirt and climbs in the bath, while the
water is still running in. She pushes her head right
under the surface, and opens her eyes to look up
at the blurry, very white ceiling, while she holds
her breath. After a few seconds, she lifts her head
just slightly, so that her eyes and nose and mouth
are above the surface, and the rest of her completely
submerged and beginning to soften. She groans
with annoyance as she hears indefatigable Daisy
run into the bathroom, scrabble around excitedly,
and drink carelessly from the toilet bowl; the
slurping sound is noisy and distinct enough for her
to make out even while she is underwater. She looks
up and catches Daisy in the act. 'Remind me never
to let that vile creature lick me again,' she says,

as Henry comes in with the coffee and the Sunday paper that she bought late last night.

'Are you talking about me or the dog?' he asks conversationally, putting the mug and the Sunday supplements on a chair next to the bath.

'Both, unless I get a little privacy,' says Lila, beginning to scrub her arms with an abrasive loofah she'd brought from home. 'Please bugger off. I said I don't like being bothered when I'm in the bath.'

'It's a good thing I'm not paranoid, I might start to feel a little rejected,' says Henry. 'Shall I do your back before I go?'

Lila is surprised into silence by his matter-of-fact suggestion, which Henry interprets as consent, and he takes the loofah and makes broad, assured strokes up and down her back. 'Mmm,' she murmurs involuntarily, as it feels unexpectedly wonderful to have someone else doing this for her. She realizes that for all the close and private moments that she has shared with lovers, she has never previously had someone scrub her back; no one had ever offered, and it had never occurred to her to ask. The bathroom was normally the place she escaped from intimacy, not sought it. She feels a rush of tenderness for Henry that she doesn't even know how to express.

'There,' says Henry, going generously right over her shoulders with his final strokes. 'I'm sorry I've been so annoying this morning, following you in here like some lovelorn puppy. It was just so nice to wake up with you; it was such a perfect moment.

I guess I just didn't want to be apart from you so soon.' He drops a kiss on the top of her damp head. 'I'll let you finish your bath in peace,' he says, leaving.

Lila sits in the bath, alone just as she had wanted, just as she always was, naked, scarred and perfected, and feels unreasonably bereft. She looks at her raw face in the bathroom mirror, and sees how stupid she has been, for such a long time. What was she doing, rejecting her lover just so she could scrub up for an indifferent, uncaring world to admire? Maintaining her beauty suddenly matters very little to her, she finally realizes that it had only ever been skin deep. Perhaps it's time to start caring a little more for herself than for the woman in the mirror, to nurture the spark of hidden fire that lights her from within, rather than polishing and perfecting the person on the surface. 'Henry,' she calls out impulsively, 'Henry!'

'What's up,' he says, returning. 'If it's a spider, you know I'm not any good with them. Can't see them, can't catch them.'

'It's not a spider, you idiot,' she says affectionately, standing up in the water and holding him close, kissing him with her damp lips as she presses her soaking body against the length of him, getting his dressing-gown all wet down the front. 'It was a perfect moment for me too,' she says, 'I'm sorry I ruined it.' She takes off his soggy dressing-gown. 'You know, you smell less than heavenly,' she jokes,

'I reckon you could use a bath,' and she pulls him in to join her.

Later, as Lila is sitting with Henry in the cooling water, while he carefully massages the emollient cream that relieves her skin over her back, arms and shoulders, he says to her hesitantly, 'I need to ask you something, Lila.'

'I know,' says Lila, who had been wondering how long she'd be able to avoid this discussion with Henry, something which her other boyfriends had never even noticed, let alone sought to mention.

Henry's capable, gentle hands continue to rub in her cream, moving over her chest and stomach; but when he reaches her thighs, he stops at the barely perceptible scars on the soft skin there. He brushes them with his thumb, just as he had the scar at her wrist. 'I know you said you didn't want me to help you, or save you. But I want to help with this, I need to. I can't bear the thought of anything hurting you, least of all yourself. I'll do whatever it takes; go with you to specialists, counselling, come over any time in the day or night when you think it might happen. I'll do anything you need to make sure it stops.'

'I've hardly done it since we've been together,' Lila replies candidly., 'You've helped already. It's just that sometimes I feel so miserable in my skin, in every sense, and I just need to take control. I will stop, I promise.'

'We'll find other ways of taking control,' says Henry. He kisses the back of her neck. 'I'm so proud

266

of you.' Lila sighs, and leans against Henry, relieved the confession she'd been dreading is over so quickly, so painlessly; with so little judgement. It feels like the opposite of a cut, of blood swirling back into her flesh, and the precise wound closing up to reveal that she might be intact after all.

Placing his arms around her middle, Henry says to her softly, over her shoulder, 'I love you, Lila Murphy.' It's something he has said to her many times already, from before they even started to make love. In the past, Lila had expected awkward, explosive passion to carry her through the first time with someone, to get them both clear of all the undignified unbuttoning and unzipping and tugging up and tugging down, all the awkward manoeuvres that physical intimacy required. With Henry it was different, sleeping with him had turned out to be as natural as holding his hand; when she'd had sex before, even in the feverish moments of climax she had always felt that some-thing was being taken from her, that she was being taken, even, in some indefinable, compromising way; with Henry, it was like he was giving her something instead, it was a gift. And when their bodies eventually joined, so simply and fluidly, with such undiluted, uncomplicated pleasure, he had said those words again, as gently as praying, as though he didn't really expect a response, as though saying the words out loud was enough for him, to know that he had spoken and she had listened.

'I know,' repeats Lila briefly. She pauses, and looks down at Henry's hands, still lightly linked around her waist. She can see the scars on her inner thighs, accusing her of something terrible, of being as cruel to others as she has been to herself. She would not fall from grace again. 'I think I love you, too,' she finally admits, so quietly she might have been saying it to herself. But she knows from Henry's gentle exhalation that he has heard; she didn't realize before that he had been holding his breath, waiting for her to speak. Lying back against Henry, Lila feels that she could cry; she had never known that she was capable of this, to be loved and to love in turn. Lying in the bath she feels perfected, no longer in the way that a scrubbed body in a mortuary is perfected, but the way a bloody newborn is perfected, swimming out of the womb with an unknown life of limitless possibility that is just beginning, with lips instinctively opening to take her first breath.

SUMMER IN A GLASS

'All the pretty girls come out in summer,' says Ravi to Asif, as they companionably clink their pint glasses. They are sitting on one of the picnic tables outside the pub, and Ravi is looking dreamily over to where a couple of secretaries are coming out of their building, shrugging off their jackets as they leave the artificial air-con environment, displaying short, sleeveless dresses and long, brown legs.

'What about your wife?' says Asif pointedly, trying not to sound prudish.

'Ah, she's the prettiest of them all,' agrees Ravi guiltlessly. He waves to the secretaries, who must know him, as they give a friendly wave back before they turn the corner, to where the organic juice bar is doing a roaring trade in the heat.

'Dears, my ears are burning,' says Matt from Marketing, coming up behind them with a glass of fruit-laden and umbrella-garnished Pimm's. 'I've always thought of myself as more striking than pretty.' He plants himself next to Ravi. 'The place is packed out today; do you mind if we share your table?'

'Sure, but you can drop the royal we, it's even camper than your cocktail,' says Ravi good-humouredly.

'A bit early in the day to be gay-bashing, you sad little fraction of a man,' comments Matt. 'And besides, my bean-counting chum, it wasn't a royal we, it was a perfectly commonplace plural, Lynn's joining me.'

During this exchange, Asif has been lost in admiration of Matt's drink, which seems a thing of utter beauty to him, like summer in a glass; he is wondering if he would ever be brave enough to order one, when he finally registers what Matt has been saying. 'Lynn? You mean Mei Lin's joining us?'

'I just said so, didn't I?' says Matt a little impatiently. 'Ah, here she comes, finally. I'm sure she hung back deliberately to make an entrance – and you accuse *me* of being camp.' Mei Lin steps out of the pub with a heavily laden tray, and looks around outside before spotting Matt at the table; she gives Asif and Ravi a grateful smile as she approaches.

'Thanks for letting us gatecrash the table, lads,' she says cheerfully, putting down the tray, and offloading two plates of sandwiches, and her own glass of Pimm's. 'Very gentlemanly of you to offer to carry our food, Matt,' she says. 'Oh, that's right, you didn't.' She winks at Asif and Ravi, before disappearing to deposit the tray back at the bar.

'But I paid!' protests Matt to Mei Lin's back.

'Besides,' he confides to Asif, 'she's much better with heavy loads than me, she's got surprisingly good biceps with all that gym training she does. I've got more of a swimmer's build myself . . .' He trails off, as he sees that Asif isn't really listening, and is glancing back at the door where Mei Lin is due to reappear. 'Ravi, I think that our young friend might have a crush on Lynn.'

Ravi laughs and pats Asif on the back. 'I think everyone on the fifth floor knows that Asif's got a bit of a crush on Lynn, apart from Lynn, obviously, and apparently you, Matt. I'd have thought that the head of Internal Communications would have been better plugged into the office grapevine. Or should I say the lurve-vine, Asif?'

'Don't be daft,' mutters Asif sheepishly.

'You're right, he's not bothering to deny it,' says Matt in delight. 'My God, Asif, are you blushing?'

'Oh, shut up, please,' pleads Asif, as Mei Lin appears back at the door.

'Are they tormenting you, Asif?' asks Mei Lin, before speaking with mock severity to Matt and Ravi. 'I've asked you two to play nicely.'

'Hi, Mei Lin,' says Asif gratefully. 'You don't normally come to the pub at lunchtime.'

'Matt persuaded me,' says Mei Lin. 'Apparently the Pimm's here is to die for, in inverted commas.'

'As is the hunky Australian behind the bar,' adds Matt.

'Well, neither disappoints, I must say,' smiles Mei Lin, sipping her own fruit-laden cocktail, 'but the sandwiches are another matter entirely.' She holds up a damp looking triangle garnished with crisps, takes a tentative bite, and puts it back down, trying not to make a face.

'Hold up, how come you've got your food already?' complains Ravi. 'Asif and I have been waiting for ages. I'm going to go and have words with the barman.'

'I'll come too,' says Matt, already draining the last of his Pimm's. 'I've run dry. And I love it when you act all forceful.'

'Only if you behave,' warns Ravi, and he and Matt wander through the swinging pub door, bickering genially.

Asif and Mei Lin are left sitting side by side at the table, catch each other's eyes, and start to laugh. 'They're quite the double act, aren't they?' says Mei Lin. 'What were they teasing you about just now?'

'Oh, nothing,' says Asif, shrugging his shoulders. He worries that he might have started to blush again, and asks, 'How's Melody?' as a distraction.

'Oh, great,' says Mei Lin. 'She's getting used to Stephen now, he still tries to see her once a fortnight or so. I might bring her with me to the Summer Party tomorrow, I don't like leaving her with a baby-sitter at the weekend.'

'You mean the CFS-CRS Summer Party?' asks Asif, who hadn't been planning to go; Yasmin was used to him being home on a Saturday. 'I didn't know you'd be coming.'

'Well, yes. Marketing always gets attached to CFS for the summer parties, because of where we sit. Matt keeps lobbying heavily for the Tax department's party instead, because they have bigger budgets, but the CFS one is usually pretty good. Better than Audit, anyway.' Mei Lin tries another bite of her sandwich, gives up, and pushed her plate over to Asif. 'Here, feel free to nibble while you're waiting,' she offers.

'Thanks,' says Asif. A thought occurs to him, and he says it out loud before he loses his nerve. 'I could give you a hand with Melody tomorrow, if you like. Just to give you a chance to have a dance and drink.'

'That's so thoughtful of you,' says Mei Lin, obviously touched. 'I think you must be the nicest guy in the office. But are you sure, Asif? I don't want to impose.'

'It's no imposition,' says Asif, chuffed by her response. 'It's a pleasure. What else are gym buddies for?' He confesses shyly, 'Besides, I always get a bit bored at the party anyway; the rest of the department always gets so trollied and incoherent. And I don't tend to drink that much because of Yasmin.'

Mei Lin nods sympathetically. 'So how is Yasmin? It must be odd for her now that school's finished.'

'Odd for us both,' shrugs Asif, 'I worry about her a bit, she's so used to having her routines. I keep imagining her at home playing *Doom* all morning and watching the same episode of *ER* all afternoon.' After Yasmin had finished her A levels, she had still gone into school, even though she didn't need to any more, and had followed her usual timetable by herself, sitting in the empty classrooms, revising the subjects that she had already been examined on, and walking around the playing fields at lunch. Neither Asif nor her teachers had tried to stop her; it just seemed unnecessarily cruel. Once school finally closed two weeks later, Asif was left with a dilemma; normally, Yasmin would enrol in the summer school programme, which meant that she'd be in a supervised environment for most of the day while he was at work, but there wasn't a summer school for students who had finished their A levels. His choice was to enrol her with the younger students, which seemed safe but overprotective, given that she was nineteen years old, and had conditional places at three London universities, or to let her look after herself at home while he was at work. Yasmin's specialists advised the latter; even though she would be living at home while at college, she needed to learn to organize her time herself; after all, she had recently shown vast improvements in being open to new experiences. Nobody dared to say the phrase 'getting better'. It wasn't appropriate, it lacked sensitivity and political correctness, it implied her Asperger's was an illness rather than a neurological state. But 'getting better' is what the specialists seemed to imply in their assessments.

They really believed that Yasmin was outgrowing some of her behavioural issues; perhaps she was ready for greater independence, if only Asif would let her, if only he would relax, as though he had been the one holding her back.

'I wanted to take some time off last week, when her holidays started,' Asif explains, worried that there might be the ghost of an accusation in Mei Lin's kindly glance towards him, in her silent encouraging nod. 'I wanted to help her set up a new schedule for herself over the summer, going to the library, walking around the park, all that sort of thing, but her psychologist thought it would be counterproductive. They all thought I was babying her a bit.' He unthinkingly picks up Mei Lin's sandwich, and starts chewing it.

'I'm sure she'll be all right,' says Mei Lin, before shaking her head and correcting herself. 'God, sorry, that came out sounding way too fatuous. Of course I'm not sure. But you're following advice and doing your best for her – you can't do much more. Sometimes you have to let go, I guess.'

'I guess,' says Asif, finding an odd comfort in repeating her words. 'At least she's got her new obsession to keep her occupied.' After her A levels, Yasmin had summarily dropped her 'To-Do' list obsession, with an abruptness that was unusual for her; Asif and her psychologist supposed that she had found doing new things to be rather more of a chore than a pleasure, and too stressful to continue. She had found a new interest almost immediately; this time it was All Things Medical. She started watching the medical dramas compulsively, and reading *Grey's Anatomy* and medical encyclopedias in close detail. Asif finds it rather morbid, especially her close fascination with deaths and autopsies, and he privately wonders if her new interest is something to do with their mother, as though Yasmin is trying to figure out the mechanics of how Mum died. He supposes it is understandable, but he is too squeamish to dare to ask Yasmin if this is what she is doing; he couldn't bear a frank and unemotional reply from her on the subject, especially if she started going into the full flow of informatively grisly detail and didn't stop.

'Oh, look,' says Mei Lin, spotting the sandwich in his hand, 'that's the one I took a bite out of. We're practically kissing.' She says it as a joke, to lighten the mood, but sees Asif looking mortified, and almost choke on his mouthful. 'Sorry,' she says contritely, slapping him on his back. 'Maybe that just sounded funnier in my head. I promise I haven't got any saliva-carried infectious diseases.'

'If it's too early in the day to be gay-bashing, it's definitely too early to be talking about fluid exchange,' says Matt, who has finally returned with a new glass of Pimm's, and falls on to his own plate of neglected sandwiches. 'Isn't it amazing how they manage to be both limp, and curling, all at the same time?' he says, holding one out for inspection.

Ravi returns with his and Asif's pub lunches, scampi and chips and chicken tikka masala that is also, somewhat untraditionally, served with chips. Asif shyly offers Mei Lin his chips in exchange for her sandwiches, and is delighted by the ready way she helps herself from his plate. When Matt and Mei Lin excuse themselves to chat to Tina from Personnel, Asif tries very hard not to stare at her slim figure, in cropped trousers and tailored work shirt, moving through the crowd; he is forced to drop his eyes quickly to his lunch when she glances back over her shoulder at him, as though aware of his gaze. He looks up from the table to see Ravi watching him thoughtfully. 'Are you sure you're not coming to the Summer Party, mate? It'll be fun. I'm bringing Asha as my plus one.'

'Well, I suppose I could,' says Asif, with what he hopes is a casual, careless air; he sees that Ravi isn't fooled for a moment. 'Yeah, I'll be coming,' he admits humbly.

'Nice one, mate,' says Ravi. 'You see, I was right,' he adds, nodding to where Mei Lin was laughing with Tina at some shared joke. 'The pretty girls do come out in summer.'

THE COLOUR OF MUSIC

My name is Yasmin Murphy, and I see music in colour, and when I close my eyes the colours are so vivid and beautiful and pure, it is like those are the real colours, and the world in my head is the real world. I know that the real world is actually the one outside, but sometimes it is easier to walk around in my world instead. And sometimes I close myself off from the real world, because there is too much happening there, and I shut myself in my room, where I know where everything is, and there is nothing new to bother me, apart from maybe something small, like a fly or spider on the wall, and I shut my eyes and play a piece of music, and focus on the sound of the colour so I don't have to walk around my own world either, so I don't have to think.

I've been having a recurring dream recently, which means having the same dream again and again, which shouldn't be that upsetting for me, because I like repetition, but this dream has become upsetting, because it is recurring in a different way from how it did before. I dream that I know I am having a dream, and that in a dream I can do anything, and so I fly around my room, where everything is familiar, and I feel safe. And before, that was where the dream ended. But now the dream carries on, and the window to the street is open, and I am pulled towards the ledge, but am afraid because I don't want to leave my room and go outside, because if I do, I know that I won't fly any more, and that I will fall. And I hold on to the ledge, and try to stop myself being dragged out. And when I lose my grip is when the dream ends. Except that it doesn't end. It starts again, and again, and again. Like a DVD on repeat. And knowing how it ends doesn't make me feel any better.

It is not a happy dream. It is not a hopeful dream. I am becoming so, so tired now, because I just want to be able to sleep, but am afraid of sleeping, because I know I will have this dream, and the dream, like my inside-outside world, is no longer a safe place to be.

SMALL MIRACLES

'Hi Lila,' says Asif, kissing his sister abruptly on the cheek at the front doorstep. 'All right, Henry,' he adds, shaking Henry's hand politely. 'Thanks for coming by and watching Yasmin for us. It's just that she's not used to being alone at the weekend. I mean, I don't mean watching, not like babysitting, I just meant . . .' He stutters and comes to a halt, thinking that he may have already talked Lila and Henry out of it before they have even walked in the door.

'No need to get your knickers in a twist, Asif,' says Lila with amusement. 'We know what you meant.'

'In fact, the timing is perfect,' says Henry. 'It got us out of having to hang around with my brothers, while they fix Lila's boiler.'

'It's so useful that Henry comes from a family of plumbers,' says Lila, adding drily, 'I might have gone out with him a lot sooner if I'd known.'

'Well, it's great that Andy and Jack have come all the way from Southwark to help us out, but if I have to hear them tell Lila any more stories about how little Harry wet the bed I might well

280

throttle them; I'm blind, not deaf,' comments Henry.

'Did you wet the bed?' asks Asif, too surprised to be discreet; it seems a very odd thing to admit to so casually.

'No,' says Henry. 'That's the point.'

They come into the sitting room, where Yasmin is both watching and reading *Grey's Anatomy*. She stands up automatically and says hello, remembering to make eye contact, albeit briefly, submits to Lila's usual overbearing hug with a slightly pained expression, and sits back down again.

'I've made some lunch for everyone already,' Asif explains hurriedly to Lila and Henry, with an eye on the clock. Lila has arrived exactly on time, but Asif is still unreasonably worried about being late; he doesn't trust the tubes at the weekend, or any day, really, but even less at the weekend. 'But feel free to order a takeaway if you don't fancy it, menus are on the fridge door.'

'Smells great,' says Lila, strolling into the kitchen, and coming back to join them. 'You'll make someone a great little wife one day, Asif.'

'Well, you wouldn't,' says Asif rebelliously, annoyed at being patronized in front of Henry. He stops and looks properly at Lila. 'You look different,' he says.

'You're saying that a lot these days,' says Lila. 'I'm not sure I should be flattered.' Asif stares at her a bit myopically, trying to work out exactly what it is that seems different; he's got used to her red, Raggedy-Ann mop of hair, so it isn't that. He realizes that it's because she doesn't have the same cosmetic sheen across her skin, and that there is a nuance of differing colour between her nose and forehead, a slight well-scrubbed redness across her cheeks; she looks less polished than usual, but unexpectedly, not any less attractive, just . . . different. 'You're not wearing make-up,' Asif realizes out loud; he doesn't say the next thing that occurs to him, as Yasmin unexpectedly says it for him.

'Lila looks like Mum today,' Yasmin says matter-of-factly, staring at Lila herself to confirm her diagnosis, before returning to her study of her programme and book. 'Apart from her hair. But she doesn't smell as nice as she usually does.'

Asif waits for Lila to explode, but she surprises him. 'Thanks, I think,' she says, looking embarrassed, but not completely displeased. 'Shouldn't you be getting to your party?'

'Yeah, I guess I should,' says Asif. 'I'll be heading off now, Yas,' he adds to Yasmin, who doesn't seem to hear him. 'I wouldn't ask,' he finds himself explaining unnecessarily to Henry, 'it's just that I promised a friend that I'd help with her kid . . .'

'I really hope you're lying,' says Lila. 'I'm not giving up my Saturday afternoon for you to be an unpaid childminder. I want you to go and get snogged senseless by the hottest thing in the office.'

282

'Don't be disgusting,' says Asif, the treacherous colour rising to his cheeks as he gets his coat. 'Thanks again, guys. I'm off.'

Lila follows him into the hall. 'Did you know that you've gone bright red?' she says with a wicked grin. 'This "friend" wouldn't be that woman at the gym you've been mooning over? The one you've been sipping platonic smoothies with on a weekly basis?'

Asif sighs. 'Remind me never to tell you anything ever again. You just make fun of me.'

He kisses Lila again on the cheek, and she whispers affectionately, 'Just get it over with and ask her out. Last budget announcement, remember?'

'You're mean,' he retorts, as if he were a little boy again. He leaves the house, and tries not to break into a run as he turns the corner, but can't help it. He really, really, doesn't trust the trains.

Asif is early at the party, and doesn't see Mei Lin anywhere. He feels cheated, and finds himself sipping a glass of champagne moodily with Matt. 'Did you know that Tax are having their party at the Kensington Roof Gardens?' Matt complains. 'And we have to drag ourselves all the way to bloody Richmond.' He waves a disgusted arm around the beautifully tended gardens of the stately home they are in, at the waiters circulating with champagne and sea breezes and South East Asian nibbles, 'I mean fair enough for a wedding, but for a *party*?'

'It's OK,' says Asif, looking around. He suddenly

decides that it is a wonderful venue, as Mei Lin is walking over to him, with her baby in a buggy, and it quickly rises even further in his estimation to the most perfect place in the world, as she kisses him warmly on the cheek in front of everyone.

'There you are,' she says to Asif. 'Been looking everywhere for you.'

'Charming,' huffs Matt. 'Don't mind my feelings.' He winks with comic exaggeration at Asif, who holds his breath, as it suddenly occurs to him that big-mouth Matt might have told Mei Lin the rumours about Asif's crush. He looks slightly desperately at Mei Lin, and is relieved to see that she is behaving perfectly normally, and shows no sign of embarrassment.

'I won't. It's not as though you're the one who offered to help me with Melody today,' replies Mei Lin. 'I think your exact words were "Keep the little poop machine a million miles from me, darling."'

'Fair cop,' admits Matt. 'Coo-ee,' he says inexpertly over Melody's pram, and then makes his escape. 'Babies,' he stage-whispers to Asif as he leaves. 'They just creep me out, it's the way they smell fear.'

Asif looks down at Melody. 'Wow, she's grown,' he says in wonder. She's practically doubled in size, and her hair no longer stands up like a shaving brush, but has become just long enough to flop down at the ends; she's dressed in a frilly orange top with baby blue jeans, from which her chubby pink feet poke out like edible sugar treats.

'Ah-wa-ya,' says Melody wisely to him.

'Nine months old,' says Mei Lin proudly. 'I can't believe how quickly it's gone. I'll be able to stop breast-feeding soon – I've only done it so long because of Stephen's asthma.'

'Stephen's asthma?' asks Asif, not understanding the connection.

'Yes,' says Mei Lin, unbuckling Melody from her pram. She sees Asif's blank face, and explains. 'You see, the asthma, combined with the eczema on my mum's side of the family, makes a bit of an unpleasant genetic heritage for Melody. The doctors told me to breastfeed for at least a year, to try and prevent her getting either of them, or to help get them less severely. There've been studies, I think,' she adds vaguely. 'Say hello to Asif, Melody,' she coos, hoisting Melody up so her face is level with his.

'Ah-wah-la-lah-LAH,' trills Melody, before bursting into a rolling peal of giggles, her smile stretching her face almost comically all the way to her ears.

'Wow,' says Asif, in awe once more at her un-diluted happiness. He feels a tug of memory as he looks at her, a vague, benign recollection of something just as pure. He's reached out for her without even realizing it, and before he knows it, Melody's nappied bottom is in the crook of his arm, while she pokes experimentally at his eyes.

'Meh-eh-eh-da,' she gabbles, and having finished with his eyes, tries plucking away his nose. Her little hand is so meltingly soft that it practically dissolves against his skin when she touches him. He realizes that Melody is beautiful, because she is loved, like he was once beautiful and loved. He has a sharp sense of loss which he knows is rather foolish; he hands Melody back to Mei Lin with a feeling of regret.

'Would you like a drink?' he asks.

'Sure,' says Mei Lin, looking at him thoughtfully. 'I don't know why I'm surprised that you're so good with children.'

'Am I?' asks Asif. 'I don't know anyone with children apart from you.'

Later in the afternoon, the music has started, and Asif is sitting on a stone bench, with Melody dozing in her buggy beside him. He's found himself thinking more and more about his mother recently, and although he's tried to avoid it, events seem to be conspiring against him. Yasmin's obsession with how people die in TV dramas, Lila's new fresh-faced look, Mei Lin's serene maternal competence, and the sausage-like cuteness of the little bundle sleeping under his watchful eye, plump arms thrown above her head. He's not sure if it's meeting Mei Lin, a woman who is ridiculously out of his league, whom he has followed like a demented puppy, but who has somehow, against all odds, become his friend; or perhaps it's the tentative possibility of Yasmin no longer needing him so much in the future; but he suddenly has a new feeling, deep down, that is so unusual and unexpected that it takes him a while to identify. It's hope. Or at the very least, the hope of hope. And with this feeling thrillingly rising within him, like a song in his heart, he is no longer sure that he resents Mum and Dad quite as much as he once thought.

Asif looks across the manicured lawn to the dance floor set up in the marquee in front of him, and watches Mei Lin chatting to Ravi's plump and pretty wife, Asha. Mei Lin sees him, waves, and begins to stroll over with a drink. Mum, he thinks, was a woman who made a great chocolate cake, but who learned to make a great carrot cake instead, because Yasmin preferred it. Mum was a woman who medicated her family with food. She was a woman who unwittingly helped prevent Yasmin suffering from either the eczema or the asthma that dogged her other children, because she realized that breastfeeding was the only way to keep Baby Yasmin quiet, and so she carried on as long as she thought she could. She was a woman who was omnipotent in her home, like God, and who never lost her temper, even when disciplining her daughter with a measured slap. She was a woman who sent her husband away, without admitting to anyone, least of all her children, that was what she was doing, and who only realized how much she missed him when he unexpectedly died on duty. She was a woman who was carelessly beautiful, but controlled in every other aspect of her life; who believed she could hide her weaknesses from her children, weeping in the bathroom where she thought they couldn't hear, and who even hid the weakness of her heart from herself. She was a woman, in the end, who tried her best, like every mother does; and perhaps her best wasn't always good enough, but didn't that make her like every other mother in the world? Mum was no angel or demon, Asif finally realizes, she was just another person; she was just like him. It wasn't fair to blame her, to resent her, or hate her in death; just as it wasn't fair to have adored her as much as he did in life. He had loved his father too, but when he died, Asif remembered asking for him less and less each night, missing him less and less, because their mother was always there, and had gradually filled the gap, becoming both Mum and Dad for them all; she hadn't had a choice. And perhaps, just sometimes, she had been right. She had been right when she told him to engage with Yasmin. She had been right when she told him that he was a good boy. She and Dad had possibly even been right to have given him those shining names; Asif for forgiveness, Declan after his dutiful father, and Kalil for friendship, as they were possibly the most important gifts he had to bestow, and receive in turn. Perhaps it is time to start being proud of his name, instead of ashamed; perhaps it is time to start being proud of being good, as well.

'You look very thoughtful,' says Mei Lin. 'I'd ask what you were thinking, but I know it's possibly the most irritating question in the world.'

'That's what Lila says,' comments Asif. 'She says that the only question that's more irritating is, "Do you love me?"'

'She must be a very pretty girl, to hear that often enough to get bored by it,' says Mei Lin, smiling. 'Here you go, cranberry juice, the only non-alcoholic thing I could find.'

'Thanks,' says Asif, sipping his drink. 'You can go back to the dance, if you want,' he suggests. 'I don't mind watching Melody.'

'I'm OK here,' says Mei Lin. 'It's a relief talking to someone who's still sober. Back there, everyone else is laughing hysterically at things that I just don't find funny.'

'Welcome to my world,' says Asif carelessly.

Mei Lin looks at Asif curiously. 'So, what were you thinking? At risk of being irritating.'

Asif shrugs his shoulders. 'Oh, nothing much. Don't let this strong, silent exterior fool you – deep down, I'm really not very interesting.'

'I've always thought modesty was an attractive quality,' says Mei Lin. Asif smiles at her; he likes her even more for being kind to him, neutral old nothing old him. As If he wasn't there.

'It's not really modesty; I'm just being honest,' he says.

'Honesty's an attractive quality too,' says Mei Lin. 'It's underrated. A little like you.'

Asif blinks and looks at her; he has that feeling again, curling in the pit of his stomach, making him feel warm and safe inside. It's hope, he's certain it's hope. 'You're lovely to say that,' he says. 'I wish it were true.' He could kick himself for saying this, but under Mei Lin's frank gaze he finds it impossible to lie. 'But the truth is that I don't have a lot to offer. I'm not underrated. I'm exactly what I seem, a mediocre accountant with problems. Some to do with my family; some just to do with me. I don't really expect any girls to be forming an orderly queue for my attention.'

Mei Lin stretches out her legs in front of her, and eases off her shoes, letting her bare feet rest on the grass. Asif notices that her second toes are a fraction longer than her big toes; on her it looks absolutely right, even her flaws are lovable. 'You know,' she says, 'there's a line in a movie, something about how a bloke being rich is like a girl being pretty; I've always thought that neither of those things would sort out all your problems, but there's no doubt that they help.' She looks directly at Asif, as she adds, 'I think the same is true about relationships. Meeting someone won't sort out all your problems, but it definitely helps. To have someone in your corner. To have someone who's there for you.'

Asif watches in wonder as Mei Lin carefully takes his hand, quite deliberately, as though she wants there to be no confusion about it. He looks into her wonderful face, and for a moment he can't see her beauty, or her narrow, merry eyes; all he can see there is hope. Her face is like a mirror. A small miracle has occurred, as Asif finally realizes, for the first time in his life, that he might be special too.

Mei Lin clears her throat, and takes a sip of Asif's cranberry juice. 'We're practically kissing,' she jokes nervously, raising her eyes back to meet his. He realizes that she is waiting for his response, and he quickly leans forward, before he can think and hesitate and ruin everything, and kisses her berry-sweet mouth with his own. Then he stops thinking anything at all, as he feels the unutterable bliss of the warmth of her lips, returning his kiss, and her hand reaching up to touch his face. As the kiss eventually breaks off, he finds that he has pulled her right into his arms. 'Will you go out with me, Mei Lin?' he says quietly, knowing what he wants, and finally brave enough to ask for it; hoping that he hasn't misunderstood, and that she wants more than just a simple kiss at a party, too.

After a long moment, Mei Lin pulls back very slightly, and leans her forehead against Asif's. 'You know, I've been waiting weeks for you to ask me out,' she says with a wry smile. 'I really don't want to make a fool of myself, because I know that this

291

isn't going to be easy. We work in the same office, and I've got Melody, and you're responsible for Yasmin. I'd rather know right now if you think that this is something you can't do.'

'I can do this,' says Asif quickly, wanting to convince himself as well as her; he's not sure before he says it, but once the words are out, he knows that it's true. He leans forward and kisses her again, with all the unexpressed tenderness he has felt for so long; he feels that Mei Lin has hoisted him out of dark, turbulent water with a competent hand, and told him, simply and without drama, to breathe. And he knows he can, because he must. 'I could do anything for you,' he adds humbly, ignoring the drunken whoops and indiscreet applause from the marquee, as their colleagues have finally spotted them together on the bench. 'Anything.' Looking into her liquid eyes, he can see that sometimes, good things can happen to good people; he can see that anything in the world is possible, even for him.

SAVING SLEEPING PILLS

My name is Yasmin Murphy, and I have researched the most effective ways to die, which would cause the least trauma to my organs so that they can be harvested and donated. I don't feel bad about this, as it's a nice gesture, and will save lots of lives and make some families very happy. Unfortunately, the most effective ways involve too much skill on my part; I don't think that I could hang myself properly, as I am not very dexterous with my hands, which is why I can't sew or knit, and I am not very co-ordinated. I would possibly just end up choking myself, which would still be OK for my organs, but would probably hurt.

I have decided to take pills instead, which isn't ideal but I think that some of my organs will be used, as long as they are harvested quickly enough, and they will be as I intend to leave written instructions for Asif, who is normally very good at following directions. I have saved up my sleeping pills for some time now, so I have enough, and am actually looking forward to having a good rest, as I haven't been sleeping well at night and even when I do sleep I have that dream that I don't like, which isn't very restful either.

I have managed to do something else on my list, which I didn't think would be possible, which is look after a baby. This is because Asif has a new girlfriend whom he met at his office, and she has a funny baby girl called Melody who laughs a lot for no reason, and only cries if she rolls over and bangs her head on something. They come every other weekend, and I like the fact that they always arrive at the same time, because the baby is on a strict routine, just as strict as mine, and eats and sleeps and bathes at the same time every day, which is possibly why she's so happy, as she never has a chance to get too hungry or tired or messy. Sometimes I play with Melody just by myself, if Asif and Mei Lin are making tea in the kitchen, and I read her board books which are very simple and bright, over and over again, as she likes repetition just as much as I do. I also make shadow animals for her, and she especially likes the sad, happy and cheeky bunnies because she laughs and laughs and laughs. I think she might even be a little simple, because she laughs so much at nothing, but I haven't told Asif that, or Mei Lin, because I know that it's not nice to say things about other people's children, even if they're true, because when people said things about me to Mum, even though they were true, she said that they weren't nice.

★　　★　　★

So now it is just a matter of waiting for my documentary to air, because Mum said that my skills come with responsibility, and I promised that I would show people what it's like to be non-NT, and think that I should see it done. My sight will be fine until then, as my eye has stopped getting worse, but I don't think I'll wait and see if it will get better, as I don't like taking things out of my schedule once I've planned them.

LOST AND FOUND

'You know, Lola, we're so glad that little Harry's found you,' says Henry's sister familiarly, patting Lila's arm as she pours the coffee, mispronouncing Lila's name yet again.

'Wait for it,' Henry mutters to Lila under his breath.

'Because, not being mean like,' Henry's sister continues, with the south-east London accent that Henry seems to have lost, 'his last girlfriend was a real minger.' Lila tries not to snort out the sip of coffee she has just taken.

'Please shut up, Ellie, that's completely unnecessary, and you know that she had a heart of gold. Besides, *Lila* really isn't interested in my last girlfriend,' says Henry.

'The hell she isn't, Harry,' retorts Ellie. 'Anyway, like I said, Antonia was a real minger, and a poncey little cow. With her A *levels*, and her *Masters*, and her *charity* work. 'Course, with an ugly mug like that, she needed to have a bleeding righteous heart to get people to notice her.' She adds conversationally, 'I never understood what Harry saw in her; or didn't see in her, if you get what I mean.'

296

'Just got bad taste, haven't you, *Harry*,' says Lila, still trying not to laugh.

'That's just it, Lola,' agrees Ellie. 'Rotten taste. Not that it's his fault, being blind as a bat these days. I guess girls like Antonia just see him coming.' She pushes back her curly frizz and grins wickedly at Lila. 'Now you, on the other hand, are like a breath of fresh air. A pretty young thing, who does an honest, simple job. Barmaid, aren't you? There's nothing wrong with pulling pints for a living.'

'I'm a waitress,' corrects Lila, the smile wiped off her face. 'Do you always belittle people with compliments?'

'What's that, love?' asks Ellie, fiddling with the plastic wrapper on a packet of biscuits. 'Here you go, dear,' she adds, shaking them out on to a plate. 'Have as many as you want, you don't look like you worry about your weight.' She smooths down her strappy summer dress over her own scrawny figure with satisfaction, and wanders back into the kitchen.

'Well, that answers my question for me,' mutters Lila to Henry. 'All the way to bloody Southwark to be renamed Lola, and then called stupid and fat. God, you owe me.'

'I know,' whispers Henry. 'Families, eh. Can't live with them. Can't escape them. Can't drop them down a deep, dark hole.' He squeezes Lila's hand under the table. 'Well, Ellie was the only sibling of mine you hadn't met.'

'You saved the best for last, I see,' Lila says caustically.

'I thought about hiding her altogether, but I thought it was only fair to let you know what you were in for,' says Henry.

'What do you mean?' asks Lila.

'I mean I've booked dinner for us somewhere nice tonight, to make it up to you,' says Henry.

'It's not so bad,' says Lila, nudging him with her shoulder, appeased.

'Oh, it will be,' says Henry, as Ellie barges back into the room.

'Did you want to see what his last girlfriend looked like, Lola?' Ellie offers generously. ''Course you do. She's on our wedding video somewhere; not sure where, so we'll have to see the whole thing.'

Lila grits her teeth and squeezes Henry's hand so hard that he winces. 'Dinner is somewhere really, really nice,' promises Henry in an apologetic whisper.

'Are you sure you can afford this?' Lila asks in awe, as they are ushered upstairs into Nobu on Park Lane.

'No, but you said that you liked it here,' says Henry. 'I thought it would be fun.'

'It's great,' says Lila, looking around at the Mayfair glitterati tucking into exquisite sashimi. 'Although I might have worn something smarter if I knew we were coming – I'm amazed they let

298

me in. You know, I've not been here in ages. Not since I went out with Wesley, he loved it here.'

Henry winces. 'I guess I deserved that, you've had to put up with lots of stuff to do with my ex today.'

'I think it's very noble the way you stuck up for, Antonia, was it?' lies Lila, who feels unreasonably envious of plain but worthy Antonia's pedigree and qualifications. 'What's she doing now?'

'Charity work, in Africa. That's why we broke up,' says Henry disinterestedly. 'It was a long time ago.'

'Hmm, charity work,' repeats Lila, realizing that she sounds almost catty. She changes the subject hurriedly. 'You know, I'm starving,' she says, ostentatiously flicking open the menu. 'Let's talk starters. They do great little crab thingies here.'

The meal is fabulous; Henry even orders champagne, despite Lila's protestations that neither of them can afford it. As Lila scoops up the last of the chocolate dessert they've shared, she can't stop herself mentioning Henry's ex again; she is uncomfortable with her jealousy, she dislikes the way it takes her over. 'You know, before I thought you were being unreasonably nice about your ex. More nice than was flattering to me, actually. But it's just got me thinking that perhaps I should have been better to my ex, too. I barely told Wesley we were breaking up . . .'

'Lila, is that you?' asks Wesley, coming up behind

her from the bar. 'It is you!' He seems delighted. He is even handsomer than Lila remembers, in a pale blue shirt and a beautifully cut leather jacket; his dark skin gleams like satin in the soft and flattering light.

'Hey there, you look great,' she says generously, painfully aware of how kind Henry was about his former partner, and not wanting to suffer by comparison. It occurs to her that this is her opportunity to show Henry that she can be noble too. 'Are your ears burning? I was just talking about you.'

'All good things, I hope,' says Wesley, raising his hand to acknowledge Henry, before turning his full attention to Lila. 'Wow, you look great too,' he says. 'Different, but great. And very comfortable,' he adds, nodding towards her cut-off jeans and thin cotton vest. He asks jokily, 'Did you leave the rest of your clothes on the beach?' Lila laughs, and notices that Henry is looking almost cross.

'Well, it was nice to see you, Wesley. Take care,' she says.

Wesley kisses her on the cheek. 'Give me a call sometime. I'm not quite sure what happened, but I know I'd like to catch up.' He adds in a low voice loaded with meaning, 'I'd really, really like it.' He kisses her other cheek, holding his lips there for just a moment too long to be discreet. He nods again to Henry, 'So long,' and heads off.

Lila laughs again, and waves briefly as she sees Wesley rejoin his waiting friends and leave the restaurant. She turns back to Henry. 'How weird is that? I talk about him, and he just appears. I suppose I shouldn't be that surprised, he was always lurking around here on Friday nights.' She stops as she notices that Henry is looking even crosser than before; his fist is clenched so tightly on the table that his knuckles have gone white. 'What?' she asks.

'Nothing,' he says. 'Let's just go.' The maître d' approaches Henry and whispers something in his ear, but Henry shakes his head, 'No, just the bill, please,' he says unnecessarily firmly. Lila sees the maître d' make a gesture to their waiter, who shrugs his shoulders and returns to the kitchen with a tray. She doesn't think anything of it; she just guesses that Henry isn't in the mood for coffee.

Henry excuses himself to go to the loo, and when he comes back he pays the waiting bill and gets up to go to the cloakroom, barely saying a word to Lila. She hurries to catch up with him before he gets to the stairs, but he doesn't seem to notice her proffered arm, and goes down himself holding the banister. 'Are you all right?' she asks, as they collect their jackets.

'I'm fine,' he says, now seeming sad rather than cross. 'I'll get a cab. Take care of yourself.' And he walks out briskly without even kissing her goodbye.

'I thought I was coming back to yours tonight?' Lila asks as he disappears through the door.

Suddenly furious with him, she storms out. 'Where the hell do you think you're going?' she yells at him.

'Home,' says Henry briefly, already getting into a waiting cab. The cab moves off and Lila is left fuming outside the restaurant; how dare Henry abandon her like that, how dare he be oh-so nice and noble and dignified in defending the coyote-ugly-bleeding-heart-little-miss-goody-goody Antonia, his irrelevant ex, but then leave Lila, his girlfriend, standing on Park Lane and looking ridiculous. Especially after they've just had a really romantic, stupidly expensive meal; he ordered champagne, for God's sake; how could he not want to sleep with her after a meal like that? Lila really doesn't want to go home, and decides not to accept Henry's mystifying rejection of her this evening; she walks to Hyde Park Corner to take the tube to Putney.

When Lila reaches Henry's place, he isn't there. The neighbour lets her in the communal front door, and she sits on the steps leading up to Henry's flat, checking her mobile too often, and wishing she had a magazine. She is beginning to feel concerned rather than angry, when Henry finally arrives. 'What took you so long?' she asks flatly, not sure how to react to him after the odd scene at the restaurant.

'I stopped in the pub for a drink. Or two. Or three,' says Henry, not bothering to question her presence. Lila says nothing; she knows that Henry almost never drinks on his own. Surprisingly, he doesn't seem remotely tipsy in any obvious way; she can tell only because he is more solemn than usual. His face is perfectly blank and Lila suppresses a wicked urge to punch him just for a reaction; she's never seen him like this before. She's aware that this is possibly the first time he's let slip that he's not perfect, that he can behave badly too.

She follows him up the few steps to his flat, saying nothing as he opens his front door. He turns and says, 'I'd ask you in, but I'm not feeling too well. I might go straight to bed.' He's about to shut the door unsmilingly in her face, when she walks in anyway. She doesn't know why he's being so difficult, but she realizes that she has no desire to leave him there on his own; in the end, Henry is just a bloke, and managing blokes is something in which Lila has plenty of experience.

'I think I know how to make you feel better. And I'm not sure we need to get as far as the bed,' she says simply, walking over to where he's standing, and pressing herself against him; she lifts her head and kisses him fiercely on his still lips. She is gratified to feel Henry respond after just a moment, and start to kiss her back just as fiercely, and then even more so, as his hands reach into her hair and he pushes her violently back against his front door. Passion, thinks Lila, isn't this what she used to long for, the explosive passion with which lovers make up after an argument? Even as she enjoys the sheer physicality of the embrace, the strength in Henry's arms as he practically picks her up, she feels disappointed in herself, and in Henry, that it was so easy for her to manipulate him. She pulls off his jacket with rough carelessness, and they sink to the floor, unbuttoning, unzipping, tugging up and tugging down. This is wrong, thinks Lila, as she feels Henry's mouth hard on hers, kissing her with a hungry desperation as though it might be their last time. It seems slightly sordid, and she feels inexplicably grubby, even though she has made violent, rushed, barely-dressed, barely-described-as love this way dozens of times before with previous lovers. 'Henry,' she breathes urgently, aware of her heartbeat, her blood rising to her skin, the agonizing exquisite tension building in her body; she needs him to know that she understands this isn't how it's meant to be between the two of them, to compromise each other in this animal way, without tenderness or meaning. 'Henry,' she tries to explain, 'this is different . . .' but she can't control her ragged breathing, and is only aware of the ambivalence of her words after she has spoken.

'You've finally remembered my name, then,' whispers Henry bitterly. 'So is this what you wanted? A quick shag against the door and on the floor. Is this how you used to do it with him?'

Lila doesn't reply. She is relieved and appalled at the simple explanation for Henry's behaviour;

it is just jealousy after all, unfounded, and irrational. Now she realizes that Henry isn't making
love to her with passion, but screwing her with
anger, something which she has been guilty of in
her chequered past, but never imagined him
doing. Jealousy has suddenly taken him over, and
made him ugly on the inside, just as it has made
her for so long, all the bitter years she has spent
resenting Yasmin. The tear-streaked image of the
terrifying woman in the changing room mirror
flashes through her memory. She is not sure if she
is more furious with him or herself, as they both
finally fall, gasping, into the blank, explosive void
of climax. Before she has even recovered her
breath she pulls back and slaps him hard on the
face. 'Don't you ever fuck me like that again,' she
hisses. 'Don't you dare.'

'Oh Lila,' says Henry, his own breath still uneven
as he pushes himself up from her, stunned sober
by her accusation. 'I'm so, so sorry.' He gets up
and stumbles through to the bedroom. Lila
straightens her clothes, and follows him, where
she sees him lying facing up on the bed, his hand
over his eyes to keep back the tears that are threatening to fall.

She sits on the edge of the bed, and asks
brusquely, 'Why have you been behaving like such
a freak?' She refuses to feel sorry for him.

'Freak?' Henry repeats with a hollow laugh.
'Appropriate, I guess.' He pauses, and asks, 'Are you
ashamed of me, Lila?'

His question takes her by surprise. 'Why the hell would you think that?' she snaps, offended.

'Then why did you blatantly ignore me in front of that guy? Why didn't you introduce me, and tell him that I was your boyfriend?' he asks, his own voice rising in response to her aggressive tone.

'I suppose I thought it was obvious,' says Lila, 'given the context. Nobody takes anybody to Nobu unless they're sleeping with them.'

'Well, he didn't think it was obvious, he was seriously flirting with you. He asked you out, for God's sake,' argues Henry.

'What does that matter?' asks Lila, irritated by Henry reading so much into such a meaningless encounter. 'It's not as though I was flirting with him, I was just trying to be polite.'

'It's more than polite to let some creep drool all over you,' mutters Henry. 'He kissed you, twice, and far too slowly. While I was left sitting there like a mug.'

'You know it was just on the cheek,' says Lila. 'Why are you bothered about Wesley?' she asks with exasperation. 'Why are you threatened by him? I mean, he's nothing like you, he's all good clothes, and expensive grooming . . .'

'And devastatingly handsome, I suppose?' hazards Henry sarcastically, not finding Lila's response slightly reassuring.

'And handsome,' agrees Lila. 'He's definitely a very handsome guy. But he's all about the surface. That's it. That's all there is to him, really. I've got no interest in him at all. He's just not my type, not any more.' She sighs, and adds, 'Look, I'm sorry that I didn't introduce you, if that's what all this is about; it just didn't even occur to me. You know I'm clueless about etiquette.'

'Oh,' Henry says inadequately. He says nothing for a long moment, and then sits up to speak. 'No, I'm the one that's sorry, I really am. I've blown it now, haven't I? I've ruined everything. I had no right to say what I said, just now, when we were . . .' he pauses as he doesn't even know how to describe what they just did, '. . . in the hallway,' he says at last, embarrassed. 'Tonight was meant to be perfect, a really perfect evening for us both, and I ruined it by being an insecure, jealous freak.'

'Well, you're still my insecure, jealous freak,' says Lila kindly, deciding that he is probably quite contrite enough. 'I forgive you.' She adds, 'Nothing terrible happened, not really, just a bad shag. You've not blown it, anything between us I mean.' It occurs to her that even bad sex with Henry is preferable to good sex with anyone else she's ever known, even someone as physically attractive as Wesley.

'You're a bright girl, Lila, but sometimes you can be really dense,' mutters Henry, rolling over towards her. 'Do you really not get why I took you out tonight?'

'If you call me dense, you're well on the way to blowing it after all,' says Lila sharply. 'And I know why you took me out. You were meant to be

307

making up for inflicting your god-awful sister on me all afternoon.'

Henry shakes his head with frustration. 'I took you out because I wanted to propose to you tonight, and I inflicted my god-awful sister on you because I wanted you to know what you were in for with my god-awful family,' he bursts out.

'What?' asks Lila. 'Propose? With a ring and everything?' Sitting in Henry's spartan bedroom, so soon after the unfortunate events of the night, she has to resist the urge to laugh; the idea just seems so preposterous.

'Of course with a bloody ring; I'm not the one who's completely clueless about etiquette,' says Henry sulkily. 'The waiter was meant to bring it over in a glass of champagne until your disgustingly handsome ex ruined it by slobbering all over you.' He sighs. 'I know that I overreacted, but I just felt like such a prat, like I'd got us all wrong. And I know that it's stupid to be jealous, but I've never felt this way about anyone before. I dream about you at night, you know; I dream about the way your voice changes when you smile, the scent of your skin. I dream that I'm holding you in my arms when you're not beside me. I dream about being with you for ever. I was there trying to ask you to marry me, and it looked like you didn't even want to admit to him that you were dating me.' He pulls the ring out of his jeans pocket, and puts it on the bed next to her. 'It was my grandmother's,' he says.

'Oh,' Lila says, unusually lost for words. She looks at the ring, and picks it up carefully. 'That's pretty,' she says. 'OK, then.' For a moment it seems as though she might be about to say something else, but doesn't.

'What?' asks Henry, raising his head. 'Did you just say OK, as in yes, or OK, as in something else that doesn't mean yes?'

'Who's being dense now?' says Lila. 'What else does OK mean?'

'God, how I love you,' says Henry impulsively, and he drops to his knee at the bedside, and takes her hand, holding it gently against his mouth to kiss. 'I've never known anyone as creative and moody and funny and wonderful in just about every way. I'm certain that I don't deserve you, but I'm going to do everything I can until I do,' he promises. He takes the ring from her, and gently pushes it on her finger. He is still holding her hand as he rejoins her on the edge of the bed.

'You were an idiot tonight, but you know I love you too,' she confesses. 'Why else would I have waited on your steps this evening, and followed you up to your door?' She turns her face towards him, so that her lips gently meet his. 'You can start making it up to me right now, if you like,' she says, and sighs blissfully as he folds her in his arms, and kisses her slowly, and carefully, before they melt effortlessly back on to the bed. There is no compromise, no anger, no sense of being used or taken; there is only the giving of gifts.

She feels clean once more, as absurdly pure as a fairy-tale bride on a hillside, holding wildflowers and dressed in virginal white.

How unlikely, she thinks, how impossible, and how miraculous, that they have found each other. She realizes that it is even easier for her to be with Henry now that he has shown her that he has flaws too, now she knows that he can be just as vulnerable and overcome by the irrational darkness of emotion, and that he really will sometimes need forgiving, just as she does.

THANK YOU LISTS

'I have news,' says Lila as she walks in the house with a bottle of champagne. 'Really big news.' She kisses Asif on the cheek, and looks around the sitting room expectantly. 'Where's Yasmin? She must be excited about the documentary airing tonight. She's almost famous.'

'Not really,' says Asif. 'She's in her room, and said she didn't want to be disturbed. She's been in a funny mood all week. Funnier than usual I mean.'

'Was it her A level results?' asks Lila, 'I thought she got what she was predicted?'

'She did,' says Asif. 'It wasn't that. She was pleased with the results. Pleased they matched the predictions, anyway. It would have been a disaster if she aced History instead of getting the B she expected.' He sighs, and Lila can see his state of habitual worry returning with the tension around his eyes. 'I asked her which college she was going to accept for university, because she had three conditional places, and she just muttered something about how it was irrelevant. Mostly or wholly irrelevant, I think her exact words were. And her making eye contact has really regressed recently, she was barely looking at me.'

'It's being off school,' suggests Lila. 'She's got out of the habit of being around people, being at home alone all day, watching telly and playing *Doom*. It's not surprising if her social skills have gone a bit downhill.'

'I told them that this would happen,' says Asif, exasperated with himself for trusting too much in Yasmin's specialists. 'They told me that I was babying her. That I was the one keeping her in her routines. Well, they didn't say that exactly, but it's what they implied.'

Lila realizes that she is still holding the bottle of champagne in her hand, and feels slightly foolish; as though she's turned up at a funeral in a party frock. She refuses to accept feeling foolish; she has every right to bring champagne, she has every right to celebrate with her family, it shouldn't always be about Yasmin, not any more. 'Speaking of poor social skills, didn't you hear? I've got news. Can we get Yasmin down, I want to speak to you both?'

'You can try,' says Asif, still too distracted about Yasmin to take in properly what Lila is saying. 'I've tried every half an hour since the morning, but she's not having it. Maybe you'll have better luck.'

Lila puts the bottle down on the coffee table. 'As if, Asif,' she says resignedly. It is obvious that if Yasmin hasn't been responding to Asif, she certainly won't to Lila. 'Well, I may as well tell you now and Yas later. I wanted to tell you guys before tonight, before the documentary airs, because I didn't want to steal Yasmin's thunder.' Lila smiles wickedly, and corrects herself, nudging Asif complicitly. 'Well, maybe I do. A bit. But I won't.'

Asif looks up from the armchair into which he has slumped; Lila has finally got his attention. 'So what's the news?' he asks. He hasn't a clue what it might be.

Lila sits down opposite him and holds his hand, looking directly at him with a frank openness that Yasmin has never been able to emulate, even with her careful mental counting of Mississippi One and Mississippi Two while she holds his gaze. 'I'm engaged!' Lila finally whoops. 'I'm getting married!'

'Oh, my God, that's so, well . . . wow,' hesitates Asif, absolutely shocked and realizing that he is muttering nonsense in order to buy time, while he flails mentally for the right response.

'I know!' shrieks Lila, hugging him boisterously.

'I mean, congratulations. He's a lovely guy,' says Asif, having finally located the appropriate formula, with some relief. Unfortunately he loses his advantage immediately, by asking unthinkingly, 'It is Henry, right?'

'Of course it's Henry,' says Lila, pulling back affronted. 'Who else would it be?'

'I was joking,' lies Asif, covering his tracks poorly. 'God, you're sensitive.' He tries to think of what

Mum or Dad would say to the news, what a normal big brother would say; perhaps he should ask after Henry's honourable intentions, but that seems a bit redundant now that he's proposed. Perhaps he should ask how Henry intends to support a wife, but that seems ludicrously old-fashioned and slightly offensive to Lila. He is not sure that he is brave enough to ask the obvious question, and his discomfort is apparent enough for Lila to notice.

'What's up?' she asks, disappointed by his reaction. 'Aren't you pleased?'

'Of course I am,' says Asif. 'He's a great guy. I guess I'm just a bit worried that . . .' Asif cannot bring himself to ask what he intends, and sidetracks unconvincingly, 'Well, you're a bit young aren't you? And so's he . . .'

'So now I'm too immature to get married,' huffs Lila. 'How bloody rude. And he's not some naïve kid that I've trapped, he's twenty-six. He's older than you.'

'That's not what I meant,' admits Asif. 'I meant that, well, he's a great guy and all . . .'

'I think you said that already,' interrupts Lila crossly. 'But?'

'But isn't he a lot to take on?' Asif finally comes out and says it, more through bumbling than bravery. 'I mean, you'll have to take care of him. You've only known him for six months, but if you get married, it'll be for ever. It's a lot of responsibility.'

'Isn't that a bit hypocritical coming from someone who's just started dating a single mum with a baby? Isn't that a lot of responsibility, too?' retorts Lila.

'Yes, but I'm used to it,' says Asif tactlessly. He realizes what he has said a bit too late, and glances nervously at Lila, not sure how she'll react. He is vastly relieved when she starts laughing.

'You're right, you are used to it. But don't worry about me looking after Henry. It's more the other way around. He looks after me – whether I want him to or not, actually.' Asif looks sceptical, and Lila finds herself justifying what she said, not because she has to prove anything to Asif, but just because she wants him to understand. 'I don't just mean stuff like getting my boiler fixed. He thinks about things that really matter to me; I mean, he got me an appointment with a new consultant dermatologist who prescribed me some fantastic antihistamines, that really take the edge off my itching, especially at night. It's insane that all these years, my skin felt like it was on fire underneath, and none of my other doctors thought to try me on them; apparently they use them on hayfever sufferers quite often. My skin might still look pretty bad, and get pretty rough, but at least I don't feel it inside all the time. And he's helped me realize that I should go back to art college, because life's just too bloody short to spend it waiting tables and not doing the thing that I love.' She gives Asif that frank gaze once more, and touches his arm. 'But the thing is, none of that stuff really matters. What matters, is that I love him, Asif. I really do.' She doesn't say that he loves her; with natural vanity, she assumes that Asif already knows this.

'Oh Lila,' says Asif with relief, 'I'm so, so pleased for you.' He holds out his arms, to hug her, and realizes that Henry has succeeded where he has failed. All the time that Asif was looking after Yasmin, why wasn't he looking after Lila, or even noticing that she needed a little bit of looking after, too? Why hadn't he ever fixed her boiler, or got her to consult a different dermatologist from the one who just kept prescribing stronger and stronger skin-melting steroid creams, or persuaded her to go back to art college? In fact, he thinks, still holding Lila, that she has failed as well. Why couldn't she do all these things herself without a Henry; why couldn't she have looked after Asif, a little bit, too? He remembers what Mei Lin said about relationships; falling in love didn't make everything better, it didn't make all one's problems go away, but it certainly, undeniably, helped. But he doesn't know where that leaves Yasmin; he doesn't know whether Yasmin ever yearns for romantic love the way other teenagers do, he doesn't know whether she would ever be capable enough to give and receive in the way that a relationship requires, when even something as simple as offering a hand to hold could be fraught with

316

difficulties. He suspects that if he were her, he'd want to hide in his room too.

'Well, look at us now,' says Asif, finally releasing Lila. 'You've met Henry, I've met Mei Lin. Aren't we lucky?' His voice has a slight edge to it, and Lila looks at him sharply, and impatiently.

'Oh fuck you, Asif,' she retorts. 'Sometimes I don't think you're any better than sodding Raingirl upstairs. In fact, you're worse, because she doesn't choose to be the way she is, and you do. Did you really think that we'd both be single our whole lives just so Yas wouldn't feel left out? Did you think we'd shudder in our miserable little circle of three and turn away any chance of hope and happiness on principle?'

'I didn't mean any of that,' protests Asif, uncomfortable with Lila's sudden fury, and at how quickly she always reads him. 'I said we were lucky, I meant it.'

'Good,' says Lila, taking a deep breath and trying to calm down; she hasn't called Yasmin any names for months, and is annoyed with herself that she did it in anger. 'Because it's not just about luck. It's about choice. We've all been dealt a pretty poor hand, you, me and Yas, but we had to make a choice. We could choose to stay unhappy, or we could choose to live. I've made my choice, Asif, and you have too.' She stands up, and looks reproachfully at the bottle of champagne that she couldn't afford, but she has eagerly brought over, to celebrate her good news with her family.

Couldn't it once, just once, have been all about her? Just for twenty minutes on a Saturday afternoon. It didn't seem so much to have asked. 'I'll come back tonight to watch the documentary with you both,' she says. 'We can have the champagne then.' She feels mean for leaving things with Asif on such a sour note, and says, appeasingly, 'The documentary should be really interesting. Henry says that they hired some swish SFX team to do a visual simulation of Yasmin's synaesthesia the way she explains it; there's a sequence of her playing one of Mozart's piano concertos, and the music is all in colour.'

Asif accepts the olive branch, smiles uncertainly, and walks her to the door. They kiss goodbye, a bit more formally than usual, and Asif finds himself saying something as she reaches the front gate; he hasn't planned to say anything, but the words just fall out, tumbling one after another like children at a playground, precipitate and unstoppable. He looks down at the doormat, as though he is just saying it to himself, 'You know, recently I've been thinking a lot about when we were kids; I guess being around Melody brings it all back. I think I blamed Yas for a lot of the things that went wrong with our family. I think we both did. But the truth is that things weren't perfect before she came along. Mum and Dad already had stupid arguments about lots of things just to do with us, whether to boil our eggs for seven minutes or ten, whether or not to cross the road with your buggy when the light had gone yellow. Lots of petty things that turned into massive fights, with Dad yelling and Mum clamming up and not speaking to him for hours. Even on that first morning we visited Yas in the hospital, when she was born, they had a fight, because Mum found out that Dad had brought us straight to see her without giving us breakfast; he was tired and didn't think it mattered, but Mum was tired too, and furious with him. What I'm saying, is that we don't know whether they'd have stayed together if Yas wasn't born; we don't know if Dad would have gone back on active duty and got himself killed anyway, we don't know if Mum's heart wouldn't have still given up in her forties. We just don't know.'

Lila has turned around, and is about to say something to Asif, when she sees a slim ponytailed figure behind him in jeans and a T-shirt. She has no idea how long Yasmin has been there, and neither does Asif, who is utterly mortified when he follows Lila's gaze over his shoulder. 'I've written you a list, Lila,' says Yasmin, holding out several pages of closely typed text.

'Thanks, Yas,' replies Lila, walking over to her and kissing her hello with her usual oppressive bear hug. Yasmin accepts it passively without shrinking away.

'You smelled nicer when you wore make-up,' says Yasmin. 'I liked the smell of the stuff you used to put on your face.'

319

'It was a Dior foundation,' says Lila. 'I'll get some for you, if you like.' She glances at the list. 'Is that what this is? A sort of shopping list?'

'No,' replies Yasmin eventually. 'It's a thank you list. I've written one for Asif too.' She pulls another set of pages out of her pink folder, and passes them to him; Asif's list, Lila notes, is much longer than hers.

'Great, well, thank you,' says Lila. 'I'll see you tonight, we can have some champagne when we watch the documentary.'

Yasmin absorbs this, and then says, 'I don't think I'll feel comfortable watching the documentary, but I'd like to know that it's happened. I'll just stay in my room.' She adds, neither rudely nor politely, just pragmatically, in a colourless voice, 'I won't drink champagne either. Alcohol doesn't mix well with my sleeping pills; it might make me throw up.' She turns and goes back up the stairs to her room.

As Lila sits waiting for the tube at Finchley Central, she takes out her list, and looks at it. It really is a thank you list. Yasmin has detailed all the occasions for which she has a reason to thank Lila; it goes back some fourteen years, starting from when Yasmin was just a few years old. Thank you for reading me the *Meg and Mog* books, Lila read, Thank you for giving me your Little People Mini Circus when the batteries ran out, Thank you for teaching me the actions to 'The Wheels on the Bus', Thank you for letting me wear your pink flip-flops in the garden, Thank you for telling Marty Tennant to leave me alone when he was rude to me in the playground . . . the list went on and on, right up until . . . Thank you for helping me buy new underwear, which was something Lila had done with Yasmin last week on Asif's request, as the local M&S had so much choice that even a neurotypical person could struggle to find what they wanted. Lila is touched that Yasmin has remembered all these things, but has no idea why she is being thanked for them now. As the tube comes in, Lila thinks about Mum; she remembers how Mum had always taught her to say, 'Thank you for having me,' when she left someone's house.

LEARNING TO WALK

Asif is stretched out on the parched summer grass of the park; even in the dappled shade of the trees, he feels slightly drunk and sleepy with the sunshine. Propping himself up on his elbow, he tickles Melody, who has rolled boisterously out from under her parasol, and is tugging the laces on his trainers with hungry interest. 'Best not to chew those, munchkin,' he says firmly, 'they're not good for you,' and places her back in the shade, handing her the bright plastic rattle ring that she has just thrown away.

'Ai-yi-yi-DAH,' complains Melody, giving the rattle ring an experimental chew, before rejecting it decisively, and rolling back out of the shade, this time towards the picnic basket, which she drums with her tiny feet, cackling uproariously. 'Ah-ha-ha-la-lah!' she practically sings.

'Living up to your name, I see,' says Asif to Melody, picking her up again, and this time propping her up on his lap where she can't escape, his hand around the comforting roundness of her firm belly. He glances over at Mei Lin, who is frowning adorably at something on her laptop. She is wearing glasses, which Asif didn't even realize she needed before they started going out.

'Do you think it's odd that she's not crawling yet?' asks Mei Lin distractedly, glancing up at Melody and Asif as she taps out something on the keypad.

'Crawling's not a big developmental milestone, some babies just go straight to walking,' says Asif. 'It's really not a big deal.'

'How do you know that?' asks Mei Lin, clearly impressed, looking up from her work.

'Just something I read,' says Asif modestly, tickling Melody on her toes to make her giggle again.

'Did I tell you that someone thought she was a boy, the other day, at the supermarket?' Mei Lin says carelessly.

'Only twice, or maybe three or four times,' teases Asif. 'You know, it really doesn't matter when she's as happy as she is. That's what makes her beautiful. That and being loved.'

Mei Lin looks up at him gratefully. 'Of course you're right,' she says. 'You make me feel very shallow sometimes.' She adds jokingly, 'But from now on I'm going to dress her aggressively and exclusively in pink until she gets more hair.' She carries on working at her computer, and finally breathes a sigh of relief. 'I'm done,' she announces decisively, 'that's the last one checked, I just need to email the changes over to the printers now.' She taps efficiently at the keyboard, before looking up apologetically, and propping her glasses up on the top of her head. 'Sorry about this, it's a real bugger having to work at the weekend. I really thought I'd have finished before I came out today, but the States were late sending the artworks over.'

'Don't worry,' says Asif, putting Melody back down in the shade, and propping a couple of cushions around her so she can't roll to freedom too easily. 'It's lovely that you managed to come out.'

Mei Lin smiles, and leans over to kiss him lightly on the lips. 'I had to come out,' she says. 'I wanted to see you.' She takes a sip of the chilled wine that Asif has thoughtfully packed, along with strawberries dipped in chocolate, an indulgence he learned to do in college. 'This is just gorgeous. It's a shame Yasmin didn't want to join us. Melody loves it when Yasmin does those shadow puppet animals for her.'

'It's a bit too sunny for Yasmin,' says Asif. 'She won't even go in the garden when it's like this, not if she can help it. She just wants to stay at home today; she's barely left her room.' He can't help himself adding anxiously, 'She did something strange earlier this afternoon, she gave me a list she'd written, thanking me for all sorts of random things. Pages and pages of it; it must have taken her hours. Yas always does things for a reason, but this just seems so odd; I can't work out why she's done it.'

'We can go back to your place, if you're worried,' offers Mei Lin sympathetically.

Asif shakes his head. 'It's OK. I can spend an hour or so out; Yasmin's just playing computer games in her bedroom; it won't matter to her if I'm sitting in the kitchen, or ten minutes away in the park. She's waiting for the documentary to be aired this evening.' He fiddles with his wine glass indecisively, before confessing, 'Lila sort of told me off today. I think she was probably right. I need to strike a balance between worrying about Yasmin and worrying about myself. I think I might have avoided relationships in the past because of Yasmin.' He adds with a touch of humour, not wanting to embarrass Mei Lin by his sincerity, 'Besides, I've just met this fantastic woman, and I really, really, don't want to blow it.'

'Oh, I think you're doing just fine,' says Mei Lin, squeezing his hand at the compliment. As she leans forward to check on Melody, her glasses fall off her head, and are seized gleefully by her daughter, who promptly starts chewing the ends. 'Not for you, Baby-Boo,' she says, and tugs them away from Melody's surprisingly strong grip with some difficulty.

'I like you in glasses,' says Asif. 'Most people look awful wearing them, but they suit you.'

'Thanks,' says Mei Lin. 'I barely need them, to be honest. I started wearing them at meetings so senior management would take me seriously. I wanted to look cleverer than I actually was.'

'Do they work?' asks Asif with interest. 'I could do with some help in looking clever. And I have difficulty getting Hector's PA to take me seriously, let alone management.'

'Try mine,' says Mei Lin, sliding her frames on Asif's face, and kissing him pertly on the nose. 'Very distinguished and serious,' she says. 'You look like Clark Kent.' Asif inspects his reflection in Melody's mirror-bug toy, grimacing at the distorted four-eyed geek that greets him, and pulls them off. 'And now you're Superman,' Mei Lin adds flirtatiously.

'I think you're making fun of me,' complains Asif, obviously unconvinced. 'There's no need to be cruel.'

'I'm not making fun of you,' says Mei Lin, trying one of his dipped strawberries. 'You should enjoy being young and attractive while you still are – you might be bald and pot-bellied in twenty years' time. I like the fact that you're modest, but sometimes you take it too far.'

'There's no need to be kind, either,' says Asif. 'It's really sweet of you, but I know what I am. There are beautiful people, like you, there are regular people, and then there are people like me.'

'That's just ridiculous,' comments Mei Lin bluntly. 'Of course you're nice-looking. And it shouldn't be so hard for you to believe; in fact, you look a lot like your dad. I've seen that dashing photo of him in uniform in your sitting room.'

'Oh, Dad,' says Asif dismissively. 'He always looked great in photos, but I don't remember him being that handsome in real life. His teeth were a bit dodgy, actually.'

Mei Lin refuses to be diverted. 'Well, there's

nothing wrong with your teeth. And the first thing I thought when I met you was that you were cute. Well, the second thing. The first thing I thought was bugger, someone's come in and now Melody's screaming and my boob's hanging out. You rushed in looking really stressed, all clumsy and wild-eyed, and then you just stopped stock still and stared at me; you looked so shocked that it was sort of funny, sort of charming, really.'

Asif looks at her in wonder. 'You remembered,' he says. 'I thought you'd barely noticed me.' He hangs his head, and admits, 'Don't laugh, but when I first saw you, I thought that you were possibly the Most Beautiful Woman in the World. I thought that you were so perfect I might have imagined you; that's why I was so pleased when I saw you walking into the lift that time.'

'Now why would I laugh at that,' says Mei Lin, clearly touched. 'Besides, you know I'm shallow enough to be flattered by outrageous compliments.' She pauses, as she takes in what he has said. 'So what do you think of me now?' she asks. 'It's a hell of a fall from the Most Beautiful Woman in the World, it's not like there's any other way to go.'

'I think,' says Asif, not bothering to hide his embarrassing sincerity this time, as he looks into Mei Lin's sunlit eyes, 'that I'm very glad you turned out to be real, after all. I think I might be the luckiest guy alive.'

'It turns out that you're far too genuine to be charming,' sighs Mei Lin. She adds with a slightly mischievous smile, 'I don't know about the luckiest guy alive, but I can tell you with certainty that you are about to get very lucky indeed,' and she leans forward and kisses him warmly. Asif feels the reassuring weight of Mei Lin's body against him, and as he returns her kiss, he feels only undiluted happiness and hope. He feels he knows everything there is to know about the world by holding Mei Lin in his arms. Here is Mei Lin's back, curving gently into his embrace, here is her silk curtain of hair falling against his face, here is her full lower lip softening against his, here are her precise white teeth that taste both smooth and sharp, here are her supple, capable hands, that can soothe an infant and rescue a man from drowning in his own anxious fears. For the moment, for this perfect moment, what he holds in his arms is enough.

He knows that he will return home, and his responsibilities and worries and self-doubts will return, but he will cope with them, somehow. He will find a way to manage them, because he finally believes that he is greater than the sum of their parts. Asif has said that he is lucky, and he is now certain that he means it. He is lucky not just because he has chosen life, but because life, in a ludicrous, wonderful twist, has finally chosen him too.

LEAVING HOME

Lila is at home in her Finchley flat in the evening, putting piles of clutter into cardboard boxes. A quarter of her sitting room has now been transformed to a patch of grey carpet and six neatly stacked cardboard cubes, which look bizarrely out of context, like a baby giant has left his play blocks in the room by mistake. The buzzer goes, and she presses the button to let in Asif and Yasmin.

'Hi there,' she says kissing Asif and looking past him for Yasmin. 'Don't mind the mess, not that you have a choice.' She sees that Yasmin isn't there, and looks questioningly at Asif. 'I thought your text message said that we were going to watch the documentary here, instead of at home.'

'It did,' says Asif. 'I misunderstood what Yasmin wanted. She texted me while I was in the park; I thought she meant that she wanted us all to watch it here. In fact, she just wants you and me to watch it here, and for her to watch it at home, alone.' He looks a bit worried as usual. 'Is that weird? Or normal? If it was me, I'd probably be a bit embarrassed to see it with other people, even family. But Yas doesn't normally get embarrassed.'

'It's a bit weird, but whatever,' says Lila. 'I thought it was odd that she wanted to come over here; she normally says that being in my flat makes her head hurt. We'll go back to the house afterwards, I still need to tell her my news.' She looks at her work in the living room with a complicated pride at her progress, turning chaos into stacked, manila order; it was like the opposite of art. 'Would you like a glass of wine?' she offers.

'Yeah, cheers,' says Asif, a bit gloomily, already missing Mei Lin, suddenly reminded of the wine and kisses they shared just a few hours earlier. 'It is weird, isn't it? Something's not right. Maybe Yas is freaked about being Almost-Famous. The TV producers had lined up a radio interview for her to do next week, and she didn't say she wouldn't do it, not in so many words, but she just said that it was wholly irrelevant. It's becoming her catch-phrase.'

'You could spend your whole life looking for stuff that wasn't wholly irrelevant and not succeed,' says Lila, pouring out two generous glasses of red wine, and passing one to Asif. He takes a few steps into the living room, and is stopped short by an enormous canvas of swirling technicolor propped up against the front of the sofa.

'God, that's amazing – is that really one of yours? It's like a cross between a Pollock and a Riley.'

'Since when did you know who Pollock and Riley

are?' asks Lila, amused rather than offended. 'I think I'd rather you said it was completely original. And why wouldn't you think it's one of mine?'

'Mei Lin and I went to the Tate Modern last week,' admits Asif. 'And it just doesn't look like your usual sort of work, it's just so, so . . .'

'Pretty?' suggests Lila, with a trace of sarcasm.

Asif nods. 'Beautiful, even. Just purely beautiful,' he says with complete sincerity, wishing he was eloquent enough to explain more; the flowing colours in the painting are like something from a dream.

Lila smiles, pleased with the compliment, even though she's not sure it's fully deserved. 'I'm glad you like it; I've spent days and days working on it. But you're right, in a way, it's not really original, so it's not really one of mine. It's more of an exercise in interpretation; it represents a few seconds of Mozart's Piano Concerto No. 18 in B Flat Major.'

'The one that Yasmin played for the documentary?' asks Asif. 'So this is how she described the colour of the music?'

'I asked Henry for a transcript of the interview,' says Lila. 'I thought it was about time I looked outside of myself, and tried painting experiences that weren't my own for a change. Empathizing, is what they call it, I think. The challenging bit was doing the textural changes that Yasmin described; they obviously couldn't do that on the TV sequence. If you run your hand across it you can feel the differences; I've used everything from sandpaper to sequins.'

'It really is amazing,' repeats Asif, gingerly brushing his fingertips across the surface. 'How weird to think that this is the sort of thing Yasmin feels and sees when music is played. No wonder she's always so distracted; the colours are so vivid, they make everything else look grey.'

'That might be because everything else here really *is* grey,' says Lila drily, sitting down on the cleared patch of grubby carpet in front of the sofa.

'Are you tidying up?' asks Asif, sitting beside her, and nodding towards the neat stack of boxes in front of them. 'Or is that some kind of new art installation, too?'

'Neither, I'm packing,' says Lila lightly. 'I'm moving in with Henry. No need for us both to be paying rent, we're saving for a deposit for a place of our own.'

'So you're leaving Finchley,' states Asif numbly, wondering why he is so surprised. He knows that there's a wider world than Finchley, he lived in it once, for a few months at college. It just seems strange to him that leaving is so easy; just a matter of packing boxes and driving a transit van to another address.

'I'm not going that far,' says Lila, still trying to sound casual, wondering if she is lying. The other side of London suddenly feels ridiculously distant, an ocean away instead of just across the river; she wonders if Asif realizes this too. 'I'll visit. And you guys can visit too. You'll like Henry's place, I mean our place. It's much tidier than mine, for the moment at least.' She turns on the TV, and they catch the tail-end of the trailer for Yasmin's documentary that has been playing all week. 'An extraordinary journey into an extraordinary mind,' intones the narrator, over a close-up of Yasmin, her clear hazel eyes seeming both sensitive and confused. The commercials start, and so Lila hits the mute button.

'She looks different on TV,' says Asif. 'Bigger.'

'TV adds ten pounds,' says Lila. 'Everyone knows that.'

'I don't mean that, I mean, like she's a bigger person, more important, stronger, wiser,' Asif struggles to explain. 'It's like that's the real her, and the person mooching at home is just some scrappy imitation, just fading away.' Asif isn't sure if he is making sense, and so he gives up and sips his wine.

'She's just really photogenic,' says Lila. 'Some people look better in photographs than they do in real life. Just like Dad.'

'Did you read your list?' asks Asif. 'It's a lovely gesture, but what was all that about? I've no idea what's going on in her head recently. I mean, I never did, but now she's just so unpredictable.'

'The routines were for her, not for you,' Lila says pointedly. 'I think unpredictable is good. You seem to be looking for things to worry about; I'm happy, you're happy, and Yas is happy. She wanted to do this documentary, remember. She wanted to show people what it was like to be her. She said that she wanted a legacy.'

'Who wants a legacy at nineteen?' mutters Asif, before complaining, 'How long do these ad breaks go on for?'

'And you shouldn't be so suspicious about the thank you list,' Lila carries on. 'You know that Yasmin likes lists. It's just a nice thing for her to have done.'

'I suppose,' says Asif. 'Maybe she takes after Mum more than we think. Mum was always quite particular about getting us to say thank you, wasn't she?'

'Yeah, freakishly particular. Especially when we left someone's house,' says Lila unthinkingly.

As Asif hears her careless comment, he is vaguely aware of a rising discomfort in his gut, as though the niggle of doubt he has felt there ever since his arrival is setting into solid stone. 'What did you just say?' he asks uncertainly.

Lila replies a bit impatiently, 'It's something Mum always said, to say thank you for having me before leaving someone's house, remember?' Her eyes widen as she takes in what she's just said, and they look at each other with a flash of comprehension just as the titles of the documentary finally start. Asif leaps up, knocking over his wine across Lila's glorious technicolor canvas.

'Christ,' he cries in panic. 'She's leaving. I think she's leaving home.' He fumbles for his phone, and glances in guilty dismay at the red stain dripping down over Lila's work.

'Forget that,' Lila says about the painting, after having jumped up herself. 'Let's just go.'

Asif nods, relieved at her decisiveness. 'Can we take your car, it'll be faster,' he says, racing out the door.

Lila grabs her keys, and bangs her front door behind her; she shouts down after Asif on the stairs, 'Do you think she's running away? Where would she go?'

'She might not be going anywhere,' Asif yells back. 'That's what's scares me. Remember what she said about the sleeping pills.'

'Oh fuck,' cries Lila inadequately, and races down the stairs and out to the street, hurriedly unlocking the car. She gets into the driving seat, with Asif on the passenger side already on his mobile.

'She's not picking up, it's not even going to answer-phone,' he says. 'Shit, shit, shit. I really hope that we're just being paranoid about nothing. I'm trying the neighbours.' After a while he swears and hangs up.

'Not there?' Lila says. 'Try the guy who runs the corner shop, get the number from directories.'

Some fifteen minutes later, during a hair-raising drive where Lila has broken the speed limits in at least three residential areas and run a red light, they screech to a halt outside the house. There's no space to park on the cluttered street, nowhere even to double park, and so Asif leaps out and runs into the house, while Lila goes around the corner to park in front of a neighbour's garage entrance.

As Asif hurriedly unlocks the front door, he hears the TV on in the front room; perhaps Yasmin is watching the documentary after all. His panic subsides, until he walks in, and sees that the documentary is showing on the TV, with the film of her playing Mozart on the piano while computer-generated colour ripples past her like water, but that Yasmin herself isn't there. He runs upstairs, and without knocking, pushes open the door. Yasmin is lying on her bed, with her arms folded across her chest, her eyes closed. And looking down at her, perfectly at peace, all that Asif can think of is that wizened, blanket-wrapped baby in the curved plastic cot, his father telling him, 'She's your baby sister, Yasmin,' and Asif stretching out his hand to her cheek, to say, 'Baboo.'

'Yasmin,' says Asif softly. 'You've not done anything yet, have you? You haven't taken anything yet?' There is a saucer of pills by her bed, and a full glass of water.

Yasmin opens her eyes, and shakes her head. 'No, the documentary's not finished yet,' she says.

'Thank God,' says Asif, starting to cry with relief. He hears Lila running up the stairs, and calls, 'It's OK. She's OK.'

Lila runs into the room, takes in the scene, the pills, the water, the prone figure of Yasmin on the bed, and starts shouting in panic and fury, 'What the fuck did you think you were doing!' Her face becomes puffy and red as she shouts, with hot angry tears brimming in her eyes but not quite falling.

Yasmin looks at Asif with the water-face, and Lila with the red-blotch eyes, and realizes that she won't be able to do what she planned that evening. And she feels a vivid emotional distress so deep that it colonizes her, so much so that she is inhabiting the distress instead of the other way around, and all that she can see is red with orange blotches, and she puts her fingers in her ears, backs to the far edge of her bed in the corner of her room, and starts humming. She stares at the plate of pills with absurd regret; she hates taking something out of her schedule once it is planned, and she had been looking forward to a really good, dreamless sleep.

'Why?' asks Asif, still sitting in her room, when Yasmin has calmed down, and he has persuaded a furiously distraught Lila to go back downstairs to do the same. 'Why would you do that? Why would you even think of it?'

'I'm not happy,' says Yasmin in a small voice. 'I don't feel hopeful. I just want to be able to sleep.'

'Do you know why you aren't happy?' asks Asif, wanting to hold her hand, or stroke her hair, but not daring to touch her.

'I don't know. It mostly started when I began to go blind,' says Yasmin.

'Who said you were going blind?' asks Asif in astonishment.

'No one, I self-diagnosed. I'm losing vision in my left eye. I have Stargardt's disease, like Henry. Although it stopped getting worse three weeks ago.'

Asif looks closely into Yasmin's pretty, hazel eyes. 'We'll take you to a specialist,' he says. 'It might be something treatable, like a cataract. You should have said.'

'It wasn't relevant,' says Yasmin.

'What about Lila and me?' asks Asif gently, trying not to let reproach tinge his voice. 'Aren't we relevant? How did you think we'd feel, if something happened to you?'

'I didn't,' says Yasmin frankly. 'It didn't occur to me.' She adds, 'I'm sorry. For upsetting you. That wasn't what I wanted to do.'

'I'm sorry too,' says Asif, 'if I ever made you feel that you didn't matter, that we wouldn't care if something happened to you. I know you're not easy, sometimes, Yasmin. I know that you know that too. But you're my little sister, and I love you. I've loved you ever since I first saw you in the hospital.' As he says this, he realizes that it is true. It was complicated loving someone who made your life harder, it was complicated loving someone who controlled your life through no fault of their own, but there it was. It was alienating, it was isolating, but in the end, it was still love, flawed and fragile, just as they were. It might yet redeem them all.

'I need you to listen to me, Yas,' says Asif, 'and try to understand. We're not the luckiest people in the world, we've had a lot to put up with, with losing Dad, and then Mum, and the Asperger's, and everything, really. But we've still got each other, you, me and Lila. Lila said something clever today, Yas, something relevant, mostly or wholly relevant, if you like. She said that we've chosen life, Yas, and so can you. You can be happy, you can be hopeful, you can get a good night's sleep, I really believe that.' Asif hears a soft footfall outside in the hallway, and is aware that Lila must have calmed down and come back up the stairs. He suspects that she is hovering indecisively at the door, but he doesn't dare to turn and look.

Yasmin says nothing for a long time, and then states in a matter-of-fact voice, 'Sometimes believing something is enough to make it happen. If you're depressed, and you believe that you're being treated for it, even if you're not, you can make yourself better. There was a study in 1999 by the World Health Organization.' She gets up and pushes the plate of pills over to Asif, still feeling that sense of regret. 'I don't know what I'm going to do tonight, now. I don't like taking things out of my schedule. I didn't have anything else planned.'

'That's OK,' says Lila suddenly from the doorway, her eyes still red and blotchy, but her voice surprisingly soft and composed. Asif looks back at her; she is outlined by the light behind her in the corridor, and as she speaks again, her competent tone reminds him of their mother, who stood so often at that same doorway. 'We can make some plans now, if you like. Together.'

Early next morning, Asif and Lila go to the hospital with Yasmin for a set of emergency appointments, and return with her revised prescriptions. While Lila goes to the pharmacy to get the medication, Asif stays with Yasmin, watching as she makes her usual cup of mid-morning tea. She pours a cup for him, as is her habit, and he accepts it, as is his. Camomile cat pee, he thinks ruefully, amazed at how delighted he is to be sitting here with Yasmin, having a cup of tea in the kitchen. How normal it feels. How close it came to being gone for ever, the tea, the ponytailed head bending over the cup. He knows that Yasmin failed in her suicide bid, and that he and Lila succeeded in preventing it; but it still feels, once more, that they are the ones who have failed. It is obvious how much help he needs, for Yasmin and himself, that he should no longer pretend that he can manage on his own; the first step to getting help, he realizes, is admitting how much he needs it.

'Asif,' says Yasmin suddenly, 'I've been thinking about what you said last night. I have something to say to you. I love you too.' She says it prosaically, without any sentiment, but she remembers to look in his eyes. Mississippi One, Mississippi Two.

'You don't have to say that,' says Asif, pleased

340

despite himself, 'if you're not sure that you feel it. If it doesn't really mean anything to you. You don't have to say the words just for my sake.'

'I want to say the words,' replies Yasmin. 'I want to say the words I love you, because I want to mean what they mean. Maybe love isn't the same thing for me, inside, as it is for you. But I want it to be. That's why I said it.'

'Thank you, Yasmin,' says Asif, trying not to cry again, and not quite succeeding. Yasmin was right, sometimes the words could mean as much as the thing that they meant to represent. Sometimes words were just as real. Sometimes the words were enough.

He puts out his hand instinctively, on the table between them, and Yasmin carefully puts hers on top of it. He feels that he has walked into her world, and she has walked into his. He wishes impatiently that Lila would return, to share this with them. He wishes that Mum and Dad and everybody who ever meant anything to them could all be there, sitting at the table with them, having tea, holding their hands, inhabiting a world filled with those who have chosen life, with all its unfairness and lunatic irrationality, with all its endless potential for happiness and hope.

'Does this mean I'm getting better?' says Yasmin; if the words hadn't come from her, they might have sounded sarcastic. Instead she seems quite genuinely interested.

'Oh Yas,' says Asif, swallowing back his tears,

which he can see are making Yasmin uncomfortable. 'No one's trying to get you better, not in that way. We want you to be happy, but we don't want you to have to pretend to be someone you're not. You're fine, you know. Just as you are. I mean, you will be. We all will.'

THE FUTURE ACCORDING TO YASMIN MURPHY

My name is Yasmin Murphy, and I have a recurring dream. I dream that I know I am dreaming, and so can do anything I like, and I start flying safely around my room, but am scared of being drawn to the open window, because outside, the world is strange and unfamiliar, and I fear that I will fall.

I have learned recently, that you do not have to be courageous to die, like my dad was. Dying can be something that is very easy. I have learned that you have to be courageous to live, because living can be something that is very complicated, especially if you are alone. I am not alone, I have Asif and Lila. They have not always been happy; they have not always been hopeful for the future, but they have chosen to live anyway, because they are courageous. And I can be courageous too; I can choose life.

I believe that I can be happy.

I believe that I can be hopeful for the future.

⋆　⋆　⋆

So tonight, when I have that dream, the dream where I know I am dreaming, I won't be scared of falling from the open window. Instead, I will go to the window and look out into the strange and unfamiliar world. And I will leap from the window, and I won't just fly. I will soar.